KINGSWINFORD SUNSET

BY THE SAME AUTHOR:

SHE'S ALONE
BOTH

Kingswinford Sunset

Richard Bruce Clay

THE RING OF THE NIBELUNG

Music by Richard Wagner
English Translation and Introduction by Andrew Porter
© 1976 by Andrew Porter
Text reprinted by permission of Faber Music Ltd

KINGSWINFORD SUNSET

1: Martin Icement

In the shed. In the shed. I am. In the shed. Nothing to worry about. I'm just in the shed. There's a tape recorder. Just a tape recorder. It works. See? It works. Shouldn't be surprised. It's an old one. They made things simpler in those days. Less to go wrong.

No. That's not the way to think about it. That's not the way to think about it at all. Nothing's gone wrong. Yes, yes, there's been the sad stuff. There's always the sad stuff. But it's over now. All over. Over and done with.

I'm in the shed. It's a bit dusty. And the window... it's a bit mucky. Ought to clean it... Can see the garden through it, though. Can see the garden. But not the house. The house is on the opposite side. Can only see the garden. It's like the house isn't there at all. Everything's all right.

There's a workbench under the window. And the tape recorder's on the workbench. There's no electricity in the shed. Put batteries in the tape recorder, though. New batteries. Got a pocket full of new batteries. Big fat batteries. The right sort for the recorder. Surprised they still make them. It's an old recorder. You'd think they wouldn't make the right sort anymore. But they do. Big fat batteries. The right sort.

Better not to mention all this money... all this money that's been getting spent on batteries. Better not to say anything. You know how things are. Just keep the batteries in here, in the shed. Everything's alright in the shed. The tape recorder makes a noise. A quiet little noise. Kind of a hum. Kind of a hiss. And now and again, the wheels make a tiny little squeaking. That's all. Sounds as good as it did when it was new. But you don't see cassette tapes around anymore. Time was, you used to see them all over, but not now. Went into WH Smith's the other day, and they didn't have any. I got some, though. I bought some from Bilston Market. I didn't say I'd gone to Bilston Market. But I did go. And I bought some batteries. Bought some big fat batteries. Bought some batteries and brought them back here, to the shed. And I'm taping things, now. Taping the things I say. I can say anything here, in the shed. I can say anything. And I can tape anything. Anything and everything.

I can go right back to the time I bought the tape recorder. Sixty-nine or Seventy, I think. November, I think. I know it was foggy in the mornings back then. Back then, there was always fog in November.

I liked taping things. I'd go around with the recorder and collect the sounds things made. I remember walking past an electrical sub-station, over and over and over again. Over and over and over again. And I'd tape the sound it made. And tape the way it changed as you got nearer to it and further away. And I kept a collection of tapes of things. Loads and loads and loads of things. All gone, now. Threw them all away...? Must have done. Must have thrown them all away. You know how things are. Surprised that the tape recorder still works.

A bit later, I met Mick and his lot. I was still living with Dad. Working in the shop. I'd let my hair grow. Dad didn't seem to mind. I don't know what Mom'd have had to say about it. Not the sort of thing she'd have let me get away with, I don't suppose. Not the sort of thing at all. But she died a while before then. When was it? I forget.

Friday nights, I'd started going down the pub. Used to get blind steaming drunk down there. Blind steaming drunk. Well. You do. I knew a few blokes from school. Some of them turned up, now and again. Mainly it was blokes I'd met in the pub. There was Mick, of course, and Steve, and Pete and Nige, and Kev and Nick and Neil. The first year or so was the funniest. We used to get absolutely blind steaming drunk. And the funniest thing was Mick. The way he used to take the piss out of Neil. Neil used to reckon he was in some sort of a 'band.' Silly bugger. He had longer hair than the rest of us. Silly, silly bugger. He used to take things way too seriously.

'You take things way too seriously,' Mick'd say to him.

'Who's taking things too seriously? I'll be out on Sunday.'

'Not the same. It's Saturday that counts. Saturday's the day that shows you've got commitment.'

'And I'll be out next Saturday.'

'Won't be the same. Won't be like you've been showing willing.'

'Stop taking the piss. You know I've got a gig...'

But Mick had stopped listening to him. Mick stopped listening as soon as he mentioned anything to do with that 'band' thing he was in. Mick didn't have time for stuff like that. He was a great laugh, was Mick. Mick was all for getting the beers down your neck. That was what showed commitment. That was what it was all about. All this 'band' stuff, Mick couldn't be doing with it. It got on his nerves. Especially when he heard the name...

'What?!'

'It's the name of a play,' said Neil, 'by Schiller.'

'You prat!'

'There's already a band named after a play by Goethe – Faust. Why not name your band after one by Schiller?'

'We don't want to know who these people are, you wanker. It's just pathetic! The Death of Wally..?'

'The Death of Wallenstein.'

'It's pathetic.'

'We like it. We think it's got the right air of ominousness.'

'Who's this *we*?'

'Me and Dave, mainly. Old Wilf joins in on percussion, now and again. We could really do with a good solid drummer, though. And a keyboard player. I reckon if we got hold of a really wild and wacky keyboard player...'

'Pack it in!'

'...it'd be a real blast. But we might have to wait a bit for one to turn up...'

'Pack it in, I'm telling you!'

Mick gave it to him straight. He wasn't having anyone getting in the way of a good time being had. All this 'band' stuff, it wasn't what was wanted. It was getting in the way of getting the beers down your neck. He was a great laugh, was Mick.

I don't think Neil came out with us much, after that. Maybe he really did... start playing gigs with that 'band' thing he was in. I don't know. Don't suppose it ever amounted to much. Don't suppose it lasted very long.

So Mick got a good tight bunch of blokes together. Blokes with commitment to the beer. After a bit, we started to go to other pubs. Sometimes, five or six in a night. And we'd get drunk. Blind steaming drunk.

Pubs were great, in those days. You had Watney's. You had Double Diamond. Round here, you had M&B, too. And you had Banks's. Some of the places were starting to sell that new lager stuff but that wasn't what was wanted. Woman's drink. If woman's drinks had been wanted, some poncey wine bar would have been the place to go. No. Pubs were what was wanted. Man's drinks were what was wanted. Mick said.

You could smoke in pubs, back then. None of your smoking ban rubbish. I used to get though a packet of Silk Cut every Saturday night. Sometimes, I'd have a Castella.

Around Seventy-two, I started working up the MEB. Meant I didn't have to work Saturdays. This was great. Mick was starting to get some really long pub crawls sorted out. We'd do a lunchtime session – three or four pubs, that'd be. Then, when closing time came, we'd nip back to Mick's, where he'd have stashed a few bottles of Woodpecker or Strongbow, or maybe a couple of Watney's Party Fours. Then when opening time came, we'd be off again.

After a while, when I got the Cortina, we started going a bit further afield. Up to Dudley, say, or out to Hagley, Clent or even Belbroughton. Only then we had that smash-up and I got the two-year ban. Pity about that. Great laugh, though.

By then, I wasn't doing any more tape recording. Didn't seem like there was any point. Hanging round power stations, taping the noise they made. No. I sometimes wondered why I'd done it in the first place. Just seemed okay at the time, I suppose. But... but I wondered if I should have done anything with the tapes? Played them to anyone, maybe? I couldn't think who, though. No...

10

Couldn't think who…

Things went on the same way for a bit. It was a great laugh. Then one of the others, Nige I think it was, came up with this bloody stupid idea of going down London or somewhere and trying out the pubs there. We'd be wasting good drinking time on the bloody train. It was a stupid idea. That's what Mick told him. Mick wasn't having any of that sort of stuff. For Mick, it was all about the beers. He was a great laugh, was Mick.

I don't think Nige came out with us much, after that.

Then there was that one bad time. Nick got hold of this bird – I don't remember what her name was – and she came out with us. Mick wasn't happy about that and, to be fair, I don't think Nick's bird was very happy either. Mick started to take the piss, and Nick went a bit out of order over it all. There was some trouble and we ended up being kicked out of the pub. It was the Market Hall in Kingswinford. We got banned. Mick went back, a few days later, and sorted things out, but we never actually went in there again. That was the last time Nick came out with us.

When Kev got hold of a bird, he just disappeared. The way we heard it, his bird knew Nick's bird and they'd both been laying the poison down, telling Kev it was us or her, and Kev had to make his mind up one way or the other. Kev went with her. That's the way Mick said it had happened. But Kev always was a prat, anyway.

Things stopped some time in Seventy-five. Mick had been reading up on this new thing, the Campaign for Real Ale. He'd checked it out and decided we needed to start drinking better quality beer. Sensible. So he sorted out this crawl, which missed out all the Banks's and all the M&B pubs, and just went in the ones that did better quality beer. So we went on this crawl. I suppose we walked about five or six miles, that Saturday night. And we drank – three pints, I think. Or maybe it was two. But I think it was three.

Steve and Pete weren't very happy.

The following Saturday, we were meeting in the front room of the Leopard in Kingswinford. We were going to Kinver, where they did Batham's and Simpkiss Ales. It was in the summer, and it was light outside and the sunlight shone through the pub window and made the air inside all golden.

Steve and Pete said they weren't coming to Kinver. They said they just wanted to get the beers down their necks. They said they couldn't be arsed going all that way. They said it wasn't worth it. That's what they said. Mick told them they weren't showing sufficient commitment to the beer. They told him to fuck off. Then they left.

And then there was just Mick... and me.

I told him his idea seemed sound enough to me. Going to Kinver to get the decent beer seemed sound enough to me. I was all for it, it seemed sound enough to me.

He told me to fuck off. I don't know why he told me to fuck off. But I fucked off. And on the way out, I looked back. And he was sitting there staring at his pint, and there was only him, now. And the barmaid had cleared my glass away, though I don't think I'd finished my pint. Seemed a waste, that – not having finished my pint. And having it tipped away. Seemed a terrible waste.

And I turned, and was going to walk out, but there were these other two people in the bar. And one of them was older, maybe fifty or sixty. He was a man – the older one. He was a man. He had a posh voice and he wore a posh suit. They were having a row, these two people. They were really hating each other. But their voices were quiet. They were almost whispering. It was weird how you could hear the hate in them, just from the whispering.

And the older one – the one who was a man – he got up and as he walked past me, on his way out, he looked into me and I saw his eyes. And they were blue. They were wide. They were frightening.

Then he was gone.

But there were other eyes looking at me and they were just like his. Younger, but just like his. They were blue, too. They were wide, too. They were frightening, too.

And I waited, as those younger eyes came over to me and looked into me, and there was nothing else but those eyes. And after we were married, they were still the same. They were still blue and they were still wide and they were still frightening. You know how things are.

Soon enough, we had the... kids... around the time I bought the Vauxhall. And soon enough, we moved up here from Pensnett. It's nicer here than in Pensnett. Houses are more expensive, though. Our place has three bedrooms; it's detached and there's gas central heating. They say you can get broadband here too, but I wouldn't know. I don't really know about broadband. All this new stuff. All this new malarkey. We're right next to the wood here, which is the edge of the countryside. In the afternoon, we're always in the shadow of the wood. Cally Wood.

Not long after, I bought the Peugeot. And we also got the Nissan. Obviously, it was needed. You know how things are. And things went on for a bit, like that. All very nice. But then, we had the sad stuff. Which was to be expected, really. The sad stuff always comes along, sooner or later. Can't not have the sad stuff. Things had been alright for a while, so we had to expect the sad stuff. But I thought we'd got over it. You know, sad stuff will happen so, shoulder to the wheel, nose to the grindstone, get back on with things...

But then...

Then...

He was a great laugh, was Mick.

2: Mary Maitland

There's nothing else like the stink of a dead junkie's bedsit and, really, you wouldn't want there to be. It's a rotten greasy treacle that sticks to everything. *Everything,* though, doesn't usually mean very much. If it can be carted down Cash Converters for an extra bob or two, it will have been. What was left in Alice Icement's place was a change of tie-dyed clothes, a bed with a blood stained mattress and a sleeping bag I'd sooner not describe, two unwashed plates, three washed plastic forks and a little black plastic CD rack with three discs in it; anything to play them on was long gone.

So getting the place cleared out took about ten minutes.

Curtains, sleeping bag *(urgh!)* and clothes went into a bin bag for the tip. Polly put some coins in the electric – how long since anyone had done that? Then she washed the plates and the work surfaces. I'd brought a vacuum cleaner and I did the carpet. The cleaner was one of those orange-red 'Henry' type things that's designed to look like a cartoon character. It made doing the vacuuming a bit of a laugh, back home. Not here though.

The bathroom was shared with other tenants. Some of those tenants – bless them – kept it clean, so we didn't have to touch it. That left us with the mattress on the bed. Half a sniff of it was enough to tell it needed getting rid of, so we covered it with taped-together bin bags and got the door open to carry it downstairs.

'I'll take the bottom end,' breezed Polly.

She sounded confident but she was a little thing – not quite five foot – and she didn't look like she'd seen the inside of a gym since leaving school. The doubt must have shown in my face but it only made her more determined

'Okay,' I began, 'one… two… three… *hup!'*

A good deal of frantic shuffling, an annoyed grunt and Polly dropped her end.

We tried again. 'One… two… three… *hup!'* This time, Polly's end stayed up. There was a bit of nervous scuffling as she went

14

backwards towards the door. At which point, it all got a bit too much for her and, wobbling from side to side, the mattress hit the floor, forcing her to her knees and leaving her gasping for breath, with her frizzy hair in a right state and her specs knocked skew-whiff.

'Are you sure you don't want me to take that end?' I asked.

'No,' Polly snapped. She sounded quite bolshie about it, so I didn't argue.

The third time, we finally got it out of the door but I was beginning to worry that Polly was going to fall backwards down the stairs.

'Can I help?'

The door to the flat opposite had opened and a big Indian-looking chap stood there in a male nurse's uniform.

Polly was still a bit flustered, so I got in there with a 'Yes please', before she could turn the offer down.

'I just came in,' he explained. 'You clearing Alice's place out?'

As he said this, he got hold of the front end of the mattress – without letting Polly feel she was no longer in charge.

'That's right,' I replied.

'Terrible business,' he sighed, as we steered the thing down, step by step, 'but I guess nobody was much surprised.'

'No,' Polly sighed back, finally reaching the bottom.

We got it loaded up into my fiancé's van, then went back and did the necessary mucky work with the kitchen bin. Then Polly had to nip outside for a fag break. The nurse introduced himself as Sharukh.

'You seem used to shifting heavy stuff,' he said.

'Ladies' keep fit every Monday,' I explained. 'My sister runs it. She's into that sort of thing.'

Polly reappeared, still flushed and a bit short of breath. Without being asked, Sharukh helped us out with the mopping. Neither Polly nor I had seen him before but, it turned out, he'd known Alice as well as anyone in her last months. I think she'd nicked a fair bit of stuff off him but she wasn't the first smackhead he'd known, so he'd expected no different.

'Knew she wasn't going to last long when she gave Rufus away,' he said. 'One of her old schoolmates had him. Alice loved that cat.'

'Yeah,' Polly remembered, 'Helen the vet had him. Alice wanted to be a vet too, when we were at school...'

Be thankful for small mercies, I suppose – think what the place would have smelt like if there'd still been a cat in it.

Finally, the CDs – forlorn little trinkets. But nobody much bought CDs anymore and she'd have made no smack money from these: *Jurassic Shift* by Ozric Tentacles, *The Sensual World* by Kate Bush and...

'Oh sweet Jesus,' I whispered. At that moment, I really needed His help.

The Adventures of Antidisestablishmentarianista Jones by The Death of Wallenstein.

'You alright, Mary?'

I pulled myself together. 'Okay, Pol. My brother-in-law's in this band. Alice told me... her dad used to know Neil, the guitarist. I didn't think she liked that sort of stuff herself, though.'

Polly drew herself up to her full height and attempted a tone of bossy reproof. 'Mary, by the time you knew her, she didn't like much of anything.'

This had been too true.

After we'd finished, Sharukh invited us in for a cup of tea. He worked at Russells Hall Hospital but his family lived in London – a mom and dad who'd have been horrified to hear he was down among the druggies. He wasn't the sort who got fazed by it, though. In his line of work, as in mine, it was important that you weren't.

'So how did you two know Alice, then?'

Polly and I looked at each other. I nodded to her to go first.

'I was with her at school,' she said. 'Summerhill in Kingswinford. We left seven years ago.'

'Nice place,' Sharukh said, softly, leaving unspoken the obvious question: *How did she end up here?*

Polly just shrugged and nodded back at me, as if she felt she'd said enough. She was a shy girl, not used to being asked about herself.

'I worked with Alice,' I said. 'I mean, I work for the Council. I find homes for people...' My voice trailed off as I searched for a polite way to put it.

'You find homes for the sort of people who most people don't want to live next door to,' Sharukh laughed, softly but ruefully.

'That's right. I found Alice this place.'

'You got to be friends with her?'

'I tried to keep in touch,' I sighed. 'I liked her – and it felt... like the right thing to do. I hoped she'd find herself a job or something.'

It sounded ridiculous, now.

'You go to church?' Sharukh asked. Then, looking apologetic, said that it wasn't his business.

'No no, that's fine. I do. My dad... er... used to be a pastor...'

Yeah, my dad was the priest who stabbed that writer to death, I thought, *but I won't burden you with that right now, Sharukh.*

'Pastor's daughter? Thought you must be something like that,' Sharukh smiled. 'Was it you who found Alice?'

'It was me,' said Polly, and her voice trembled.

Polly Gauvain was not the person best equipped to deal with discovering a dead body. I'd first met her the day Alice had moved in here, when she'd helped us with the decoration and cleaning.

Despite Alice's heroin, her string of lousy boyfriends (abusive or just plain useless) and her terrible self-loathing, Polly had looked up to her. In fact, Polly had always seemed loath to express an opinion on anything until Alice had given her verdict; maybe this had been the pattern of their friendship from the start.

Polly sometimes said a bit about her own mom, who sounded as shy as she was. And there was one time when she'd mentioned 'my brother Colin', then looked horrified with herself and shut up about the matter. I'd wondered if this was the same Colin Gauvain who you'd see on *Channel 4 News*, whenever they needed the opinions of somebody loud-mouthed, right-wing and obnoxious. I'd never found a nice way of asking. Nothing much about boyfriends, though I gathered there'd been a few. Nothing at all about her father.

Sharukh sipped his tea, looking at Alice's little CD collection.

'What about her mum and dad?' he asked. 'Didn't they want to come over and check things out?'

'Don't know about her dad,' Polly replied. 'I only spoke to her mom. She didn't sound like she cared tuppence. Alice used to say as much.' She frowned a little. 'But she has a brother, somewhere in Handsworth or West Brom. I haven't seen him for years.'

'That's weird, though,' Sharukh said. 'You'd think her mum... I mean, isn't she a headmistress, somewhere?'

I looked up. This was a surprise to me. Now that he said it, though, the name 'Icement' had sounded familiar when I'd first taken Alice's case.

'Whereabouts?' I asked.

'Think it might be over Tipton way,'

Round by my mom and dad's old place. Where my mom still lived. I'd be meeting Alice's mother sooner or later, because I'd recently taken on the job of doing talks about drugs in school assemblies. Hmm...

Sharukh made us one more pot of tea before we headed off to the tip. As the steel pot lid clunked down, he looked out the window.

Then he looked again.

'That don't look like good news,' he muttered.

'What?' Polly moved to join him. A cold beam of light had sneaked through a gap in the clouds and was reflected dazzlingly, from the lenses of her specs.

'Posh car out there,' Sharukh explained. 'Black Audi. Been there since I got back. Think there's someone in the front. He ain't gonna be on no mission of mercy. Not round here, not in a car like that.'

I felt uneasy – the haunted feeling I got when things weren't right and which I'd reluctantly learned to trust. I got up and peered through the flat's lace curtains, down into the narrow street.

Sharukh was right: a big, expensive black car that I wouldn't have recognised as an Audi. But, apart from my own little Renault, I knew nothing at all about cars, so I was happy to take his word for it. It was out of the price range of this part of town and any exceptions were likely to be the sort of people who had sold Alice the stuff that killed her.

The tinted glass made it hard to be certain – but yes, there was someone in the front.

After a moment, the car started up, its engine very quiet, and moved off. There was no reason to think the driver had noticed us through the old-fashioned lace and yet, suddenly, I really needed that second mug of tea.

***

'What sort of person drives an Audi?' I asked my fiancé, Ryan.

We were round his place. He creased his brows and sipped his cocoa.

'Woman in her thirties, forties,' he mused. 'Primary teacher, two or three kids. Votes Lib Dem, reads the *Guardian*...'

That didn't sound right.

'How about a black Audi?' I asked.

'*Black* Audi? Hmm... That'd be different. Bloke, most likely. Audis are fuel-efficient, but he wouldn't be interested in the green side of things. It'd be efficiency for efficiency's sake. Not a bugger you'd want to mess with. Plays his cards close to his chest.'

'Tinted glass?'

'Yeah, he would have tinted glass, yeah...'

That sounded more like my guy. Not a person you'd want to mess with. No. Definitely not.

He might have been a daft sausage, my Ryan Sheepshanks, but he knew his motors. What was more, he knew the psychology of his motors. You did get to know the psychology of your motors if you had the bits of half a dozen vintage Land Rovers, in various stages of loving reassembly, all stashed away in a row of lockups in Brierley Hill. It also helped if, at the back of your parents' house in North Yorkshire, there was a grassy field and, in that field – a garden of earthly delights for your countless little nephews – you and your father had two partially-reconstructed JCBs, a 1930s steam engine perched on a set of rails only slightly longer than itself and a lovingly restored Matilda Tank.

Motors, then – anything Ryan told me about them was pretty reliable.

'Drug dealer?' I asked.

'Probably not,' he said. 'At least, not smack.'

I looked up at him, puzzled.

'No,' he explained, 'that lot would go for something a lot flasher – a top end Merc or Beamer, if not yer actual Porsche or Ferrari. Just to rub their homies' noses in their own inferiority.'

'Hmm... I see. Still, an Audi's a funny sort of motor to be parked outside Alice's place.'

His arm went over my shoulder and my head rested on a big melon of bicep – got by spending every spare moment hoiking bits of tank or steam engine all over the shop.

'Alice?' he asked.

'The girl who died. Cleared her place out this afternoon.'

'That where you found those CDs?'

'Yeah. One of them's by Death of Wallenstein. I think it might belong to her dad. Apparently, he used to know Neil.'

'Didn't her dad want to come and pick it up himself?'

'No. Don't think things had been too good between them for a long time.'

'If the girl was into smack, they won't have been, will they?'

'No. I reckon I ought to drop it in to him, though.'

'You sure?'

I paused. 'Hmm... No, I'm not. You never can be.'

'People can be funny buggers.'

'True.'

Very true. And especially true, it turned out, of Martin Icement.

The place where Alice had grown up was a long straight road on the very edge of the West Midlands. A thick old wood loomed over the houses to the west – the back gardens on that side would rarely be out of its shadow. Beyond the wood was open countryside, all the way to the Welsh Mountains. If you ended up here, most people said, you'd done all right: the semis were nice and the detached houses were even nicer, all less than sixty years old. You'd not see much change out of two hundred grand for any one of them. A place like this was about as far as most people could ever hope to get from the sort Sandwell bedsit where Alice had ended her life. All the same, round here you could live next door to someone for twenty years without ever talking to them.

It was a warm evening in April when I pulled up. Outside three of the houses, blokes were washing their cars. Outside another two, blokes were mowing the lawn.

Martin Icement was one of the blokes washing his car. Our conversation didn't last very long:

'Mr Icement?'

He made a peculiar little noise. I wasn't sure what it meant, so I tried again:

'Mr Martin Icement?'

That peculiar noise again. This time it sounded a bit more like a 'yes'.

'I'm very sorry to be bothering you right now... I know things must be difficult but... I thought you might want these. I knew Alice. I found them in her flat after she passed away. I thought one of them might belong to you...' I offered him the little CD case. 'I think you know one of the people in the band...'

Terrified, he drew back from the disc and stood trembling. After a horrible effort, he managed to get a few words out:

'Oh no... *Aha...* Oh no no no... *Aha...* I couldn't... *Aha Aha Aha.* Oh no I couldn't...'

It took me a moment to realise that the hiccoughing *'Aha'* noise was meant to be a polite laugh: I'd never heard anything less funny.

'Do you know when her funeral is going to be?' I asked.

He grimaced and was silent.

I'd been standing with my back to the house. I hadn't heard the front door open. But I did hear a level female voice say, 'It's on the fourteenth. Eleven o'clock, at Sandwell Crematorium. You'd be most welcome. Thank you for helping Alice.'

By the time I turned to look at the speaker, she'd closed the door again. All I could see was a greyish silhouette flickering away behind the misty glass.

Mrs Icement, Alice's mom.

I'd be very welcome, would I? It hadn't sounded like it. But I was going, all the same.

I turned and tried to thank Alice's dad but he'd already got back to washing his car, more frantically now – desperate, it seemed, to wipe me from his consciousness.

I was beginning to feel daft, standing there. Martin's soapy cloth squeaked like a mouse in a trap as he pummelled the car windscreen. Was this grief? It might have been, but to me it felt more like fear.

I looked down the road: blokes doing the mowing, blokes washing their cars – little or no eye contact between them.

Then, out of the corner of my eye, I saw Mrs Icement again. A face in the front window, very briefly. Too briefly for me to be sure what she looked like, though I sensed pride, dignity – and something darker. But she hadn't been looking at me.

I turned up the road, following her gaze, and at the end was a house, detached, not much different to half a dozen others in view. And the lawn was neat, but it didn't seem to have been mowed; it was as if the grass was terrified to put a blade out of place. And the car was clean, but it didn't seem to have been washed; it was as if the dust was terrified to settle on it.

And the car was a black Audi.

3: Satansfist

You know the sort of place: arse-end of town, Victorian redbrick; sometimes there's a nice original bar but that's usually long-nicked. And the choice of drinks is enough to assure you that you're being treated with contempt.

You know the sort of people: there are three or four types. The first lot's lives have proved pointless – so they've crawled in there to die. The second lot have the idea that the first lot's despair is a subtle wisdom – that might rub off if you get sufficiently pissed alongside them. The third lot just want to get off their heads. There may be another sort, dotted about in the afternoon – relics from earlier years, before the air in the place became unbreathable to anyone but the hopeless: usually quite old, sometimes very old, unaware of the decline in drinks, surroundings and company. They spend the day staring down into their Johnnie Walker Black Labels, dreaming of a time when the label was Red.

On certain nights, early in the week, a foreign element invades: little groups associated with a 'hobby' or 'interest'.

In this place, on Monday nights, you got the darts team; on Tuesday, there were the bridge players. On Wednesday, alas, it was poetry night.

I wouldn't have gone near the place, if it hadn't been for The Cunt.

It hadn't been me who'd turned round to him and said, *'Here, Cunt, me old matey, you can write poetry, you can!'* But someone had. Because he'd suddenly started beavering away and had recently squelched out a malodorous litter of versiform abortions that I'd somehow managed to read through and now had to sit through. What was on telly, Wednesday nights? It had to be better than this.

Things were slow to start. I walked in the place about eight, making no apology for looking like I could have bought it eight times over. Taste, as much as expense, accomplished this: the leather coat went down to my ankles, the matching trousers clung to me with the fervour of a wretched lover. And I worked out. And it showed.

The Cunt was there already, and gave me a pathetic smile. The organisers – an ill-adjusted couple in their mid-thirties – drifted in, grizzling over which of them was responsible for 'the event' not having been 'promoted' in the local papers. Their dishonesty was obvious: if the evening became popular, there'd be the danger that someone halfway decent might take the stage and make them look like the tossers they were. The stage – yes! – the place had one! It was about six inches off the bar floor, had two acceptably bright footlights and would have been big enough to accommodate a stripper on a Saturday night – assuming she was economical with her movements.

Three more losers shuffled in, clutching sheaves of crumpled, stained paper. One looked autistic, the others were dribblers. One of the dribblers brought along a bitter-eyed, bitter-mouthed woman of about fifty. Turned out, she was his care worker.

Two more appeared from somewhere and that was judged a good turnout. The last of the long-time regulars looked up from their M&B Milds, glanced at each other with horror and went into the lounge.

Off we went. One of the organisers – the female – took the stage and read a long, four-iambs-to-the-line, clangingly rhyming atrocity informing us that Nuclear Weapons Were Very Bad Things. By the time she'd finished, nukes seemed, to me at least, like the least worst option.

She followed this up with another, structurally similar piece about how The War In Afghanistan Was A Very Bad Thing. *Slaughter ragheads now,* I chuntered under my breath.

And she finished off with that ever-popular old fave at gatherings such as this: Men Were A Very Bad Thing. At least she got that right. Ho-hum.

A few announcements, off stage she went, introducing the first of the dribblers, who shuffled forward, smelling of piss and looking like shit. Dribbler One behind the mic, began thus:

> *'I bastard 'ate*
> *Them bastard wogs*
> *They come over 'ere*
> *They tek ahr jobs*
> *This place am agooin'*
> *To the God dogs*
> *So I'm movin' to Kingswinford*
> *Kingswinford, Kingswinford,*
> *I'm movin' to Kingswinford.'*

Much, much more in this vein. And a rare pleasure it was *not,* to hear the old hometown thus bigged up.

Nonetheless, these were clearly not the sentiments the organisers had in mind when they set the evening up. Amusingly, they began to squirm.

Sighs of relief when Dribbler One finally waddled off. Premature, as it turned out, because the place's NF Old Guard, sensing a sympathetic viewpoint, had reappeared in the bar, hoping for a few dollops more of *Mein Kampf* from the moronic. They weren't too happy when The Cunt took the stage and began to inflict his bum-ache.

It must be said, he didn't look too bad. If he had, I wouldn't have gone near him in the first place. 'Like a young Lou Reed' or 'a young David Gilmour' were two opinions I'd heard from people unashamed to reveal the contemptibility of their musical taste. The lace and the feather boas, the frilly shirts and the hair down to his arse (always immaculately washed and conditioned), I could have lived without but, in general, I'd done well this time. You wouldn't know he was gay; you certainly wouldn't know he was such a wretched little slag...

So it wasn't prejudice against his sexuality that provoked the response he got. It was, I'm afraid, all down to the standard of his material:

'Er... This is called... er... "The View from Saturn's Moon:"

*'It must be really dark out there. No sun
To speak of – scarce more than a star, its light
A distant lantern, telling you you've run
Too far from home, and that feels far from right.
Now, cautiously, away from capsule camp
You tread the ground that's really frozen air
Towards the low horizon. A vast lamp
Begins to be revealed, for here's where
The banded archway rises 'gainst the black
And then, within, a sphere so stately vast
Its white gold grandeur half the sky fills. Lack
Of chance of getting home? This trip's your last?
Perhaps, but is this sight not worth your death?
Thank God for it with your last frozen breath.'*

'You're shit! Fuck off! Bring the other bloke back on! At least he talked some sense!'
But The Cunt did not fuck off.
'Er... This one's called... "Schroedinger's Christ."'
And off he went; more of the same – only blank verse, so worse. The Old Guard were looking around for things to chuck.
At which point, my phone rang.
I glanced at the number: not one I recognised. I went outside to answer it.
'Hello?'
'Lee?'
'Who is this?'
'Don't try mucking me about, Lee; this is your mother.'
I couldn't be arsed remarking how blandly unmemorable her telephone voice had always been.
'Oh. Well. What d'you want?'
'Your sister's just died.'
'Mother, don't take the piss.'
'Well, if that's going to be your attitude...' – and silence. The frigid retard had hung up. Fine. If she thought she could fuck me about

26

like that, she'd got another thing coming... Then again, I supposed it was possible that the stupid twat of a smackhead *had* finally OD'd. I wasn't going to ring back to find out more so I supposed I'd have to check it out in the local paper. Shit! The worst thing about it was that I'd have to put up with the humiliation of buying the *Express and Star* – Dudley edition, even.

Re-entering the lounge, I found that the Old Guard had finally chucked something at The Cunt, giving him a nice little Jackson Pollockoid gash across his forehead, which did look rather fetching.

The organisers looked around for me and, as if wanting to provoke the Old Guard further, tried to push him into my arms. The gaffer of the place collared them and snarled that, from now on, they'd better take their evening elsewhere. They looked devastated and triumphant at once: he was providing a perfect little stage for the tawdry drama of their victimhood.

Meanwhile, Dribbler One was being accosted by some of the Old Guard who asked him why he didn't start running the poetry night himself? He grinned back at them, blissfully imbecile. The Care Worker (who belonged to Dribbler Two) tried to thrust herself into the conversation, suggesting that this would not be a good idea at all. The Old Guard began to eye her with M&B-infused, Jurassic malice. Some of their younger associates had shown up, Carling-soaked and Cretaceously aggressive. I couldn't see her escaping at least one broken leg before the end of the evening.

'Let's get out of here,' I said.

The Cunt looked at me, close to tears and with no will left but to obey.

I turned from him, knowing he would follow. Nobody noticed us leave or, if they did, they didn't care.

'Don't bring me out to one of those things again,' I grated, knowing that he would. He could never resist the opportunity to be humiliated.

He sniffed.

'I won't,' he croaked.

We went and found my car.

At home, we went to bed. We didn't have sex that night; there was nothing about him left to defeat, so what would've been the point? The gash on his forehead wasn't as bad as it had looked at first, so there was no need for hospital. I washed it with TCP and put a plaster on it.

***

Thursday, we were both at work for most of the day. I had the chance of a nice little commission to design a mural in Merry Hill and, spending most of the day schmoozing the folk with the money to pay for it, I'd convinced myself that I'd got the job by four o'clock.

Cringing, I dropped into a newsagent and bought an *Express and Star*. Leafing through it in the car, I quickly found the little article: 'Twenty-four year old Alice Icement... Flat in Wednesbury... Heroin overdose...' Ho-bloody-hum. Couldn't you have made a more original job of it? Why did you always have to be so bastard predictable?

Then again, why do any of us?

Sighing, I telephoned the number I'd been called from the previous night. Dad answered in his chronically terrified little voice.

'Hello, Dad. Is Mother in?'

I was advised that she was not.

'Do you know when the funeral's going to be?'

Dad's wretched squeaking informed me that, no, he did not know this - that he 'left that sort of thing to Mother'.

'Dad, that's shite and you know it. There'll be letters from the funeral directors in the sideboard. If you can't remember, look it up there.'

There was a broken little silence. Then I heard him shuffling off, presumably in the direction of the sideboard. Then:

'Fourteenth. Eleven o'clock. Sandwell Crem.'

'Right. I'll be there.'

I broke the connection. I did this with a touch of guilt. Dad had few pleasures. One of them was failure: failure to communicate, failure to get things done, failure to remember such trivia as the date of his daughter's funeral. It didn't matter – any sort of failure gave him the closest he ever got to a kick. But this time I'd fucked it up for him and he hadn't even succeeded in failure.

The fourteenth? Some way off. They were probably doing an autopsy, though the cause of Alice's death should have been obvious to any fool. An autopsy: the idea felt strange. An autopsy for Alice. Why should that bother me? We'd not known each other for years. If we ever had.

Back at our place, The Cunt was looking a bit more appetising. He'd got back from work before me and smartened himself up into something approaching shaggability. I did him the favour of stripping for him, which he savoured. Then I went to the drawer where we kept the gloves, choosing the best black leather ones with chrome spikes. His trousers were, by now, around his ankles. Glancing at the large jar on the bedside table, I noted we needed to splash out on more Vaseline.

'Come here…'

He hardly moved. He quivered a little and made pathetic, terrified noises.

'I said, come here!'

He began to shuffle, the trousers around his ankles making his movements ridiculous. After a minute or so, he was at my side.

'Now. Bend over.'

No response. Terror had shrunk his pupils to pinpricks. He began to snivel. I loved it when he snivelled.

'I. Said. Bend. Over.'

He moaned. It was a moan of terror and of lust. This was what he wanted.

'Cunt! Slag! Piece of shit!'

That's what I called him. That's what he was. That's what he wanted to be. Shaking with abject fear, he stood before me, bent forward and reached behind him to part his buttocks.

'Cunt! Slag! Piece of shit!'

I looked hard at the viciously-spiked black leather glove. The thing he feared. The thing he desired. Then I looked at his puckered opening. It spasmed and flexed, terror and need at war within it.

'Cunt! Slag! Piece of shit!'

It was time to remind him why I was known as SATANSFIST!

4: Mary Maitland

God bless my two little nephews! I was babysitting them for a couple of days while their mom was away at a women's self-defence convention and their dad was on tour (four dates, mostly in Nottingham) with the band. Mattie and Luke, aged six: a pair of twins further from being identical had never walked the face of the Earth.

'I think Mattie's going to be a gardener when he grows up,' I said, half to myself. I was doing the washing up, looking out the kitchen window as Mattie thrust his little spade into the vegetable patch.

'He is,' Luke replied from the lounge. His piping voice never suited the Deep Seriousness he always seemed to intend. He kept most of his attention on *Stephen Hawking's Universe* – which he was reading as if he understood it completely. I'd had a look at it and couldn't get past the introduction. Luke had taken no notice when I'd told him to get out into the sunshine with his brother but I couldn't be cross with him: he was in a world of his own.

'I,' the grave little astronomer announced, 'am going to establish a dialogue with Extra-Terrestrial civilizations.'

Well then, poof to careers advisors – both of them had their employment sorted (A part of me almost wished that was just a joke).

I looked back at the frying pan I was Brillo-padding: still a long way from lunar module shiny.

Luke, of course, wasn't only digesting physics – that would have been a shameful under-use of his busy little intellect. No, he had the telly on too, and had half an eye on an old movie from the seventies. It was one of his dad's fave DVDs – science fiction, of course.

We were getting close to the end and one of the characters was getting carried off by a set of twinkly disco lights. Back in the seventies, people seemed to think that aliens from other worlds would have a thing for disco. Out in the garden, Mattie looked up. Dropping his spade, he lumbered back towards the open French windows.

'Take your mucky shoes off, Mattie, before you...'

Too late. Muddy footprints, muddy handprints, beige carpet. We were definitely going to have to change that carpet.

'Phoenix Ast'oids!' Mattie cried, as he gazed, rapt, at the twinkling on the screen.

Luke glanced at him, glanced at the screen, then got back to his Hawking. Nothing strange about the scene as far as he was concerned.

Looking at the pair of them, though, something seemed odd to me. Mattie gazed at the screen for a minute or two, his mouth hanging slightly open, his eyes wide. Then he turned his head to his brother and stared for a longer moment, his expression changing to one I'd not seen on his face before, and I only saw once after. It was an unreadable look, not one you'd expect from a six year old lad with learning difficulties. But there was a touch of wonder in it.

He nodded his head, once, slowly, like a marionette. Then he seemed to come back to himself.

'Phoenix Ast'oids...' he whispered again, softly.

I got back to Brillo-padding the frying pan.

Things didn't lose that feeling of strangeness in the weeks that followed. Alice's funeral wasn't for another fortnight or so but my invite to speak at her mom's school had turned up and I was going to have to do that first.

I got there just after eight on a grey spring morning. Sixties-built schools in Sandwell tended not to look nice. My first impression of this one, though, wasn't too bad. True, it looked like it was made of Lego – they all did. The paint and the brickwork were cheap. The kids in such schools – and I'd been one myself — weren't expected to do very well.

But it was quiet in the playground. The kids were standing around talking. That's right, *talking* – as in *not shouting*. Some of the lads were playing football. They seemed to be taking particular care that the ball only went where it was supposed to... There was no danger of it whacking the back of my head by accident.

I locked the car and followed a sign to reception. I smiled at a couple of the footballers. To my surprise, they smiled back. But their smiles looked a bit... I don't know – a bit functional. There was no cheek in them but no feeling either.

Inside, you got the usual reception area with the low padded chairs nobody ever sat on and the big yucca plants in red clay pots. A woman behind a thick pane of glass looked up at me. There was neither welcome nor hostility in her face - just blankness.

'Hello, I'm Mary Maitland,' I said. 'I'm guest speaker in your Key Stage Four assembly. I think I need to speak to Mr Chiselhurst.'

Her face stayed blank. Her voice was just as emotionless: 'Please take a seat. Mr Chiselhurst will be with you shortly.'

The rarely-used chair creaked as I sat. I needn't have bothered because Derek Chiselhurst was through the door within seconds, brisk and efficient and full of apology for keeping me waiting. He was everything you'd want an assistant head in a tough inner-city school to be: early to mid-forties, handsome, spent a lot of time in the gym or the squash court or something. Good at his job. He was a bloke I'd be happy to work with but I'd be much cannier about ever starting to think of him as a friend.

He led me along corridors. There were a lot of notices on the walls, proclaiming exam successes, but very little in the way of pupils' art. Such pictures as there were, were very humdrum stuff. Still lifes, mostly - the GCSE grade awarded (A-Star in every case) was noted on a little label on each frame.

Mr Chiselhurst didn't give me much time to look, though. Within a couple of minutes, I was in the conspicuously tidy staffroom and somebody had gone to get me a coffee.

'Will I be meeting the Head Teacher?' I asked.

'Maybe not,' Mr Chiselhurst replied. 'She's quite busy today. Someone from the Department's in to see her.'

'The Department?'

'Department of Education. This is the most successful school of its type in the country,' he smiled very brightly. 'Everyone wants to know how we do it.'

I wasn't surprised at this: I'd heard their GCSEs were sky high.

'What's your five-or-more A to C percentage?' I asked.

'Ninety,' he replied.

That sounded good. In fact, given the catchment area, that sounded close to incredible. I nodded, and I could tell from Mr Chiselhurst's posture that he knew he'd impressed me.

An expressionless classroom assistant gave him a message from Mrs Icement. He shot off, telling me he'd be 'back in a mo'.' Left alone, I looked around a bit. There'd been a lot of departmental meetings the night before; laminated notices, saying when and where they were held, covered a big blue board at one end of the room. A good deal of coffee must have been drunk but the washing up had all been done, dried and put away. And my coffee, when it turned up, was offered to me in a clean mug. Have you ever been in a school staffroom? And forced yourself to look at the kitchen sink? And at the state of the crockery? If you haven't, you might not appreciate how odd this place was starting to seem.

Polite conversation in hushed tones. A sense of urgency, but no rush or panic. I heard 'CAFS procedures,' 'BOBS data' and two dozen other acronyms discussed in a most respectful manner. The snarly resentment-bordering-on-rage you get – rightly – from most teachers in relation to such stuff… it just wasn't there.

I went to the window and looked out.

Kids coming in at the sound of the bell: all neat, nobody fighting, nobody raising their voices.

'Miss Maitland?' Derek Chiselhurst was back. 'If you'd like to come down to the hall, I've a couple of prefects who're ready to help you set up.'

I necked my coffee and followed him. It was a bit of a relief to get out of that staffroom.

Derek Chiselhurst was different from the others. He was the charmer, the face of the place. He was there to talk to people like me so we'd walk away with a favourable impression.

He introduced me to the prefects he'd mentioned – two Year Eleven girls. They weren't the chatty, confident sort who usually get such jobs. They spoke when they were spoken to – in quiet little voices –

they avoided eye contact and they tried to hide behind their long hair. And there was something wrong with their mouths: the lips were tight and narrow – mouths that looked like wounds.

Efficiently, they set up a screen, a laptop and a projector: these girls were very competent. As speakers went, I was pretty low maintenance. I wasn't a born preacher like my dad or my elder brother, but I could talk to a crowd well enough with just myself and a basic PowerPoint, or even – at a pinch – with just myself alone.

'Thank you for your help,' I smiled at the girls. They made grateful, frightened noises and shot off.

I found a chair at the side of the stage, sat and waited until Mr Chiselhurst reappeared, a silent column of teenagers not far behind. There was a pin-stripey bank-managerial woman at his side who looked like she ought to be in charge of Business Studies but who he introduced as the Head of Drama.

The staff lining the hall during assembly were all very well dressed – rather expensively, in fact. And the men all had those pricey but horrible-looking short haircuts you see on the less sympathetic, loudly pro-Tory sort of police officer.

So I gave my talk about the things I'd seen drugs do, and it was a good talk because, thanks to people like their head's daughter, I knew exactly what I was talking about.

I'd expected a bit of kerfuffle when they heard what my job was. Teenagers can be horrors for gossip and I assumed they knew what had happened to Alice. I thought that, when I started, they'd be twisting round to see if Mrs Icement had come in and, if she had, what the look on her face was like.

I thought wrong.

They weren't completely inert. No teenager can be dead still, perched in a group of eight hundred, on a hard plastic chair – the sort that's either orange or brown: you'll have sat on a few of them. There was shuffling, sneezing, sniffing – lots of sniffing – and the odd noisy fart. That's a school assembly for you. They all had their spotty little faces pointed in my direction as I tried to plant some notion that These Things Can Kill You but, it seemed to me, I could have told them the sun was black and I'd have got the same passive acceptance.

I ended my session on time, or maybe a minute or two early; you go quicker in front of a quiet audience. Bank-Manager-Head-of-Drama took the stage and droned announcements at them. Then, row by row, they quietly left the hall.

The two little prefects rematerialised, wordlessly helpful as before. Inside two minutes, I was packed up and ready to go. I thanked them and they stared blankly back at me.

Derek Chiselhurst was at my elbow, still all smiles, and I sensed it was now a priority to get me off-site sharpish. The two prefects evaporated once more and the corridor outside the hall was as quiet as the Moon. The kids, with crushed resignation, had accepted the inevitability of Lesson One, in a way that a couple of thousand eleven-to-sixteen year-olds *just don't do*. Then:

Click Clack.

Shirley Icement's heels weren't high. But they weren't so sensible as to be conspicuous. They measured each pace across the hard, plastic-coated floor, regularly and deliberately, as she approached us, silhouetted by the cold morning light from a window behind her.

Click Clack.

At last, I got to have a good look at her. And she was worth a good look: a woman in her mid-to-late fifties, pale-grey-suited, pale-grey-haired. Hawk-nosed and elegant. Very, very hard-mouthed, though, and the flesh of her cheeks was sucked in against the determined shelves of the bones of her skull. About to reintroduce myself, I was cut off by her terse, disciplined smile.

'Hello, Miss Maitland. I am sorry I was unable to listen to you. I know your talk will have been appropriate. I must thank you again for the work you did with Alice.'

She permitted herself a little sigh. It was a very disciplined little sigh.

'I will see you at the funeral, I expect.'

I managed a quick 'Yes', in reply.

'I must go and collect our other visitor from the staffroom. Please contact the secretary if your expenses haven't been sorted out by the end of the week.'

By the end of the week? That'd be quick, I thought.

There were questions I wanted to ask but, before I had worked out what they were, she was gone. Ten minutes later, in the car and on my way back to the office, I could not stop thinking about her face.

It hadn't been like Alice's: Alice was her father's daughter. But there was something in it that I knew – perhaps from another face, perhaps only from an old photograph.

It was something to do with evil – and something to do with my family.

I thought she'd sensed my recognition. She'd dealt with me effectively enough – got rid of me before I had a chance to ask anything. She'd wanted me out of there and out I'd gone.

But I didn't like being *dealt with*. I especially didn't like being *dealt with* by people who needed my help but wouldn't admit it. Because, whatever it was that had made Alice Icement want to numb her life with heroin, it was in her mother, too. And, if somebody didn't do something, a little bit of it would wind up in every one of the two thousand-odd kids in Shirley Icement's care.

God had put me into the world to try – not always successfully – to stop stuff like that from happening.

***

The fourteenth came around: Alice's funeral. Sandwell Valley Crem was a tall pyramid with high windows. It was the sort of space that made people feel their prayers were getting somewhere. Now me, I didn't think I needed architectural contrivances to know where my prayers were going, but I knew there were people who did so it wasn't my place to criticise. I went with Polly Gauvain and we showed up late. Polly had insisted on driving and, at the last minute, had lost her car keys. I say late – we were just in time for the service. I was surprised at how many people had turned up.

In the car park, I'd noticed that black Audi again.

Shirley was in the front row. Next to her was Alice's dad. Next to him, there were a couple of long-haired guys. One of them I recognised, as he raised his black mane to re-tie it into a ponytail, as Alice's brother. Lee, she'd said his name was. He had his mother's beauty. Every plane and curve of his hawkish face was perfection. The other guy, chestnut-haired and with gentler features, whispered to him softly and submissively. A gay couple? They wore long leather coats, frilly shirts, tights or leggings and leather thigh boots – all black. Courting disapproval, it seemed to me.

In here, the force of Shirley Icement's presence was diffused. It seemed to drift up into the high bright space above the congregation, softened by the afternoon light from the big windows.

Not so the driver of the black Audi. He'd been waiting in his car and came in last of all. He sat behind us. Shirley Icement glanced round and seemed to notice him. She gave no sign of recognising Polly or me.

I decided I wanted to take a look at him.

Which I tried to do.

And which, at first, I was unable to do. And this, to me, was very surprising.

There are people in the world who have the knack of making you do what they want. And sometimes, you're not really aware of it. I'd come across a few of these people and some of them had made the mistake of trying it out on me. Apart from my dad, none of them had ever got away with it – until now.

Becoming quietly angry, I told myself that this bloke, whoever he was, wasn't going to get away with it either. I remembered the breathing exercises my sister had taught me, quietly did them, then calmly turned and smiled.

I saw a stern megalith of a man, well into his fifties, suited in dark brown with a brown leather coat. His face was long, straight-nosed and heavily lined under a mop of grey-streaked brown that, while washed and combed, seemed to have a life of its own. The eyes, hazel, shone with surprise. An ordinary-looking woman in her mid-thirties was not someone he'd expected to defy his will.

Beside me, I heard Polly make a noise. He didn't register her. I nodded at him and turned back to the service.

The priest, who I knew quite well, showed the polite sensitivity I'd expected. Alice's dad looked a bit confused. He kept glancing at his wife, searching for some clue as to how he ought to behave. She gave him none.

Eventually, it was over and we made our way out into the brightness of the afternoon. Sandwell Valley was green and English and, looking at it, I was able to pray for poor Alice who'd never in her life been granted the wonderland she deserved.

Jesus grant it her now. Jesus grant it her now.

Polly disappeared into the loo. While she was gone, I noticed Black Audi Bloke speaking to Shirley Icement. Their faces matched in severity and lack of emotion. I wasn't close enough to overhear much, but I caught her introducing him to someone: 'Our neighbour, Harry Ronsard.'

Harry Ronsard...

When she came back, Polly was very quiet. We were just getting back to her car when the Audi pulled out and headed for the main road.

'Wow,' Polly murmured.

I turned to her. I didn't like what I saw. Polly had been giving herself a hard time over Alice, as was only natural. Her self-respect was running low, and the look on her face was vulnerable: eyes wide, mouth open, prominent teeth making her look like a love-struck bunny rabbit. Tough-looking blokes had a bad effect on people like Polly, I thought, especially at times like this.

'He's got a bob on himself,' I grumbled.

'*A bob on himself:*' arrogance, ambition, the Pride of Lucifer.

I looked back at Polly; my words had not sunk in. She was still staring after the disappearing Audi, slack-jawed, wide-eyed, adoring.

I sighed. Harry Ronsard, Black Audi Bloke, was trouble. But getting Polly to understand as much might be beyond me.

'Do you know who he is?' Polly asked, her whisper hoarse.

'No, I don't...' I made myself reply. I heard the dishonesty in my voice; I hoped Polly didn't. I wasn't going tell her that he was a neighbour of the Icements. I wasn't going to tell her where to go looking for him. And I wasn't going to tell her his name.

'D'you mind if I have a quick fag?' she asked, nervously. I sighed but had to admit that today was the wrong day to be giving up.

She consumed the tobacco in hasty, sheepish little drags, smiled guiltily at me and moved to get back into the car.

She said little as we drove off but I could almost smell the infatuation through the cigarette smoke.

'Would you like to come in for a cup of tea?' I asked as we pulled up outside Ryan's.

She blinked, as if coming out of a trance and said that'd be 'nice.'

Ryan was working on something in the back yard. It was a big black thing with a boiler and a chimney and a lot of coal dust. Turned out, it was an old lift engine from a disused mine. And the daft sausage was getting it working – not because he had any use for it but because this was the sort of thing he just loved doing.

'Hey, Mary love, will you fish us out the Number Two Chinese Laundry Spanner?' he asked, without turning.

I'd been with him long enough to know which tool that was.

'Ta love,' he said as the big end of it landed in his outstretched palm.

It was only then that he registered we weren't alone. Turning, he said 'Oh – 'ello,' and I made the introductions.

I got the kettle on and he went back to his spannering. Polly and I stood in the kitchen doorway.

'How long have you been together?' Polly asked.

'Going on eleven years, all told,' I replied, 'Long story. We've been intending to tie the knot for most of that. Family bother put it off for a while. Then I got cold feet when I found out I couldn't have kids.'

Polly looked distressed. Ryan made a dismissive noise.

'But, as he says, I've got two nephews by my sister, a nephew and two nieces by my older brother and, as for Ryan's sisters…'

'*Enthusiastically* fertile,' Ryan said.

40

'Yeah, so…'

Ryan found something to wallop with a hammer. Nothing could spoil his mood when he was walloping something with a hammer, but the cheerful musical clanging made conversation difficult; we moved back into the kitchen.

'So, as far as the next generation's concerned, our families have got it all pretty sorted.'

Polly couldn't shake off her expression of pity. But there was something else in her face, too. Ryan and I had got to the stage where our relationship was like a huge and lovely joke. Polly seemed to sense this and she looked at us with an expression I knew from many an alcoholic who was being offered a drink of plain water: thinly disguised terror and revulsion. What was between Ryan and me, to Polly, looked like poison.

After she'd gone, I continued to worry about the bloke in the black Audi. I thought I should find out a bit more about him.

Where did you go, round here, if you wanted the background to any local mystery or dodginess? One place only: Dave Calper's bookshop.

Dave Calper, bass player in The Death of Wallenstein, had been running his little second hand bookshop since the seventies and, by now, was pushing seventy himself. The shop was part of a terrace of cottages in Brettel Lane, Amblecote, dating back to the 1740s. Dave was Rock Music itself – one hundred per cent pure. Long white hair, droopy moustache and wide, staring eyes.

You went into the paperback lined gloom and, if you'd been in more than twice before, you were a regular and you qualified for a mug of tea. True, the mugs looked a bit grim and the brew was strong enough to make most people wince, but it was all part of the 'Dave's Place' experience.

So, the following Saturday afternoon, I was sipping my dark brown spoonmelter and asking him if he knew anything about Harry Ronsard?

'The bloke with the murals!' was his surprising reply. 'Used to be a builder. Packed it in when his wife got sick…'

Forty years in the West Midlands and Dave still talked pungent East London. My sister reckoned he sounded 'cultured,' but I couldn't hear it.

'Murals?'

'In his house. All over the walls and ceilings. He got his neighbour's lad to do them. Lee Icement.'

I must have twitched a bit at that, which Dave spotted straight away. 'D'you know him?' he asked.

'I knew his sister Alice. Professionally. She died a few weeks back.'

'Yeah, I heard. Smack, was it?'

No reason to hide it, so I gave a little nod. 'What's these murals, then?' I asked.

'Lee painted them a few years back. Not the sort of stuff you'd think he'd do but he was pretty young back then – maybe seventeen, eighteen. Harry had just lost his wife. Lee used to come in here quite a bit, after art books. He started off with the Burne-Jones illustrations for William Morris: knights, damsels and dragons. That stuff really got to him. You should see that black dragon he put in Harry's lounge!'

'You got to see them?'

'Lee took me round there to show me 'em. Just the once, though Harry didn't seem to mind. Harry came to one of our gigs a while later, which was odd. Wouldn't have thought it'd be his cup of tea...'

'These murals, though, they don't sound like the sort of stuff people put on their walls in Kingswinford.'

'Bloody right they're not. Harry's got a thick set of lace curtains, though, so nobody notices, and I don't think he has many visitors. Just his daughter, who's a dyke. She had a fling with...'

He paused a little.

'Don't tell me,' I sighed, 'your seductive keyboardista.'

Dave nodded. The Death of Wallenstein's keyboard player. My sister's ex. Who'd also had a brief and unwise thing with my elder brother. And with many many others. A right madam.

'There was something about Harry's family, though... let me think,' Dave mused. Then he scrambled over book piles into the back and logged on to his clunky old computer. I picked up a book about black holes and flicked through it, deciding to get it for Luke.

'Bloody Hell!' Dave cried, suddenly, 'I knew there was something but... Bloody Hell!'

'What is it?' I asked.

Dave was looking at a genealogical website which told us that Harold Lewis de Lantenac Ronsard had been born in 1947 (older than he looked) to Henry David Ronsard and Genevieve Audrey Ronsard *née* de Lantenac.

'The guy's a de Lantenac!' he whispered, horrified.

'What's that mean?'

'His family... His mum's family. Ultras, old French nobs. Go back hundreds of years. Bad reputation. Not like de Sade: it's all in the name of God and King and Country. But go looking in French history – anywhere you find a pile of bodies ten feet high, all butchered in the name of Jesus, there'll be a de Lantenac not far off.'

I thought about his words, holding them up to the image of the man I had briefly and wordlessly met. They fitted. Too well. A man who lived in a house with fantasy on every wall and ceiling. A man whose family had a history of mass murder – and mass murder in the name of some perverted idea of God: the worst kind of murder of all.

'Watch it with him,' Dave said, levelly, turning away from the screen. 'Don't judge anyone by their family but this guy... He's got some very bloody roots...'

'I'll be careful.'

And I left the shop, clutching little Luke's black hole book to me as if its rationalism was a shield.

5: Dave Calper

'Who's going to put him back together?'

Nobody answered.

'We're going to have to send him somewhere to have him put back together.'

Still nobody answered.

Then there was a noise like somebody swallowing hard.

'Come with me, David,' said Gran.

And she took my four-year-old hand in hers and pulled me away.

I didn't argue. I was a quiet little kid.

There was no doubt it was her son's left hand: he'd lost the ends of two fingers in a factory accident and the skin where they'd healed was shiny, like it was polished. Poor old Gran – she must have wished there'd been a chance I could mistake it for somebody else's. But no – it was Dad's. If she'd not had me to look after, she'd have gone searching for other bits of him. There must have been a fair few scattered across the bluey-grey cobbles of our street, all mixed up with bits of Mum and bits of the neighbours and bits of the houses and bits of the V2. As it was, Gran walked quietly away, face very still, not holding my hand too tightly, but just tightly enough for me to feel like I was going to get taken care of.

Thanks a fucking bunch, Werner.

Whatever it was that Gran had swallowed, that dull afternoon in '44, she somehow managed to keep it down – pretty much for the rest of her life. Soon I stopped asking who was going to put Dad back together. Over the months and over the years, an awareness that nobody could ever do it soaked in, without me noticing. I didn't cry about it. Couldn't. I didn't have space inside me for the feeling that was needed to do that.

Instead, I remained a quiet kid.

1956 and there was Elvis, and I bought a guitar and practised and learned all the Scotty Moore parts. But it was an acoustic guitar and I practised upstairs, so I didn't upset Gran. I started playing with bands and made a lot of friends. Gran never minded that – when you don't have any family, you learn to value friends.

It never meant that much, back then. The tunes were a laugh and you got to pull the birds. You even wound up making a few bob and since it was more fun than driving a forklift, I said ta-ra to the forklift. But it didn't seem like it was anything life-or-death.

Then came '64.

Then came the Wolf.

Don't know if I'd heard the records before I saw him live. If I had, I'd not been paying enough attention. Everything from that night is a complete blur apart from the music itself so I'm sorry, I can't tell you what venue it was or anything. When his band started up, the music straight away pulled me from the bottle blonde I'd been chatting up and nailed my eyes and my ears to the stage. This was going to hurt and I knew it.

Mr Chester Burnett, Mr Howlin' Wolf, started singing; his music strode into my head like it owned the place – which of course it did – and started opening up new spaces. It wasn't gentle about the way it did so; it knew it needed not to be. And the Wolf's first harmonica solo kicked its way into the core of me and explained to me, very very clearly, exactly how I'd been feeling for the past twenty years about seeing my dad's severed, bloodless hand on the cobbles.

After the show, when I tried to walk out, I fell over. Some of my mates had to carry me, laughing at how pissed I was (I'd had one pint). My legs kept giving way, there were tears streaming down my face and, they reckoned, I was singing, wordlessly, the tunes of every harmonica solo the Wolf had played that night.

By the time I got home, I could just about stand up. I went straight to bed, slept like a log and made it down to breakfast by seven.

Gran looked at me over the teapot. Then she looked again – harder. 'Heard some… strange music last night, Gran…'

She was quiet for a bit, still staring at me. There was a look on her face… I don't know… I've got no word for it apart from 'relief.'

'I'm glad you managed to get home all right, David,' she said.

And from the sound of her voice, she'd been waiting for me to get home all right for a very long time.

Eighteen months later, she was dead.

During those eighteen months, I'd switched from guitar to bass. Not sure how that happened but it probably had most to do with what vacancies were coming up in what bands. And by then, John Entwhistle and Jack Bruce were proving the bass didn't have to be in the background anymore.

I splashed out on a big old stand up acoustic, though I was never going to be no Danny Thompson. Then the whole psychedelic thing kicked off and I was there from the start. I knew Syd – vaguely. One day, June '66, he gave me a ring and asked me if I wanted to get down to Sound Techniques? 'Cause there was a session going on there done by a bunch of ex-Westbrook geezers. Course, I was there like a shot – I mean, anybody with anything to do with Westbrook, always gonna be worth a listen. And it was AMM and they were doing *Later during a Flaming Riviera Sunset* and all that stuff. It still sounds a bit weird to most people today but back then – bleedin' 'ell!

After, I was heading back to the tube with Syd and he was saying he might try out something like what we'd just heard and I said, 'Okay, mate, you've got a bloody good electric blues band on the go but do you really think you can mix it up with stuff like that? I mean, that was some scary shit, man!' But he was saying, no, he was sure he could get it to work. And I remember I said to him 'Well, I suppose if you got it right, there might be a bob or two to be made out of it…'

Understatement of the millennium? Just a bit.

And it was about then that I met Wilf Reynolds.

A percussionist, he was doing Latin stuff, working with some of the big bands – Jack Parnell in particular – but he'd been into people like Skip James, Robert Johnson and Muddy Waters a long time before anybody else over here. He used to go to the States with his work, back at the end of the war and in the late forties, early fifties. So even though he was a good twenty years older than us, he liked the right sort of thing. Everybody else his age was screaming about how

46

depraved the Stones were, but he'd just shrug his shoulders. He'd got wa-ay dirtier versions of any of their old blues covers. By people like Muddy, John Lee and, of course, the Wolf.

So anyway, here was me and Wilf, and we got a nice little rhythm section together. Plenty of work around at that time but out of the blue we got offered a gig at what was supposed to be this massive new psychedelic venue in Birmingham.

Now Wilf didn't think it was going to come to anything but, thing was, he came from West Brom and had kids still living round there. So in spite of his misgivings, we decided to chance it and move on up the Mercian Metropolis.

The highly anticipated psychedelic whatchamacallit lasted about six months. Bleedin' Kozmik...

Once it had all imploded, though, Wilf was finding he was really comfortable living upstairs at his daughter's and I had my own reason for wanting to stick around... Well, her name was Miriam. Though, back then, she was calling herself 'Starshine.' We did that sort of thing in those days.

By the time Starshine-and-me was a thing of the past, Wilf wasn't too well. He lasted until the mid-eighties but he didn't play much after about Seventy-two or Seventy-three.

So, all things considered, I might have moved back down the Smoke, if I hadn't met Neil.

Except, to start with, it wasn't just Neil – it was Neil and Martin.

Neil wasn't that great a guitarist at that stage, but he had a very open pair of ears. Chuck anything decent at him and he'd spot what was worth picking up on.

Martin was the intense one. On his tape, he says he never knew why he was making those field recordings. It's not true; he knew exactly what he was after. I'm not saying he was lying though. By the time he recorded that tape, he'd spent a long time forcing himself to forget anything apart from the joys of getting mindlessly pissed. But, when I knew him, he was into those recordings. He only ever used a cassette player – God only knows what he might have done with a decent reel-to-reel. But he knew how the thing worked, and he found no end of different ways of over-dubbing, slowing down, speeding up – things you weren't supposed to be able to with cassette. I could imagine him in a corner of the stage, behind his nest of cassette decks and reel-to-reels and God knew what, making that stuff a massive part of the music. But then he and Neil met that bloody Mick Anderson and it all went downhill fast. It did no good me or Wilf telling Martin that the guy was just a loud-mouthed pisshead. Or that he'd collected a little clique of the sad, the broken and the insecure, and taken it upon himself to do their thinking for them. Neil clocked what was going on pretty quick but he hung around for Martin's sake. Once it was clear Martin wasn't budging, Neil bailed out.

So that was about Seventy-three. Sad times for us. We'd really wanted Martin on board and we were gutted he cut us off the way he did. And though we never gave up hope that Wilf would get well enough to start playing regularly again, we always knew it wasn't going to happen.

By that time, to earn a bob on the side, I'd opened up the bookshop. Art books and music books were a speciality. I knew how to shift second-hand sheet music, which not a lot of dealers could, so I did all right.

Neil and me kept it going over the years, though we never got that recording deal we were after. By the time we were able to put our stuff out (cassette only, to start with) we had a tasty back catalogue to choose from. Sound quality wasn't too bad either, on most of the stuff. Okay, okay – that does not apply to *Live at JB's, February 4th 1976,* but, if you've still got one of the bloody things and want your money back, just get in touch and spare me any further embarrassment. Please.

We had a couple of singers with us at different times during the 80s, but neither of them lasted. Then, in about Ninety-six, we were sweating away in Dave Donovan's rehearsal space, just round the corner from mine, and the door opened. We were a bit surprised by this – in Donovan's, when the door's shut, daylight's in short supply. If someone lets the stuff in unexpectedly, it can be pretty disorientating. Bloody hell though, in walked this lad, fourteen years old, with a flute and a cheeky grin.

'So you're the band, then,' he said.

And I recognised his voice from..? From where exactly? We looked at each other, and at him, and we realised he'd been at a couple of gigs, lately, lemonade in hand and trying hard to blend into the background.

And it was Andy.

Wilf's grandson – Andy.

Well, we'd got the old team back together, hadn't we? No stopping us. Five or six years as a three piece, loads of gigs around Stourbridge and Birmingham. A few down in Worcester, too. Mostly good. We got to do some support slots at the Robin and made a few decent contacts.

Then in 1998, I met Martin's son.

I was in the front of the shop and it felt like the temperature had suddenly dropped a few degrees. I looked up. There was this kid, seventeen or eighteen, scowling his way through a book on the Pre-Raphaelites. He was having a hard job knowing how to take it. You know that look people get when they're born to love something but they don't know how to go about it? The games they play with 'irony' and 'denial,' and all the other names we give to what we should be calling plain old 'bollocks'. He was trying to curl his lip into a sneer but it was refusing to twist the way he wanted and that was driving him bonkers.

'Burne-Jones is a better painter than a lot of people give him credit for,' I said.

He turned round, trying to look cool. And, I'll be honest, making a better job of it than most people of seventeen manage.

'Not really my sort of thing,' he drawled, 'But my neighbour's asked me to do something along these lines for him. Arthurian. Heroic.'

The mix of irony and relish he poured on to the word 'heroic' was a giveaway: *'You're gay,'* I thought, *'And you've got the hots for this neighbour of yours – got 'em good and proper.'*

49

'Burne-Jones is a good place to start, if you want *heroic*,' I told him. 'What sort of thing's your neighbour after? Oil on canvas? Woodcut?'

'Murals.'

'Ey?'

'Murals. On the walls. On the ceilings. He wants me to cover the whole place with them.'

'Murals of King Arthur?'

'That's what he needs. I told him what I had in mind. He reckoned it sounded alright.'

'You're telling me your neighbour just came up to you and told you that he wanted you to cover his walls and ceilings with Arthurian murals?'

'Pretty much. It was my sister who actually gave me the message.' He paused. 'It does sound unlikely, doesn't it?'

His blank matter-of-factness spooked me. And, the more I looked at him, the more I sensed something familiar. Something a bit worrying…

'He's an unusual man,' he explained. 'I sometimes think he doesn't belong on this planet.'

'If he wants his whole house covered with Arthurian murals, I guess that's fair comment.'

He grinned at that. And I grinned back. I was starting to like the lad, despite being nervous of him.

'Where does he live, then?' I asked.

'Barratt Road, Kingswinford,' he said.

My mind went blank – for quite a while, to be honest, because that piece of information took a bit of processing.

'Kingswinford?'

'Yes.'

'Kingswinford?'

'Yes.'

I struggled to find the words to explain how astonished I was.

'A bloke wanting murals of King Arthur all over his house may or may not belong on this planet,' I finally said. 'But he definitely –

definitely – doesn't belong in bleedin' Kingswinford.'

He laughed. I laughed.

'It's my fondest hope,' he drawled, 'that the neighbours will be so shocked, their haemorrhoids will burst.'

***

Let me tell you about Kingswinford.

Back in the 1950s, there'd been a move afoot in England to clear everybody out of inner cities. The old back-to-back houses and tenement blocks had been breeding grounds for cholera, TB, you name it. But what really got folk moving was the immigrants coming in – mostly the Irish at first, but the Afro-Caribbeans and the Indians weren't far behind. There was bound to be bother, and you got the predictable bunch of villains – an evil sod called Powell was the worst of them – out to stir it for their own advantage. The upshot was that the inner-city whites upped sticks and moved out to the suburbs – where nice new estates got thrown up all through the fifties, sixties and seventies.

They moved out of fear. Fear of who and what they didn't understand, which is a bad reason to go looking for a new home. And they moved, family by family, in dribs and drabs. Many many communities smashed themselves up that way – brother in Solihull, sister in Sedgley, mum and dad still in Smethwick – and they were never put back together.

In these new places, these nice little semis, folk lived next to people they didn't know from Adam, and had jobs half an hour or an hour away by car. With the telly, there was no particular reason to step out of their front doors once they'd got home in the evening.

The birth of English suburbia – mile after mile of sealed up dwelling capsules full of frightened, isolated people. No good was going to come of it.

Kingswinford was one of those suburbs. South of Wolverhampton, West of Birmingham. A little village in the Domesday Book, swamped by the spread of the big towns. And living in the shadow of...

Yeah, now I've got to tell you about Cally Wood.

I'm not saying the place is evil. Definitely not. I'm not even saying it's haunted. Well, maybe not exactly.

But it is... funny.

There are places that tend to... take what you bring to them and give it back to you. But give it back in a concentrated form. You go there on a summer evening, look west, out over the fields to the Shropshire hills. There's nowhere more beautiful. And listen to the noise the wind makes. It kisses your ears. It cleans your head.

Five hours later though, after it's got dark, you do not want to be there. You may think you ain't superstitious, you don't believe in ghosts, but you try spending a night on your own up in Cally Wood. You'll've changed your mind by the time the sun comes back up, for a cert. In the meantime, you'll've shat yourself.

Shat yourself? At what?

Look at the name, kiddies, look at the *name*...

Back in the seventies, when I first moved in round here, I noticed the name 'Cally' aerosoled on a few walls and billboards up Kingswinford. Thought it was just some hard knock's name. Then, this bloke who knew his local history clued me up. It was referring to 'Cally Wood.' And it was put up there by a set of local wide boys – skinheads most likely – calling themselves the 'Cally Wood Mob.'

Up the wood was where they used to go with their Party Fours and their bottles of Strongbow to have a bonfire and shag their birds. A hard bunch – nothing in the league of the Brummie or Wolverhapton lots, but a hard bunch.

So they took their name from a wood that had got its name many years before...

Don't really know how long ago, maybe hundreds of years, but there was once a gypsy camp up Cally Wood. The north end of the place, next to where Summerhill School is now. The trees at the north and south ends are older than the ones in the middle. If they could talk...

Hmph! If they 'could' talk!

Get it right.

If they *chose to* talk.

Go have a wander round the place – you'll see what I mean.

Anyway, the lads among the gypsies used to call themselves 'Cally boys,' meaning 'hard knocks,' or 'wide boys', that sort of thing. The name stuck and it's wound up getting applied to the whole wood, not just the bit where the camp was. Sure, the name you find on the OS map is 'Ridge Hill Wood', but none of the old-time locals ever call it that. And it's kept its aura of aggro. 'Cause the gypsies, remember, the Roma were originally an Indian bunch. And, when they came out of India, they brought their gods with 'em. And who's the old Indian Goddess of Time and Death? Who's the black-faced babe with the bloodthirsty tongue? And the sharp looking scimitar and – just in case you're in any doubt – the severed head to show just what she done with it?

That's right: Madam Kali.

Not a girl you want to get on the wrong side of.

And she walks there, at night. You don't need to be Roma or Hindu to feel her. Too many people have given her name to those trees for her not to have taken root.

Now, I know you'll be laughing at the thought of a bunch of white skinheads in the seventies giving themselves the name of a Hindu goddess. Poetic justice.

And those of you who know a bit more about Hinduism might be ready to point out that there's more to Kali than death and destruction. Indeed, in the greater scheme of things, she's one of the good guys. I'm sure that's right and if you go up Cally Wood to watch the summer sun go down behind the Clee Hills, you'll see that she can't be a bad bird. But she's not the first aspect of God you want to go praying to, if you've got a wrong that needs righting. Try doing that, there'll be blood for supper.

Cally Wood's on the western edge of Kingswinford – on those beautiful summer evenings, she casts her longest shadow. The sun disappears into her leaves and branches, long before it's set behind the Clees.

There is no such thing as a Kingswinford sunset.

**

Lee Icement started coming in the shop quite regularly. I had plenty of art books and he spent a fair few quid on them. I hadn't known Martin that well, so I didn't make the connection between the two of them. Neil was sharper. We were getting things ready for a rehearsal, one Saturday afternoon, when Lee swanned in. I'd put a Paul Klee hardback at the top of a pile in anticipation of him and he swooped on it.

Neil glanced at him, did a double take and said:

'You're Martin Icement's son, aren't you?'

The look Lee shot him was poisonous.

I tried to rescue the situation. 'Your dad,' I said, 'used to be into music. Tape collages.'

Lee was very quiet. It was a few moments before I realised he was dumbfounded.

'He never got back into that stuff, then?'

Lee shook his head.

'Pity,' I sighed.

'I had… no idea he'd ever been… interested in anything like that.'

'He was,' Neil told him, 'Once…'

Lee snapped the Klee book shut and bought it. He told me to keep an eye out for any Frank Auerbach and left. In no apparent hurry.

Well, he carried on coming in and I carried on selling him the books. I didn't make the mistake of trying to talk about his family. As a result, we wound up getting on.

Around 2003 our band went from a three piece to a four piece – or a five piece, depending on the availability of Madame la Keyboard. It was just after then that I met Mary Maitland.

She was well pissed off, that first time. She came banging into Donovan's, where four of us were rehearsing. Briefly and disgustedly, she looked at the drummer. From his descriptions, I recognised her as his sister-in-law. This was before her keep-fit-kung-fu-superhero sister got her into all the exercise and self-defence. Mary was still a nineteen-stoner and not happy to be so. But even then, she *looked* as if she could do you serious damage. And we'd all heard how she'd punched the lights out of some right-wing arsehole at her dad's church. After a moment, it seemed, she decided she wouldn't be able to talk to her brother-in-law without walloping him round the head with his floor tom. To everybody's relief, she turned to me instead:

'Kindly inform your *percussionist,*' (word pronounced as if it was a synonym for *total wanker*) 'that, should he be bothered to come with me – *right now* – to the maternity unit, he will find he's the father of twin boys. And their names are Luke and Matthew. *Not...*' she paused venomously, 'Holger and Irmin.'

Much panic and frenzied apology as the drummer discovered he'd let the battery on his mobile go flat. Oops.

The gig we were rehearsing turned out to be one of our better four-piecers. I tried to get Lee Icement to come to it – not least because he was the album-cover artist we'd always dreamed of – but... well, we were nowhere near fashionable enough. I couldn't help but be happy for him though: his work was starting to get known and murals were going up on quite a few walls around the Midlands – beautiful stuff. A couple of years after, to nobody's surprise, he hooked up with Lewis Gladrell. You'd see them around the place, Lewis clinging to Lee, desperate, and unable to believe he'd got hold of a guy who looked like *that.* By now, Lee was in his mid-twenties. I still wasn't hearing anything about his family. I knew about Martin. I knew there was a sister, too. I assumed there was a mother, though she seemed especially unmentionable.

But the cold that Lee brought with him, the first time he stepped into the shop, didn't go away with his later visits. And the name 'Icement' isn't very common. So, when I read in the local paper that a girl called Alice Icement had OD'd on smack, I knew who it was.

6: Satansfist

'Harry,' simpered Alice, 'wants you to do some paintings on his walls.'

'What?'

'Murals, frescoes, paintings on his walls. And his ceilings. He asked me to ask you.'

She tipped her head to one side and gave me that stupid grin she used to pull. She thought it looked 'cute'. It looked bloody annoying.

'Harry down the road was talking to you?'

'Yes.'

'There's a first.'

She looked wounded. When 'cute' didn't work, she'd always switch to 'wounded.' It was still bloody irritating. But it suited her better.

'Harry's my friend,' she whined, pathetically.

I could have taken the piss. That would have been the obvious thing to do but to be frank, I could rarely be arsed to take the piss out of Alice. It was like kicking the shit out of a wide-eyed bushbaby when it was already dead.

I had no idea though, how she'd got it into her head that Harry Ronsard wanted me to get a paintbrush anywhere near his walls or ceilings. Because that crazy fuck had never belonged on this planet. I'd known it when I was growing up and everything I'd seen of him since his wife died suggested he was getting worse. Him and his hatchet-faced bull dyke of a daughter.

So I suppose, it was ghoulish curiosity that led me to follow Alice as she skipped and pirouetted up the road to Harry's. This was 1998, and she still had one of those crappy 'walkman' things with a cassette in. She was pirouetting to Ozric Tentacles. I swear people ought to be shot for listening to Ozric Tentacles.

At Harry's place, she stopped listening to Ozric Tentacles. Because Harry had Wagner on – full blast.

Ever hear how Wagner wanted to stage *The Ring*? At the end of the final opera, he wanted the Palace of the Gods to burn down. He wanted the whole stage to burn down. He wanted the whole theatre to burn down. He wanted the singers and the orchestra and the audience and old Frau Scheisskopf who sold ice cream in the interval to fucking die!

You can't argue with that – that's class, that is. Wagner is music that's in love with death. I've always loved music that's in love with death. Do you suppose Ozric Tentacles have ever contemplated massacring their entire audience? No bastard way – the pathetic wankers.

The weird thing was, as the Wagner came to an end and the strings played the last tune of the whole nineteen hours, I looked at Alice. And, for a second, the tune seemed to be about her. Though I could tell she did not like it.

Harry was standing on the hearthrug in the front room, taking in the music and taking in my reaction to it.

Every inch of wall and ceiling was pure, brilliant white. And my paintbrush could resist all that Dulux virginity about as easily as my tongue could resist a cute twink's arsehole.

'Hear that?' Harry snarled.

'Loud and clear.'

'Understand it?'

'Yes.'

'Really?'

'One hundred per cent.'

He paused.

'I want it on my walls. And on my ceilings,' he growled.

'No problem.'

'Really?'

'Really. I'm fucking good, I am.'

His eyes narrowed.

'I don't like swearing,' he said. 'Swearing is disgusting. It wants stopping.'

'I swear a lot.'

57

'Not in my house, you don't.'

I paused. And I looked at the walls and at the ceilings.

'It's a deal,' I replied.

At the extreme right corner, about half a centimetre of his mouth twitched briefly upwards. This was as close as he ever came to a broad grin.

'I thought it might be,' he said.

On the way back to Mum and Dad's, Alice had Ozric-bastard-Tentacles back on her fucking Walkman. I swear I'd've strangled her with the headset lead if I hadn't had more important things to think about.

White, white space. To me, it was yearning for images of big guys with big muscles and big fucking longswords. Yeah... Yeah... I reckoned I could cope with that. I knew I'd have plenty of commissions that would be far less appealing.

So – research. Back then, the internet wasn't much good so I headed down the nearest second-hand bookshop. 'Burne-Jones,' recommended Dave the bookseller, so Burne-Jones I checked out.

Christ, that beggar-maid's a slag, isn't she?

Poor old King Cophetua! He hasn't got a fucking chance! All those wide eyes and tits half hanging out! But don't be taken in, Cophie, me darlin'! She's got all her orifices bunged up with chastity, though she'll string you along for decades, vaguely implying that you might – eventually – find your way up one or two of 'em!

And the slut in *Love among the Ruins* is worse! She doesn't even make the effort to get her bloody tits out. And the guy in that one is gorgeous! You would. The lot of you – I don't care what you think your sex or your orientation is – you bastard well would!

So I got into the paintings of Burne-Jones – I think you can see how.

Round to Harry's I went, with paints, brushes and a few sketches, Alice skipping along beside me. This time she'd got Kate Bush on the Walkman: again, music deserving the death penalty – with the possible exception of *The Dreaming*.

I stood before a big white wall, looked at it, looked at it a bit more, looked at it a bit more still, and kept my mouth shut. Alice was twittering away at Harry and he didn't seem to be taking any notice of her. Then, to my surprise, he turned round and gave her another one of those twitches of the corner of his mouth that he used instead of a smile. He must have liked her, somehow, because his face rarely compromised in its utter contempt for change of expression.

I began to flick through my sketchbook. There was a fair attempt at a Sir Lancelot, influenced, I must admit, as much by the movie *Excalibur* as by anything from the tradition itself. I got out a blue pencil and held it, an inch or two from the Dulux. Here was the moment when I expected Harry to balk. Somebody bringing mystic Camelot to his pristine Kingswinford white wall? Unacceptable, surely! But he said nothing. And Alice had gone quiet, too. I didn't turn round. I drew the first pale blue line – the muscular curve of Lancelot's spine, from arse to neck. The pencil made a soft scraping.

And I was off. Half an hour later, the outline of a figure had taken shape and I knew I'd captured the flow and the movement of the colossal, beautiful thing I wanted to create. I was making him and I was falling in love with him at the same time. You do, at times like that. Reality is such a pile of wank by comparison.

I turned, finally. Harry and Alice had not moved. Harry's face was immobile. If he hadn't liked what was happening to his wall, he'd have let me know by now. He didn't fuck about. Alice's face – very weird, this – was just as immobile as Harry's. Her eyes might have been beggar-maid wide, but there was nothing slaggy about them. She was looking at the pale blue lines and what those pale blue lines were creating and, just for once in her pointless life, she was understanding. Fucking unbelievable.

'I reckon,' Harry rumbled, 'we can leave you to get on with it.'

Alice smiled at him. He nodded at her. And they left me to get on with it.

Two weeks later, I'd been spending most of my time round Harry's and I was getting close to having his front room sorted. The same, however, could not be said of my 'A' level assignments. My mother took enough notice of my existence to make it clear that This Would Not Do At All, so, to keep the frigid old bag off my back, I regretfully cut the amount of time I was spending up the road, enough not to get kicked out of that bloody grammar school.

'I knew you'd get on with Harry,' Alice chirped, one afternoon, just after I'd done what was necessary to get into Falmouth.

'We don't *get on*,' I sighed. 'It's just that he's got enough sense to realise that I know what I'm doing.'

She smiled at me as she stuck something typically shite by Suzanne Vega into that bastard Walkman.

'For you two,' she said, 'that constitutes getting on.'

I forget what had brought her round to Barratt Road, that afternoon. She'd moved out a couple of years before to go and live with some foul-smelling crusty who claimed to be a poet. Mother had been less appalled by this than I'd expected. In fact, she gave no indication of having noticed enough to give a shit.

I looked up at Alice from my sketches. There were getting to be quite a few of them.

Murals from Mordor, frescoes from Gormenghast, metal lighting fixtures like the shields of Hengest and Horsa's invading armies – you name it, I was coming up with it. And the world I was depicting was one where I knew Harry would feel at home – not a mountain range (and there were lots of mountain ranges) without a dragon brooding, not a lofty tower without a damsel in distress. The dark woods all had plenty of giant spiders to keep you going, and the port towns no end of bloodthirsty buccaneers.

But, for me, the centrepiece remained that drop-dead gorgeous Lancelot I'd first come up with – dark, curling hair, wide jaw, all in black leather that clung to his muscles in a way that never failed to give me a stiffie. That figure was completed now, and almost three-dimensional. Even Alice was impressed; given her apparent taste in men, I hadn't expected that at all.

'I think,' she went on, hesitantly, 'you might have saved Harry's life.'

She must have known how unlikely that would seem but I didn't let my face give away my incredulity.

'You didn't see him the day they took Christine into hospital,' she said. 'You've never seen anyone look so lost.'

'You're talking rubbish. Christine was just a doormat.'

'She was a quiet woman, yes. But he loved her.'

The idea of 'love' and Harry Ronsard did not seem credible, and I said as much.

'I spent a lot of time with him after she died,' Alice insisted. This was one of the very few times I heard her insist on anything. Thought, identity and individual choice were things she gave little sign of feeling she had any right to. That was why she wound up making such a good smackhead.

I'm sure she was hoping I'd ask her what she and Harry had found to talk about? Bollocks to that – I didn't want to know.

I worked on the murals over the summer. They were completed just before I fucked off – to land like a tactical nuke in the middle of Falmouth's awestruck gay scene. Alice went round to Harry's and looked at them, just after I'd finished. She came back to ours and gave me a wan little smile. It looked as if she was happy with what she'd seen but it also looked as if she knew her life's work was complete. Self-indulgent bollocks, I suppose, but I still felt a bit sorry for her, especially when she tried to get Mother and Dad to go up the road and see. Dad came close to shitting himself with terror and Mother disappeared up her own arse with contempt. That was the only time I ever heard Alice tell Mother to go and fuck herself. Before actually storming out. With an actual slam of the front door. Would you believe it? In Barratt Road Kingswinford, too! Whatever next? Bloody-jawed dragons and shaggable knights in armour suddenly seemed far less incongruous! So let's give Alice a wretched little round of applause, shall we? Yes. For the one brave thing she ever did in her wretched little soon-to-be-smackhead life.

The first week of that September had me counting the days before I kissed Kingswinford byebye. The one thing I'd miss was my own artwork – the murals on Harry's walls.

And, perhaps, Dave the bookseller.

The bloke had cultivated the persona of a pretentious hippy well enough that few people realised there was a brain in there. Apart from Harry and perhaps Alice, Dave was the only person I wanted to see those murals. I asked Harry if he'd mind my bringing him round to look at them. Harry agreed, indifferently, and Dave turned up, hair ponytailed and clothes a bit less dusty than usual.

Quietly, he went from room to room, taking in everything I'd done.

'It's a bit... Roger Dean...' he murmured, at one point, then hesitated. 'Nah, nah... That's not it. More like... Patrick Woodroffe...' he sighed. 'I dunno. You wanna be careful...'

I didn't ask what he meant. We were interrupted.

I hadn't heard the Harley.

No, that's a stupid thing to say – you can't fail to hear a bastard Harley – I hadn't registered the sound of it. I thought I heard Harry mumbling to someone downstairs as Dave stood, transfixed, by a crocodile-jawed sea monster snarling at a (seriously hot) bare-chested barbarian on the wall of the spare bedroom.

Harry Ronsard was suddenly at my shoulder. Together with the former occupant of that spare bedroom.

Charlotte Ronsard wasn't much shorter than her dad and, ever since I could remember, she'd been coming round to visit Harry and Christine on the fuck-off-and-die Harley. In biker's black leathers and a Jodie Foster T-shirt. In yer face, to say the least, but Harry didn't seem bothered.

She had the same face as Harry. Same eyes, too. The mane of black hair she'd got from her mother. Standing there, together, they looked a right pair of killers. Killers from a different world – some other Earth, far in the past or future or some parallel dimension or maybe somehow, all those things combined, where there were dragons and witch-queens and hordes of marauding zombies and big bastard spaceships. And there the pair of them would be, facing up to the lot with only their whacking great broadswords. And it'd be even stevens as to which side would come out on top.

But I'd tamed them. Both of them. With what I'd put on those walls. Their faces told me that. They looked at what I'd put on

Harry's walls and they were in love with it.

'Good stuff, Lee,' Charlotte murmured, no overt feeling in her voice.

Harry just nodded, silently.

Dave looked at them, then back to the murals, worried and perplexed.

As we left, he looked up at the wood that overshadowed Harry's house. In the distance, an ice-cream van played 'Greensleeves.' Dave seemed to shudder a little.

'What's the matter?'

'Oh... nothing. Ever hear some of the old stories about that wood?'

'No.'

'Oh. Well. Maybe another time.'

'It's okay – I know what the problem is.'

He turned to me, his face a question.

'You looked at Harry and Charlotte, right?' I asked.

'Right.'

'And you looked at the murals I'd done?'

'I did.'

'And it was hard to tell where Harry and Charlotte ended and where the murals began?'

'It was.'

'You think I've shown them themselves as they really are.'

'You have.'

'And you think that's dangerous.'

I kept my voice quiet and even. It wasn't easy. At that moment, I wanted to rub the mediocre face of Kingswinford into the world I'd painted. I wanted that face to be ripped off by broadswords and dragonjaws. And I wanted to scream with laughter like a deranged wizard.

Which was a bit on the peculiar side, because I'd never really gone in for that sword and sorcery bollocks.

'Dangerous...' Dave murmured, 'Yeah, dangerous...'

He turned and looked up, once more, into the shadows of Cally Wood.

7. Polly Gauvain

It wasn't necessarily a scream.

It could have been a wonky vacuum cleaner. Or somebody drilling a hole in a bit of brickwork. Or, even if it *was* a scream, you'd have been daft to think it was a real scream. People were well off in Kingswinford: they could afford home cinema systems that made pretend screams – horror movie screams – sound like real screams. In Kingswinford, you assumed that, unless you could be absolutely sure it was a real scream, it must be only pretend. Not a real scream, then. I was being silly for thinking it might be.

I had to ignore the nagging voices at the back of my head...

Polly, it can get very quiet round here...

I had to ignore them when they reminded me what this place was like...

Apart from a few old ducks who don't get out much, most of the houses have families living in them. Dual income families, Polly, with kids at school. So, between eight in the morning and four in the afternoon, there are very few people around – very few potential witnesses.

Had to ignore them when they reminded me what that meant...

If you wanted to get away with murder, Kingswinford, mid-week, between eight in the morning and four in the afternoon, would be the place and the time to do it. Right now, Polly, it's two thirty pm on a Wednesday.

But that still didn't mean it was a real scream...

It was, Polly, and you know it – because you've heard a scream like that before. Heard it here, in Kingswinford. And it was a real scream then...

It was, perhaps, my earliest memory. I'd been about three or four. I had a feeling that, before then, my mom had never seemed sad – at least, not as sad as she'd always seemed afterwards. But I did remember her and my dad talking to each other and my mom crying. I did remember my dad saying:

'Better this way...'

and:

'Think of the children.'

and:

'You'll be provided for.'

and:

'Don't be so pathetic.'

and I did remember that, after saying these things, my dad had gone away. And my mom had screamed. It had only been the once that she'd screamed. Only the once, as my dad walked out for the last time and she knew she'd never be able to pull him back. My mom was a quiet person, you see. But, from then on, even when she was completely silent, I could sense that the scream had stuck to her. It never went away, but it hung around her like a cloud of tiny little particles of grey metal.

By the time I went to school, I'd got used to it being there. I went to Summerhill School, which was where I met Alice.

Alice was pretty, back then. She had that bright, flowers-in-the-sunshine look that my mom had used to have. Alice said she wanted to be a hippy and get rid of all the nuclear weapons. She listened to weird music. I didn't like it. I used to ask her why she didn't listen to Take That or to New Kids on the Block like everybody else? She'd just laugh at me.

You wouldn't have thought she'd wind up a junkie. She did her homework, played netball for the school and never did drugs. True, a couple of weeks after we did our GCSEs, the pair of us made the traditional trip up Cally Wood – with three or four bottles of

Woodpecker and half a dozen grebos – and offloaded our virginities, but it was Alice who'd remembered to bring the Durex. Sensible Alice.

She used to come round our house, on the way home from school, and stop to watch *Grange Hill* and *Byker Grove*. She'd go home when *Neighbours* came on. She always wanted to be back when her mother got in. But that wasn't going to be until six or seven – her mother always used to work late.

She used to come round at the weekends too, sometimes. We'd do our homework. My brothers, Colin and Tim, had moved out to university. A few years later, we started to see Colin on TV. He was making loads of money. We got to be quite proud of him, though he never came to see us.

Now and again, we'd hear from my dad. Usually at Christmas. He was enjoying life in Texas and his new wife – who was about Colin's age – had had the baby. Once, he wrote that I ought to come over for a visit. Never happened, though.

My mom used to get a sort of a grey, washed-out look on her face when she read his letters. She'd give them to me and I'd keep them. She didn't seem to want them back.

Alice used to cheer my mom up a bit. But I never went round hers. Neither did anyone else. This wasn't strange. In Kingswinford, there are a lot of people who keep themselves to themselves. Some weekends, they get visits from relatives but mostly they don't see much of anyone; home is a place where they eat, where they watch telly and where they sleep. They do their living in the places where they work and the places where they go shopping.

But some of our mates were pissed off about never getting to go round Alice's. They wanted a chance to get close to Lee; he went to King Ed's in Bartley Green – the grammar school – so we didn't see much of him. He was drop dead gorgeous from the age of about twelve. Alice used to laugh about that.

'He's got Mother's looks,' she said, once, 'Otherwise they'd be taking the piss out of him for going somewhere so posh – hormones trump inverse snobbery!'

She was right – she usually was about stuff like that. A few hearts broke when it got back to us that he was gay.

I relied on Alice and I carried on thinking of her as 'sensible', long after she'd started to go downhill. I never really stopped thinking of her as sensible, right up until the morning I dropped round and found her front door off the latch. And what was left of her, skin turned the colour of ear wax and so very still. I'd phoned an ambulance, waited quietly and wished I could find the strength to get loud and fierce and upset. To weep, to wail, to scream...

To scream.

Yes, the voices were right: I did know what screams sounded like.

And, now, this had been a scream.

I'd come for a walk in Cally Wood. I'd wanted to spend some time remembering Alice.

I'd meant to go into the wood through the gulley, then turn left and walk to the south end, the Lawnswood School end. Then, I'd climb to the top of the ridge and walk to the north end, the Summerhill School end. When I'd looked at what was left of my old place (they'd been about to knock down the last bit of the school I'd known and would soon be rebuilding it), I'd maybe go and see if Alice's dad was in; he'd looked as if he needed the sympathy...

Then, as I was halfway up the gulley, I heard the scream.

I looked up the road to the far end, where it turned left into Lawnswood Avenue.

And I saw the black Audi.

And then, suddenly, I didn't need to think at all.

In fact, it seemed much, much better if I avoided thought altogether. Thought came from the head. What I wanted came from the body.

Not rushing, I walked towards the house. From outside, there seemed nothing special about it. But the memory of the man who I knew lived there burned into my insides.

With his face like Stonehenge, he made this place into a stern and ancient monument. And I wanted to be here. I wanted to be where he was. It wasn't a desire I needed to explain. Explanations were things that belonged in the mind and, now, I wasn't interested in the mind.

I was outside. He was inside. There were other people inside, too, I could hear their movements, but I didn't care about them. I waited for a long time. Then I crunched down the gravel at the side of the house, towards a doorway of rough, brown wood that led into the back garden.

I thought about opening it. I thought very long and hard. But it wasn't going to happen. It would need me to make a decision. And it wasn't my place to make decisions. Decisions were things I wanted to leave to the man who lived here. He was the man who was going to take all those problems – uncertainty, individuality, thought itself – and make them go away. I was fine with that. Horrible, nagging voices in my head – I'd never liked them, anyway.

It was very quiet. I think, somewhere in the distance, an ice-cream van was playing 'Greensleeves'.

The wooden door opened. He stood there. His trousers were brown corduroy, his shirt pale ochre. Both were blood-stained.

I was shivering, very badly. I could smell something – I thought it might be blood. Was it blood? I didn't care. One look at this man and the question was meaningless. All questions were meaningless. Meaning itself was meaningless. There was only the total, overpowering sensation of being here with him.

I wanted to worship him. I wanted to be on my knees, abject and utterly, utterly mindless.

He reached out his hand, and delicately held my chin between his right thumb and forefinger. I could feel the power behind the delicacy.

And he said, 'No.'

Cruel! Cruel! Cruel!

And he said, 'Leave here, now.'

Cruellest! The only command of his I could not obey!

Which he knew. And there was, perhaps, something like the ghost of a smile at the corner of his mouth, in acknowledgement of it. Because there was something between us, something reaching to our roots, deep within our own beings and down through the generations, that made this meeting inevitable.

'Come back another time,' he said.

Which was what I needed to hear.

Still not wanting to leave, I opened and shut my mouth a few times, stupid and fish-like.

'What's your name?' I asked, finally.

'Ronsard. Harry Ronsard.'

'Ronsard?'

'Yes.'

'That's a French name.'

'Yes.'

'My name's Polly Gauvain.'

'Gauvain's a French name, too.'

'Yes.'

Another silence, then:

'Come back another time,' he repeated. 'But off you go for now.'

I stood for a moment, then I obeyed. And around me, I could not see Kingswinford. I could only see him. And I didn't want to see Kingswinford; I wanted to see only the world in which Harry Ronsard belonged.

8: Harry Ronsard

'Alice died,' Lee says to me. Just like that. And he's acting like it doesn't bother him. Acting well, too – well enough to fool almost anybody – certainly well enough to fool himself. But not well enough to fool me.

I'm just getting in from work. He's standing there, with his daft long leather coat and his daft long hair.

'How?' I ask him.

'Heroin overdose.'

'Come in.'

And he does.

'Know who's the supplier?' I ask him.

Just for a moment, he's surprised I'm asking. Then he looks at me as if he's giving himself a kick. Because, despite his daft ways and his daft clothes, he's not stupid. Somebody's done for his sister, and she was a sweet kid who didn't deserve it. He knows that. He may not admit as much, but he knows that. And it's going to be me who tracks the buggers down and sees that it's Cooper's ducks for every one of them. He knows that too. He painted those pictures on my wall. All that King Arthur stuff. I never used to bother with that sort of stuff before he painted those pictures. Thought it was for kids. I went out and bought the books, though, after he'd finished: Tennyson, Mallory, Geoffrey of Monmouth. Good stuff – read it all. Took me a long while – had to buy one of those big Oxford Dictionaries to help me get through them. Got the music, too. Always liked the music, proper music – Bryn Terfel sings Wagner. Knights of the Round Table... Good blokes, those, Knights of the Round Table. Blokes who did the right thing. My sort of blokes. There wants to be a few more blokes like that in the world. Things'd get sorted, if there were.

Lee Icement knows all this, no matter how hard he pretends he doesn't.

'We don't,' he sighs.

'D'you know where she lived?' I ask him. He gets a bit of paper out and scribbles the address down. Don't suppose he'll be going round there himself. Don't suppose his parents are going to get round there either. Like Lee, Shirley will act like the whole thing doesn't bother her.

It's a Wednesday, so it's a couple of days before I can go and give the place a look over. And, no surprises, the coppers have been and gone and somebody's clearing stuff out. Not the Icements – a couple of girls in their twenties or thirties. One's a nondescript flibbertigibbett of a thing, a bit chubby and with frizzy hair, the other...

The other, I can see as she appears and disappears into the house, is a lot more substantial. She's quite sturdy, dark-haired. She looks like someone who underrates herself – I reckon she used to be very fat, and she's put a lot of effort into changing that. She's got herself a good bloke – you can tell that, too – but she doesn't quite believe her luck. Except it's not a matter of luck. This is a good woman. I can tell it, so can any good bloke. And any good bloke, no matter what shape she was in, if he found her going spare, he wouldn't hang about.

There's something else about her, too. Not sure exactly what it is but some time, not so very long ago, she's been up against some bad stuff. She's not been alone in being up against it; she's had a good mob on her side but, I'm sure, it's been really bad stuff. She gave it a seeing to, though – no doubt. She gave it a right smack in the gob. You can tell – even from this distance. You can see it in her; it shines out.

She's in no rush to get the place cleared out but it doesn't take her long. There's a pause. And then I realise, none too quickly, that she's spotted me. She would have done, of course, she's got the gift of seeing things as they are – a rare thing. And I know I'm going to have to make myself scarce or she'll be all over me with questions.

A day or two later, I'm at home. And I'm looking up at Lee's paintings, feeling them soak into me, the way they do. That's it with a good painting – a proper painting, not like all your pickled cows rot

– a good painting soaks into you. And, if it's really good, it tells you what it is that's the right thing to do. I always listen to a good painting.

So, I'm staring at the big portrait of Sir Lancelot that's in the front room, and I get this funny feeling. I look out the front window and there she is again, talking to Martin Icement. I've never seen a woman who looked so full of what's right, who looked so... *just.* There's not much to be got out of Martin, though she spends longer talking to him than most people would. This is a woman who persists when she knows there's a wrong that needs putting right.

Then Shirley Icement comes out and says something to her.

I've got time for Shirley Icement. Because she's another one who's been up against some bad stuff – might even have been the same bad stuff as this good woman. It's done Shirley a lot more harm, though. I can tell all this, though she's never confided. Evil has a range of stinks. I can recognise every one of them.

But just before she gets back in her car, the good woman looks up the road at my place, and her eyes fix on my motor. And I'm pretty certain she's recognised it from outside Alice's place.

These are women who need help, but neither of them'll admit it. All this women's liberation rubbish – men are supposed to lie around useless and let the women solve men's problems. I tell you, all this women's liberation rubbish, all this equality rubbish, all this feminism rubbish, it was cooked up by men. Lazy men, dishonest men, weak men, all trying to get women to do men's jobs. I won't pretend to be all a woman might want, but I won't use that kind of rubbish to hide from what's a man's responsibility. Shirley's daughter has been murdered, and it's a man's job to make sure whoever did it winds up in bits, soon. Small bits, and very soon. That's a man's job, that's what is right and I will do it.

Okay, then, get round to where poor Alice died and start asking questions. The neighbours aren't going to keep any secrets from me. Just give them the right look, the look that says you mean business, and they spill their guts soon enough. It's a matter of keeping doubt out of your mind. And keeping thought out of your mind. Most people are crippled by doubt, crippled by thought. Show them someone who's got no doubt, no thought, and they straight away know who's boss. Doubt is effeminate. Thought is effeminate. Only threat is manly. Only threat and violence get things done. It might be sad, but it's the truth.

The problem is that they don't know anything. And I leave behind me a few streets full of people who've peed themselves with fear but haven't had anything useful to say. And after a few days, I begin to realise this might be a bit trickier than I thought.

I go to Alice's funeral and there's those two women again, the flibbertigibbet and the good one. When I give her the look, the good one doesn't budge an inch. I have no power over her; I like that, though it comes as a bit of a shock. And I've still got her at the back of my mind when, a few days later, I spot something that might give me a clue about Alice.

It's in one of the local free papers. Now, I'm not usually a one for free papers, or for anything 'free' to be quite honest – there's always strings attached. But this week, instead of chucking them in the bin straight away, I have a quick look through.

A band name jumps off the page at me:

OZRIC TENTACLES

AT WALLENSTEIN'S, ZANN STREET, HALESOWEN

FRIDAY MAY 2nd

DOORS: 6.30

SUPPORT: BIG BREN'S COMBO.

£15 adv. £17.50 on the door.

I remember Ozric Tentacles. Music for daft people. Nice people – but daft people. People like Alice – she used to love them. People like her, who think the world's a nice place, full of nice people who are kind and good and well meaning. Music for poor bloody fools who wind up dead with a needle in their arm. Music for poor bloody fools who could do with facing up to what things are like in the real world. Music for poor bloody fools who could do with listening to a bit more Wagner.

So I show up there, on the night, with my £17.50 in my hand and a bit more for a drink. It looks as if whoever runs the place knows his beer – there's a few on the bar that I remember from my drinking days. But I'm on the lemonade tonight; I want to keep my head very clear.

Funny place, I've got to admit. Rambling old house, been done up maybe five or ten years ago and there's a big car park out the back. The music's on in the cellar. The bands haven't started to play yet, but there's enough noise coming out of the speakers anyway.

'Hello, Harry!'

I'm recognised. I'm a bit surprised to be recognised, then I see who it is – Neil Haines. Worked for me, a few years ago. Plays in another one of these bands – the sort of stuff they're going to be playing tonight. I went to see them once, five years back. Funny thing, one of the blokes in the support band gave me a present: two swords – a falchion and a spatha. Authentic-looking, like out of the times and the kingdoms I've got on my walls. I packed them away, stuck them in the loft and haven't thought about them since. But now, of course, I'm getting close to the time when they might come in useful.

'Neil.'

'Nice to see you again. Been a while. Didn't think the Ozrics would be your cup of tea.'

'They're not particularly. A neighbour of mine used to like them. She died recently, so...'

Neil puts his head on one side and asks:

'Was it anyone I'd know?'

'Girl in her twenties. Name of Alice Icement.'

'Oh no. Any relation of Martin Icement?'

'His daughter.'

Neil's face freezes for a bit.

And next to us in the crowd, there's a shabby little specimen who twitches, very slightly, but very definitely, at the name 'Alice Icement.' He doesn't think I've noticed. All the same, little by little, he takes himself to the far side of the room and stays there. He reckons he's going to keep out of my way for the rest of the evening. No good, Twitchy, it's too late for that. I've clocked you.

'Poor bloody Martin,' Neil sighs, at last. 'How's he taking it?'

'Keeping himself to himself.'

Neil sighs again.

'Martin used to be in our band,' he says, at last, 'years ago. Before he started drinking. Does he still drink?'

'No.'

Neil sighs again. 'He'd be dead if he still did,' he says. 'The way he was sticking it away. He used to do tape effects and stuff. Real whizz kid at that sort of thing. Could have been the next Luc Ferrari.'

'Hmm… I don't know about that. Would this be the same band as has got Dave Calper in it?'

'Yes. You know Dave?' He's really surprised at this, and I suppose it's not a connection you'd make readily.

'Met him the once,' I explain.

'Well, we'd be doing the support act ourselves, tonight. But we're missing the drummer and the keyboard player – they've got a friend in Glasgow who's ill. It's been great of Bren and the boys to step in. You won't have heard anything like 'em.'

Well, the support band comes on and indeed I've not heard anything like them. Not sure I'd want to again but, to be fair, I've certainly not heard anything like them. A fat bloke with one of those Brummie accents that's three quarters Irish, shouting poetry that talks some sense, up to a point, but has way too much swearing in it. Behind him, there's a bunch of jazz musicians – some know what they're doing but all of them seem to think it's okay to make it up as they go along.

Hmm.

Not my cup of tea at all.

After they've gone off, something a bit weird happens. The piped music's back on. More jazz, but whoever wrote it thought very very carefully about it. And the words... I can't make them all out but they sound like something that just ought not to be in the world. If the world deserved words like these, then...

Then it wouldn't deserve me.

And for half a second, I'm sure there's someone back on stage, talking in time to the music and he, or she, is saying *'Forget not Me, Mine Seventh Eye,'* but when I turn round, there's no one behind the microphone and Neil, who's back at my side, says 'Westbrook, *Bright as Fire,'* as if that explains everything.

Five minutes later, Ozric Daftbugger Tentacles are on stage, telling us that 'This one's called "Become the Other".'

But I make myself listen to every over-amplified note of the whole concert. A part of me would like to think that dead Alice can use my living ears to hear it. Yes. I'd like that. That would be good, that would. And, even though I can't say I believe it, I listen to every note, just on the off chance. Because Alice deserves it, she does. You listen to your daft little tunes, my poor little braveheart. You listen to them one last time through old Harry's ears. God bless.

***

'So,' says I to Twitchy.

And he twitches a bit more.

I've got him pushed up against an old concrete bus-stop pillar, round the corner from where Ozric Tentacles have just played.

'So,' says I again. And my eyes narrow. And my mouth tightens. And my face gets close to his face.

'Tell me about Alice Icement, then.'

He makes this funny little quivering noise like those keyboard things Ozric Tentacles use. What they call 'em? Cynthia-sizer? This is all very well but it's not what I want to hear.

'Tell me about Alice Icement.' I'm speaking very very low now. His bladder understands before his brain does. It knows what I'm going to do to him if he's not helpful. The smell isn't nice at all, but I've been expecting it.

'Tell... Me... About... Alice... Icement.'

A very brief pause. And then:

'BastardfuckingbastardfuckingbastardfuckingThatcher! It was Pete bastardfucking Thatcher and his bastardfucking toyboys! They sold her the bastardfucking shit! She was trying to give up. They'd nicked a bastardfucking stash off the bastardfucking Khans! They flogged her half of it! Bastardfucking tossers! They aren't even proper dealers. You'll see! They hang round in the 'Spoons in Dudley. And the one down the road, here. Bastardfucking tossers!'

Then he's quiet, except for the desperate sound of his breathing. And I have a bit of a think about things...

'Oh-ar,' says I.

'Hmm...' says I.

'Alright then,' says I, 'you can go.'

And he does.

So a name has got coughed up. A name and a couple of locations.

A day or two later, I'm in the Dudley Wetherspoon's and somebody's helpfully pointing out the mob I want. Three people, two white, one black. Harder to know what to think about the black lad, but the whites are straightforward enough. They want to be gangsters. They want to be feared and their name for the fear they want to inspire is 'respect'. But it is not respect. They are incapable of understanding what is meant by the word 'respect' and their presumption that they have the right to use such a word – that alone has earned them the penalty that I will administer. A few more questions and I've got some addresses, too. None very far away. This, I tell myself, will be easy.

I think, for a moment, about the swords I have stashed up in my loft.

No, I tell myself, *that's not the way to go about it. Live in the real world, Harry.*

So I decide I need to enlist some help.
And the first name to cross my mind is my daughter's.
I dismiss the notion.
I start racking my brains, thinking of somebody I can use…

***

Night time, Kingswinford. I'm staring up at the castle – or palace, or whatever the proper name is – that Lee painted on my bedroom ceiling. It's been there ten or eleven years. Every other summer, Lee drops in, checks out what's faded or flaked and he touches it up a bit. Not too much, though; sometimes, paint looks better when it's faded.

I can't sleep. It's past time to be going after the bad 'uns. Every day I leave it, they might be getting some other little girl hooked on their filth. I get up, get dressed again and walk out into the night. I'm in my running gear. It's a warm enough night – the middle of May now. I head down the road to the gap between Six and Eight, passing the silent Icement house on my way. I go up the gulley, into the wood. It's very dark, here. The conifers in the middle of the wood clack together in a light wind. At the north and south ends, under the birches and the old oaks, it'll be darker still.

I head up to the top of the ridge, the clacking of the conifer trunks louder. The breeze is picking up a bit; it kisses my forehead, coldly. Along the top of the ridge, there's a path. The Welsh Mountains send me over another face-full of cold air, sharpening up everything. There's movement around me, clacking conifer trunks like petrified snakes, under the needle sharp stars.

I turn north, heading up to the end of the ridge and as I move under the thicker shade of the older trees, I sense their branches, twisted like sword-wielding arms in battle, or like black flames burning away weakness and corruption. And I know I have been made ready to do what needs to be done. I will set about it tomorrow.

***

The place I work is over in Dudley. A big warehouse of concrete and grey plastic. Noisy inside, with stuff getting carted about. We supply building materials. Our customers are people who do the job I used to do, before Christine got sick. I started there about nine years back, very junior role, but I've been promoted a few times, because I know my stuff. These days I get my orders straight from the gaffers, who aren't a bad lot, but not as bright as they might be. They've enough sense, though, to have spotted that I know what I'm doing and they let me get on with it; they've never found themselves stuck with a consignment of unsellable rubbish when they've got me to do the buying, which is more than can be said for some other monkeys.

One of those other monkeys, a waste of space called Darren Hatch, who I'd not normally give the time of day, looks like what I think I need. He's a short bloke with a Carling Black Label gut and a Beatles haircut dyed a colour that fools nobody. Stupid twerp. And his face is saggy and his skin is stained and his mouth is pinched and lipless like a dog's bumhole.

He's the sort you get in those pubs where nobody goes. And nobody goes because they know people like him are in there. Him and his mates, twisted up close to their tables, under the bright lights, while the barmaid's eyes, vicious with nicotine withdrawal and chlamydia, stab resentment at them from behind the till.

They won't do her the favour of getting out, though. She's someone they can pick on, someone they think is lower down the food chain than they are. She is a *wanker*. Because, to them, the world divides into two sorts of people: those who are more powerful than they are – *bastards*; and those who are less – *wankers*. And any other human being is, as far as they want to know, either one or the other. And nothing else.

Their conversation's on the usual lines, for a lot of the time. A bit of sex here, a bit of football there, a bit of how much they hate the wife everywhere. But it's different from most such conversations in three respects: *the bastard nigs, the bastard wogs* – and (recently, taking the place of *the bastard Irish) – the bastard Poles. Who come over here and take our jobs. Who ought to be stuck on the banana boat and sent back to Bongo Bongo Land, or something worse, know what I mean? Yeah, best not say it aloud, though. All this Political Correctness bollocks...* (As if there's any chance that Tracy the Till is about to shop them to the Commission for Racial Equality). *Yeah, coming on the EDL march on Saturday? Gonna tear the whole place apart, ain't we? That'll show the bastards...*

And Darren Hatch is the loudest, the meanest, the most contemptible. But he knows where to find others like himself. And I need the cannon fodder. Or I think I do.

So I go up to him at work. It's lunchtime and he's having a fag out the back. It's a grey day. I stand upwind of him, because I can't stand the stench of fags, not since Christine died.

'Darren,' I begin. He looks at me suspiciously. I'm a *bastard*, after all – someone to be treated with caution.

'Yeah?'

'I've got a bit of a problem.'

Caution now turns to alarm; there's any number of reasons why I might want to have a go at him. His eyes dart to and fro like cornered rats, looking for an escape route.

'Friend of mine died recently,' I tell him. 'Drugs. I've done a bit of homework. I know who sold her the filth. Got names, addresses. I reckon the lot of them want sorting out. I was going to do it myself but I was thinking, I know you and some of your mates are quite... concerned about that sort of thing.'

He's looking scared, now – what am I trying to get him into? And how's he going to get out of it without looking like the snivelling coward he is? Answer: you're not, Darren, you're not.

'I'll supply the wheels,' I tell him, 'and the blunt instruments. And nobody's going to come digging up my back garden looking for the bodies. Nice part of town. All I need is three or four extra pair of hands to make sure it all goes smoothly.'

Three or four... Painfully, the Carling-rotted Hatch brain does the maths. That makes odds of... er, let's see... four or five to one!

Hatch likes those sorts of odds! And so do his mates. And his dogsbum mouth twists into the nasty little grin it assumes when he thinks he's going to get away with something vile.

So I'm invited up their pub, that evening. Oh, the honour! And I tell them what's what. And all the time, Tracy the Till is shooting the lot of them looks. Now, these looks would send anyone with a shred of decency screaming from the place but the little Darrenistas? They're as happy as the proverbial pigs in their own muck! Tracy doesn't know what to make of me though, and her eyes go wide when I go up the bar and order three pints of the dreaded Carling and – for me – a half of M&B mild. Nobody drinks M&B mild anymore; those days are gone; those men are gone!

No they're not, Tracy. Not quite.

The mild isn't in perfect nick, truth to tell. It's been a long time since I've been out for a drink but, I'm sure, I've tasted fresher.

And I take them through how we're going to do it and if she was bothered, Tracy could overhear enough to have a right good story for the coppers, but she's not bothered.

There's one thing I don't tell them, though. Darren and chums are going to make a wrong assumption about the lads we're going to take care of. I've not lied to them, but I've allowed that assumption to go unchallenged. When the time comes to do the business, I'm hoping that their blood – such as it is – will be up and they'll not be bothered about what seems, to me, an unimportant detail. It won't make a difference. That's what I'm hoping but, as it turns out, I'm hoping wrong.

The following lunchtime, we're in my car – four of us. And the villains we're waiting for are over the road, in a Wetherspoon's. It's a Wednesday, we've booked the flexitime, it's quite sunny and I can tell Darren and his little mates are a bit nervous of being here, in the sunshine. Sunlight makes them nervous, shows up too many of their faults. The fluorescent tubes in the pub might be bright, but the Darrenistas feel they blend in there. They feel their little evils won't be seen.

About twelve-thirty, three lads come out.

'Them's the ones we're after,' I say.

And I can feel the surprise and the disappointment. Because two of them are white.

This, I suddenly realise, *is* going to make a difference. It's the difference, in the Darrenistas' eyes, between a 'necessary evil' (killing a white bloke) and a 'bloody good laugh' (killing a black bloke). And, despite the look on my face when I told them what was going to happen, they'd assumed they were being signed up for a 'bloody good laugh.'

More fool them – this is 'necessary evil' time, kiddies.

They don't say anything, though. They're not sure what to say. Each of them is scared to death of the others. More scared of the others – stupid or what? – than they are of me. So no one dares utter a thing that might sound like reluctance.

Pretty soon, they're telling me to get off after the targets but no, I take my time, I'm not going to lose them and we mustn't be obvious – not round here: the centre of Halesowen's well covered by CCTV. Eventually I pull out, follow the targets round the corner, pull up again, then wait. Again, they go round a corner and again, I wait.

This happens a couple more times, until they're well away from the protection of the CCTV.

And then it really goes pear-shaped.

Because they split up. Now I'd been hoping to do the bloody lot of them in one go but seeing how nervous Darren and his little chums have been getting, it's clear that this is not going to happen. Four to one it's got to be, then. Only the problem is, the way they split up – the two white guys go one way and the black lad goes the other. No doubt how this is going to pan out now and at this stage I don't argue with it. Do the one who's on his own. Procedurally, it makes sense. Plus, he's been daft enough to head off down a quieter street.

So I take the motor round the corner after him. I pull up, just a bit in front. Then Darren and chums nip out with a sack and a bit of lead piping. Just before the villain's face disappears into the sack, I catch a glimpse of the fear on it. Makes him look like a little kid.

Bob's your uncle – two minutes later he's in the boot, out cold, head in the sack and arms tied. Three to one odds do make that possible.

All back to mine then, cool as custard and, for most of the way, the needle on the speedo's stuck on twenty-nine miles per hour. Stuck like it was glued there. Darren and his chummie-wummies unable to understand how I can fail to floor the accelerator at a time like this. No no, lads, nice and smooth, lads – *especially* at a time like this.

Once back home, I reverse the car into the garage. Then I make sure the door's closed. One very useful feature of my house is a door from the back of the garage into the kitchen. So, without the least bit of bother from the neighbours, we're able to unload the villain and cart him into my hall, the carpet of which I've covered with bin-liners, to stop any mess. And we start unwrapping him.

The plan is, get a big plastic dustbin, stick his head in it and do his throat. Over in a minute – no pallaver. So I go in the front room, where I've left that very dustbin.

Which is the point when the bugger chooses to wake up. And he screams.

Bloody hell, he screams! It'll be a rum lookout if the neighbours actually wake up and wonder what's going on. I come into the hall and he's making mincemeat of Darren and co, as I'd expect. He's got the sack off his head and I look into his eyes. And he looks into mine.

And suddenly, I know all about this lad. Because he's just started to think about his mom.

It's a certain look people get in their eyes, when they think about their moms. He gets it very, very strongly.

His mom is a religious woman, you can tell – Baptist or Pentecostal. When he was a little lad, she took him up church – two, three times a week. And the bloke running that church was one of those old-fashioned black ministers. I've got a lot of time for ministers like that. They have some idea what it's like to let them bang the nails in. They have some sense of what's meant by 'sacrifice'.

Only this lad, for the past few years, he's been pretending that he doesn't believe what he was taught at church, that he doesn't believe if he strays from the Path of Righteousness, Satan himself will come to get him. Now he has strayed from that Path of Righteousness, well and truly. And what does he see, as I come out of my front room with my big black dustbin? He sees that I have indeed come to get him.

So now he knows that in the next second or the next century, he will be at Heaven's Gate and Alice, a bright angel, will face him and ask him what he has done that has earned his passage inside? Because if he has done nothing, my hand is at his ankle, ready to drag him down to Hell.

And he knows that he must have done works, or have truly intended to do works, in her name, that have earned that passage. And the first of those works, he knows, is to get out of here, get back round his mom's and be at her knees, begging her forgiveness.

And I know that I have made this of him, and I am honoured, that of such vile trash, I have made something noble. And he knows me, and I know him and, for an instant, there is, despite the fear, a little gratitude in his eyes.

He lunges for the door.

And he almost makes it.

It's just luck that lets Darren get the knife into the back of his neck. Then all feeling is gone from those eyes. And Alice is opening the Gate of Heaven for him, for intention is sufficient, if it is true, and as Satan I have done my job, for it is Satan's job to ensure no rubbish gets into Heaven, only good stuff, and good stuff has got into Heaven today.

But I have seen what was in those eyes in their last moments, and I am not blind to the waste. I was proud of him, this good man I had so briefly made, and I know that it should have been him at my side in what I am bound to accomplish, instead of...

...I look up, at Darren Hatch.

He's gasping for breath, Carling gut heaving his tracksuit top up and down, up and down; Royals breath scraping lungs and throat like rusty metal tearing itself apart.

And he sniggers, and says 'Done the nig nog, then, day we?'

There is blood on the bin bags that cover the carpet. There is a bloodstain on the wall; I'll have to ask Lee to come and restore it.

And it's very quiet for a moment.

Then there's a noise, a crunch of gravel down the side of the house. The three of them look terrified. I'm not worried.

'I'll go and have a look,' I tell them, and I go out the back.

I open the door to the side passage and, in front of me, it's the chubby little flibbertigibbet again, with frizzy hair. She was the one who helped the other woman, the good woman, clear out Alice's flat. And she was at the funeral. She must have been a friend of Alice's or something. This time she's on her own. I see that she's pretty in a way, but very frightened.

And her eyes are big, blue and wide, with pupils big and dark. She looks like she's about to fall to her knees in front of me, but I reach out and take her chin between my thumb and forefinger.

'No,' I say, 'leave here, now.'

She can't. I look at her and it's clear she can't. She must think she's in love with me or something, the daft little thing. Been a while since this has happened, I must say! But I can't have her going inside. So I smile at her, a bit.

'Come back another time,' I tell her.

She pauses for a moment, opening and shutting her mouth, wanting to say something.

'What's your name?' she asks.

'Harry Ronsard.'

'Ronsard?'

'Yes.'

'That's a French name.'

'Yes.'

'My name's Polly Gauvain.'

Gauvain. The name gives me a strange feeling. I'm sure I've heard it somewhere. Some story or other that Mom used to tell...

'Gauvain's a French name too,' I say.

'Yes.'

Another silence, then:

'Come back another time,' I tell her, again, 'But off you go for now.'

She stands for a moment, then she obeys.

Back inside, Darren's been looking at what is painted on the walls and on the ceiling. He stares at it, then at me, puzzled.

And he asks: 'What's all this shit, then, Harry?'

'Never you mind, Darren, never you mind...'

***

I've got the hole in the back garden dug already. Twelve feet deep, because I know there's going to be quite a few in it before this is over. The first body goes into an extra large bin bag, taped up tightly so there'll be no tell-tale pong. Then, it goes down the hole. I cover it with a shallow layer of soil, then three paving slabs to keep the foxes from getting at it.

Now for the next one.

'Okay,' I tell Darren, the following lunchtime, 'we'll do the other two on Saturday.'

The little rat's been avoiding me all morning, so I've known I was going to get this response:

'I dunno,' he says. 'I don' think it's worth it. We done the nigger.'

He's expecting me to argue. He's a bit surprised when I don't.

'Then you're gonna leave the other two for me to do on me tod?' I ask.

'You can if you want. I can't be arsed. Talked to the others. They can't either. We done the nigger.'

'Fair enough,' I say, and I leave him.

And the next time he sees me, it's late that night, somewhere between his local and his home, and he's at the other end of my arms. And those arms have got hands. And those hands are round his throat and they're not going to let go. Not as long as he's still alive. And the thing that surprises me is how weak he is. It's hardly a struggle at all. And I feel sullied, dirtied by taking the life of something so pathetic. I feel cheated at not been granted a worthier adversary.

Into the hole in the back garden with him then, and cover him with earth and paving slabs.

By the end of the week, there are four more down there with him. More to follow, as soon as I've dug another hole, because I'm getting a taste for this. The last of the drug sellers was so stupid, he thought I'd let him live if he gave me the name and address of the creature who he stole the filth off.

And I'm looking at the painting of Sir Lancelot on my wall, and I'm looking at the sword in his hand. And I remember the swords I've got stashed up in the loft.

I don't smile very often. But I can feel myself smiling now.

9. Mary Maitland

'Er... Miss - er - Maitland? Mary Maitland?'

I looked around. It had been a big bloke's voice but hushed and nervous, not sure if he ought to talk to me.

It was Sharukh. His face was solemn, as it had been at Alice's place, and anxious too. He had some new worry to bother him. The light in the front foyer of Russells Hall Hospital, as bright and airy as anywhere in a hospital ever gets, showed up the bags under his eyes.

'Hello, Sharukh. How you doing?'

'Been a bit difficult, to be honest. I was going to give you a ring about this problem we've got.'

'Talk to me now if you want. I've just been visiting another client.'

'Somebody in a bad way?'

'Pretty bad, yes.'

He sighed and there was grief and shame in his sigh.

'If that's okay,' he said, 'I mean, I've just come off shift...'

We nipped over to the café and, cups of coffee bought, we sat down. He stared at his coffee and was silent. Then he sighed again and said: 'My cousin...'

His face creased up with disgust. Then he laughed, bitterly. 'Not really my cousin. My grandma, his grandma, came from the same village in the Punjab. That makes us cousins...'

'You wish it didn't?'

He looked up at me, eyes miserable, and nodded, once.

'He's been getting in with some bad ones. He was always one for doing that. When he was fifteen, he had a photo of Osama bin Laden on his bedroom wall. Stupid!'

Difficult stuff to talk about – especially to anyone outside 'the community'. This couldn't be anything good.

He raised his coffee and knocked back a blistering mouthful.

'He in trouble?' I asked.

Sharukh nodded.

'With the police?'

He hesitated, then: 'Don't really know. His dad and mum are keeping him at home. He can't go anywhere. He can't talk, most of the time – just sits there and screams and cries. They've had to put him in nappies! He shits himself, pisses himself...' He choked up. I gave him a moment to get himself together.

'He'd started throwing a lot of money around,' he went on, 'and having posh white girlfriends. Driving round in his new BMW. *His new BMW!*' The name of a car makes a filthy obscenity if you say it with enough venom.

I knew the answer to the obvious question, but I asked it anyway. 'Smack?'

A silence. The clattering of the café around us sounded a long way away.

He nodded again.

'I see,' I said, paused, then asked, 'Had he been dealing for long?'

Sharukh shrugged. 'Don't know. Can't ask his mum and dad: they're in enough of a state, as it is. Must have been a few months, though...'

'You'd be surprised how quick that lot get rich. And you'd be surprised how easy it is to get lured into it...'

'There's no excuse,' he cut me off, softly but firmly, 'I mean, what happened to his religion? You shall not pollute your mind, it says.'

'I know.'

'That stuff's against God.'

'I know.'

'He deserved it – whatever happened to him.'

'Have you any idea what that was?'

He raised his eyes from his coffee again and looked at me.

'His mum and dad got a call from him, early morning' he whispered, 'He was hardly making no sense but they managed to work out where he was, out on the Kidder Road, the 449. His dad and his brother went and picked him up. He was in his Armani suit and all. He'd thrown up all over it. Squealing like a pig. Wet himself – they thought he was on something. But it didn't wear off. They took him home and put him to bed. They knew he'd been "out with his mates" but when they ask about those mates, he just says they're dead. All of 'em – dead.'

'Dead?'

'That's what he says?'

'And are they dead?'

Sharukh looked at me, again. 'We didn't think so,' he said. 'We thought he was just crazy – imagining things. Till this morning... This morning, the coppers fished one of them out the cut in Old Hill. Head cut off, like with a sword. Now I hear they've got this house near Enville sealed off. And Abdul – that's my cousin – he's saying the whole mob are gone the same way.'

'A rival gang, then?'

Sharukh shook his head.

'He says it was just one that killed the lot of them...' he sighed, very quietly.

'One bloke?'

Sharukh shook his head.

'Not a bloke. Not a bloke. Abdul says... He says it was the Devil.'

A longer silence.

'I know it sounds dumb,' he said, 'But if you could see the look on his face... I just... don't know what to think.'

'I don't either,' I replied, 'But I'm not the sort of person who goes around thinking the Devil works like that. He doesn't.'

'Really?' he asked, his face curious, 'I'd heard somewhere that...'

'That wasn't me. My sister... got in with a bunch who went in for that sort of thing – occultists – but they were just a load of pretentious drama queens. Real evil's what your cousin's been trading. And I do know something about that.'

'Real evil,' he breathed, softly, 'You're not wrong, there...'

'Would you like me to come round and have a chat – with Abdul?'

Sharukh stared at me and there was relief in his eyes. He nodded.

Two days later, I was upstairs in a nicely-kept terrace somewhere close to the Dudley Road in Wolverhampton. Nicely kept and smelling strongly of proper Asian cooking.

Abdul's bedroom was dim, its curtains drawn. All I could see of him was a quivering bundle under the duvet, making high-pitched, broken little noises.

Downstairs sat a grey-haired, grey-bearded man in scrupulously cleaned Kurta pyjamas. He stared rigidly at the living room wall: I reckoned he was in shock.

'Abdul's dad – very respected man,' Sharukh had said, in the car on the way here. 'Does a lot of work for the mosque. There's people who've known what Abdul's been getting into – who've gone to a lot of trouble to make sure his dad didn't hear about it.'

'Yeah. I've known that sort of thing.'

Quietly, now, I stepped into the bedroom.

'Abdul?'

I kept my voice level, firm, wanting him to feel I was someone reliable and trustworthy. It was a professional persona you learned to adopt, but I'd never known it have such a sudden effect as it did now – the noises stopped. The quivering stopped. Behind me, I could sense that Abdul's mother and Sharukh had noticed.

'Do you want to talk to me, Abdul?'

A soft, slow rustling of the sweaty bedclothes. His mom would have changed them nightly or more often but, with the state of his metabolism, they'd be stinking again within minutes.

He was facing me and I'd never seen such frightened eyes. Not Alice's when she was looking death in the face, not my own dad's when he was looking at the fact that he was a murderer. Alice had been resigned, despairing. Dad had been full of righteous anger at himself. Abdul was just scared.

'What happened to you, Abdul?'

He looked at me. Then he spoke rapidly, in what I knew to be Punjabi, which I didn't understand. Desperate, he switched to what was probably Arabic, which I understood no better. I was pretty sure, though, that he was quoting the Koran. I thought I caught the name *Shaytan* a couple of times.

It took a few moments for him to clock the blankness of my face. With a painful effort, he forced his mind into English.

'Sorry… sorry…' he croaked.

I nodded. And I decided he didn't need a soft touch.

'I'm a person who tries to help drug users. I'm like Sharukh. We clean up the sort of mess you've been making, Abdul.'

Behind me, I heard his mom make a pained little noise.

Abdul stared at me, closed his eyes, opened them, thought hard for the English words, then said, 'God is great.'

'That is true. And He's angry with you, Abdul.'

Misery in those wide eyes, again. Well deserved, but bitter stuff.

'What happened to you, Abdul?'

Another pause.

'*Shay…* The Devil,' he said.

'Where did you see the Devil?'

His breathing grew harsher. 'In Enville,' he said, 'We were at… the supplier's house. Over by Enville. Big man, the supplier. Gets it all in from Pakistan. Nobody messes him about. But the Devil come. Come for him. Come for us all. Come with swords.'

'Swords?!'

'Swords. Two of 'em. A short and a long. You wouldn't think they could kill so many blokes. But they're fast. Faster than a bullet – when it's the Devil holding them. He killed everybody. Everybody but me. Like he wanted someone left alive to send the warning…' And he lapsed back into Punjabi.

'He says,' Sharukh explained in a flat voice, '"stop all the unrighteousness, or the Devil's gonna come for you" – more or less.'

A part of me, by now, was pretty sure Abdul had been dosed with LSD.

'Big deal's going down,' Abdul gasped, 'and we hear the car pull up outside. We hear it but we don't do nothin'. Crazy. We weren't expectin' no one else. We should've checked it out but we didn't. Like he'd got into our heads right away. Like we couldn't do nothin'. Somebody gets up and goes to the door – and the supplier looks like he don't know what's goin' on, 'cause he never told that guy to get up. And for a minute I think he's gonna give that guy a real bad bollockin' – or somethin' worse. Only… only we don't hear

92

no more from that guy. I can't remember what happened then but... next thing I know, there's six or seven guys lyin' there with their heads cut off. And it's the Devil and you can tell it's the Devil and he's come for what's his own. No point tryin' to get away from him. And he does them all. Everyone but me. And he looks at me and he's got them eyes... What you call them? Hazel eyes, and they sort of burn into you. And his face – it's kind of like a skull. And he looks at me and he just nods. Like he knows I'll be the one to tell everyone that he's here! And he's comin' for the unrighteous!'

Hazel eyes? Face like a skull? My insides began to feel cold.

'What happened then, Abdul?'

'He just... left me there. Just looked me over, one more time, went out the front door and into his car. A minute later, he's gone.'

A sudden brainwave – one I hoped was wrong. 'What kind of car was it, Abdul?'

His brow knotted.

'Big black Audi,' he said.

I heard Sharukh gasp. Reluctantly, I turned to him.

'Is it... the same guy?' he asked.

'Hope not,' I said.

***

When I got home, Ryan had photos laid out all over the coffee table – three rusty-looking traction engines of the sort you get, restored and spruced up, at posher fairgrounds. These three all looked a bit knackered but, Ryan assured me, one of them was 'in good nick' and it wouldn't take much to get it in shape. I made some unconvinced noises and suggested I wouldn't relish him getting blown up by some faulty old boiler only a few months before our Big Day.

I was still less reassured by his suggestion that we might spend our honeymoon in a caravan, pulled by the lugubrious old chuffer, on a slow-paced round-the-country jaunt that'd wind up at his dad's place. This, I was assured, would be the most brilliant thing imaginable because, of course, Everybody Loves a Traction Engine!

'There's legends about this one!' he told me. 'Story is, when it was used in the First World War, some clown left the brakes off and it went careering down a hill. By the time it came to rest, it'd flattened some Jerry sniper no one knew was there!'

I harrumphed, unconvinced.

Ryan went on regardless. 'What's amazing is, that sniper had been about to take a shot at a certain Brigade Major Bernard Montgomery...'

'Where did you hear this guff?'

'...who turned out to be the future Montgomery of Alamein!'

'Well, I gathered that. Sounds about as likely...'

'It gets better! Twenty odd years later, it does the same thing again. This time though, it was in Reading. Somebody leaves the brakes off, down the hill it goes and – splat! Only now it was some fifth-columnist bum chum of Ernst Rohm's who'd been about to toss a grenade at Clem Attlee!'

'Ho-hum. I can see I'm just going to have to accept this. Your traction engine apparently goes around saving the nation...'

'On two separate occasions!'

'On two separate occasions. Yes.'

'And there's a reason why it does so!'

'I thought there might be.'

'Story is, when they were digging up some fifth-century fortification down in the West Country, they found a broadsword, fully preserved, and had it sent off to the British Museum. Only because of some cock-up in the post, it got delivered to the place where this beauty was made, and wound up melted down and part of this here boiler...'

'Oh for Heavens' sake!'

'So we've got this bloody lovely traction engine, with all its heritage and nobody – until now – nobody's ever thought of slapping a plate on the side to give it its rightful name!'

'Oh Ryan, please don't!'

'Think of it! Here, have a cup of tea, love, have a cup of tea...' He shoved a steaming mug under my nose and I sipped, gingerly, at the brown liquid sanity, while Ryan went on being bonkers: 'Excalibur! The True Excalibur! And it's a traction engine!'

Ryan eventually came down from his chuff-chuffing ecstasy, enough to take an interest in how my day had gone. When he realised what company I'd been keeping, he was as concerned for my welfare as I'd expected. But since I couldn't think of any way to take the enquiry further, I was able to promise to spend less time, for the foreseeable future, nattering to Wolverhampton smack dealers.

10. Satansfist

'Hello, Lee.'

'Harry?'

Surprising – phone calls from Harry were an annual occurrence, made to arrange a time and date to retouch the murals. It had been a few years, now, since they'd needed very much work. These days, I could afford better quality paint – less prone to fading. And Harry was a careful homeowner. Up to now, I'd got the call in July or August. Never in May. Something was up.

Sensing my surprise, Harry explained: 'Had a bit of an accident. Splashed a bit of paint on the mural in the hall. Like you to come round and fix it.'

I wasn't going to hesitate. I had every reason to love those paintings and we both knew it. Because they were good – unspeakably good.

'I'll be round tomorrow night. Seven.'

The Cunt looked kickably miserable.

'Was that Harry?'

'Of course it was.'

'What did he want?'

'I'm going round tomorrow night to touch up some of his murals.'

'Touch them up?'

'Yes. He's spilt something on them.'

He blinked incredulously. I had the feeling that I'd said something stupid.

'Harry Ronsard,' he pointed out, 'never spills anything.'

For a moment, I wanted to thump him. Then I realised that I actually wanted him to thump me – repeatedly and very very hard. Because he was right. And I'd been a complete retard for not seeing as much.

Harry Ronsard never spilt anything. He was pathologically incapable of having an accident. He was no more able to slip on a banana skin than he was able to make a joke. Or to get a joke.

'Something funny…' I said.

'Funny peculiar,' The Cunt replied.

I shrugged.

'Be careful,' he said.

I looked at him. He really was looking fucking gorgeous, I had to admit. It irritated me, because I'd just made a twat of myself so I didn't feel like shagging him or slapping him around. But he was. Fucking gorgeous.

I said nothing.

***

The following evening…

'Here's fifty quid,' Harry said as he pulled open the door.

I took the money. Never pays to be precious. But when I inspected the damage, there seemed a good deal less than fifty quid's worth of work to do. I was surprised he wanted it fixed so quickly. Could surely have waited till August. Still, with Harry, everything had to be perfect. That's the mentality you tend to have if you're the sort who drives a black Audi.

The splash of paint was dark burgundy. I didn't recognise the type at all, which was odd. I was able to scrape most of it off without doing significant damage to the mural beneath.

I'd spread a few sheets of *Daily Mail* over the carpet. (Did you expect any other paper round at Harry's?)

A bit of pale green in the background. A touch of brown for the leather and a few dabs of silver on the armoured boot of a bare chested and – because I intended him to be – extremely shaggable Nordic warrior…

Taa-daa! Perfection.

Of course it was bloody perfection – *I'd* painted it.

I'd heard the noise of Charlotte's bike but had taken no notice. The front door swung open and she stepped in, hanging her biker's helmet on the coat stand and tugging off her black leather jacket.

'Dad about?'

'Out in the back garden. I think he's decided there's a patch of lawn that needs re-seeding.'

'Hmm... Right.' She was on her way into the back but hesitated, turning to me and saying, more softly than usual, 'Bin a bit worried about him.'

Squeezing the lids back on to my paint pots, I blinked. Charlotte Ronsard had a face that was not well suited to 'worry.' It did various sorts of ferocity, implacability and desire for a bit of aggro, yes. But worry? That it left to more delicate visages.

'What's the problem?' I asked.

'He's knackered.'

I thought about that for a bit.

She was right. The lines in his face had always been severe, but they'd grown deeper this past couple of weeks. And, yes, there were bags under his eyes.

'What's he been up to?' I asked.

'Not a clue. You know what he's like.'

I frowned. No use asking Mum or Dad if they'd noticed anything strange in Harry's behaviour. *Emotional Intelligence* was neither of their middle names. Nobody else round here would do any better. They weren't into gossip. They didn't give a shit enough to be into gossip. Outside, there was the roaring hiss of strong wind in the trees of Cally Wood. I might as well have told Charlotte to ask them.

Harry came in from the garden, heavy dirty boots landing on the old *Daily Mail* pages he'd placed ready for them. The parquet tiles in the kitchen he'd laid – immaculately – himself, and I'd never seen them not looking clean.

A gush of hot water into the stainless steel kitchen sink and the squishing sound of hard-skinned hands getting washed. We joined him in the kitchen and he turned, drying his hands, to say hello to his daughter.

'Hm-hm.'

'Hm-hm.'

Never a wildly enthusiastic pair of greeters, those two.

'How you bin?' – Charlotte's opening play.

'Hmm... Alright.' – Harry's rebuttal.

'You're lookin' a bit knackered...'

'Hmmmm... I don't feel too bad.'

'You sure? Don't want you knackering yourself up.' Charlotte making a passable attempt at sympathy here.

'Hmmmm... Nothing to worry about...' – Harry doing 'casually dismissive' as only he knew how.

'Work bin alright?'

'Hmm... Hmmmm... Bit busy, now you come to mention it. Bloke quit at short notice. Had to sort things out...'

'That make a lot of extra stuff to do?' she asked.

'Hmm – not that much... Bloke was waste of space, really.'

Harry seemed annoyed at himself for having mentioned it. He glanced, very quickly, out of the kitchen window. My eyes followed his. At the bottom of the garden, under the overhanging branches of Cally Wood, there was a pile of freshly dug earth. I couldn't see where it had come from.

'I know you,' Charlotte insisted. 'You'll take on anybody else's problems.'

'No, no. No big problems. Cup of tea?'

Investigation closed. With very little to show for it. Nice cup of tea, though.

Just before I left, Harry said he had something to show us. He placed a roll of stair carpet on the dining table and pulled open the string that held it together.

Unwrapped, two swords lay in polished brown leather sheaths. When he drew them, they gleamed against the dusty old carpet, one long and straight, the second shorter, slightly curved. They had both been cleaned and polished very recently. And the edges looked sharp.

'Had these in the loft for a few years,' Harry told us. 'Decided they needed to come down.'

The two blades looked like things from my murals. I recognised the longer, straight one as the sort they called a 'spatha' – just shy of a metre long with upper and lower guards of the handle almost the same size. The mixed iron of the blade made swirling patterns in the three long fullers. The curved one was a 'falchion', its blade widest towards the point, its handle crucifix-like.

Harry held the spatha, looking at the patterns in the metal, and the weariness had gone from him. Charlotte picked up the falchion, her face suddenly alive with terrible possibilities.

And I felt as if I had created them.

And nothing had ever been a bigger turn-on.

Emerging from chez Ronsard, I shouldered my bag of paints and sauntered up to my old home. Dad was outside, washing the car. He did this a lot. He jumped when he saw me. He did this a lot, too.

'Mother back from work, yet?' I asked, not supposing that she would be.

Through a series of high-pitched, querulous noises, Dad confirmed that she wasn't.

'Okay if I hang around a bit?'

More noises, to the effect that that would be fine, coupled with a look to the effect that he didn't really think so. He needn't have worried – bust-ups between Mother and me were rare things, these days, each of us having given up on the other when I was – I don't know – maybe twelve.

I opened the side gate and trudged down the passage to the back of the house, then went in through the kitchen door.

Inside, I stood for a moment, purposelessly, before going into the lounge. The furnishings were quite ornate – Victorian looking – but there were no pictures on the walls. No mirrors, either. The silence of the place was as exquisitely polite as poison gas. I looked in the sparsely populated bookcase. Not much to see. All the fiction and history was long chucked. One book on astronomy survived: a forlorn relic of a past life – Mother had once been a physics teacher. I seemed to remember she'd enjoyed the job, up to a point, back then.

Next door, a dog started barking, loudly. An approximately human voice joined in, snarling at *'Beckham'* to *'Gerrinere!'* Instead, the barking got louder. I went upstairs and idly looked out over the privet hedge that Dad – typical specimen of Kingswinford manhood that he was – kept trimmed as neat as Hollywood pubes.

The dog was an Alsatian, hackles up and teeth bared. I got the feeling it was very afraid. Its voice was getting ragged. But it was barking at nothing. Well – nothing apart from Cally Wood itself, the leaves and branches of which were still thrashing around in the wind as if they were doing a war dance.

I wandered into the room that had been Alice's. Mother had been meticulous in her removal of all trace of the little div. No psychedelic posters, no tie-dye wall hangings. No little nest of CDs by Ozric Tentacles, Kate Bush and all the other hippy-dippy saddoes. No printed twitterings of David Icke, Langdon Tremayne, Rudolf Steiner, nor any of the yards of wanky self-help books. Whatever whimsical pinch of Middle-Earthery Alice hadn't taken with her, Mother had seen that it had got stuck in the bin. Not sent to the charity shop or given away. But stuck in the bin. A long time before Alice had heeded the siren song of smack. No fire breathing dragon or armoured warrior remained to dream of avenging her. Not here.

I went back downstairs.

In the dining room – a cramped little affair made more cramped by the memory of childhood Sunday lunches – was a sideboard. On the sideboard were two photographs – Alice and me, both taken around graduation time. They were a necessary concession; now and again, Mother had visitors. She needed those visitors not to ask questions. You know the sort of questions: *No sign of a picture of either of her kids? That's weird, isn't it? Wonder what the problem is?* The last thing Mother needed was to be thought 'weird'. And the second-to-last thing she needed was to be thought a person who had 'problems'. Mother did not need problems. She needed to be the answer to problems – all problems. Anything less was unacceptable.

So I stared at Alice's frozen face. It smiled back prettily but, to my mind, stupidly.

'Alright for you,' I said, in Mother's voice, 'alright for you, lying around the place, being dead. Some of us have work to do. Some of us have responsibilities. Some of us can't afford the time to hang around the place, being dead. There are things that need doing. You aren't going to get them done by being dead, are you?'

I laughed. It was a funny, choking sort of a laugh.

It occurred to me how important it was to Mother that there were things that needed doing. That the thought of a world empty of things that needed doing was a thought that scared her.

Why?

I turned to the photograph of myself and the face, frozen behind the glass, answered the question in a foreign language.

Quarter past seven and she turned up. All thoughts of Alice now highly inadvisable. With self-conscious efficiency, Mother headed straight for the kitchen, not registering my presence. A couple of microwave dinners got chucked in the oven, done to the ping, taken out and plonked on the kitchen table. Then she hurried back to the front door to call Dad in. On the way, she noticed me.

'Want any dinner?' she asked.

I declined.

There was a look like old ghosts on her face.

'You feeling okay?' I ventured.

She stared back at me, blankly, which I could understand, I suppose – expressions of concern for either of my parents' wellbeing had never been my strong suit.

'I've been perfectly fine,' she responded after a few seconds, predictably huffy.

I didn't press things. If I wasn't careful, I'd be accusing her of maternal grief and that would be taken as a grave insult. Plus, I sensed that this wasn't connected with Alice – not directly. Instead, I took a chance with 'You just look a bit worried.'

'Not worried,' she grated, as sympathetic as a sabre-tooth tiger with piles, 'Angry.'

I said nothing. But I put a bit of curiosity on my face, and waited to see if she'd let me know who'd been doing the angering.

'If you,' she began, 'come across a horrible little man in a grey Mercedes car, hanging round here, tell him to go away. If he talks to you, don't listen to him. Everything he says is drivel – rubbish.'

102

'What's he likely to say?' I asked.

'Doesn't matter. It's all rubbish.'

I knew that would be all I'd get out of her on the matter.

I was out of there not long after and, surprise surprise, there actually was a metallic grey Mercedes parked up the road. I wasn't sure if the driver had clocked me but the car headed off almost immediately.

Harry emerged from his front door and looked after it. I walked down to him.

'Notice him in the Merc?' he asked.

'I did, yes. You know him?'

'No. But he turns up here, now and again. He's had that Merc for a year or so. Before then, it was a Beamer.'

There was a pause.

'I think,' Harry continued, 'he thinks he's keeping an eye on your mother.'

I must have looked surprised.

'*Thinks* he's keeping an eye on your mother, I say,' Harry went on. 'But he's just a twerp trying to act big. Going to be in trouble if he thinks he can take her on. I know twerps like that. Wastes of space, the lot of them.'

I got home about nine. The Cunt had been trying to write. The bin beside his desk was full of scrunched balls of paper like white turds.

He stared at me.

'How's Harry?'

'Seems fine.'

'He say anything strange to you?'

'No stranger than usual.'

He stared at me some more.

'What's going on between you two?'

'*Going on?*'

'Going on.'

'I am not fucking Harry Ronsard.'

'I never thought you were. And if you did, it wouldn't kill me.'

I was silent.

'But there's something going on. Every time you see him, it gets into you. It gets you fired up. It's something strong.'

'I paint pictures for Harry. That is all.'

'Painting pictures is a religion to you.'

Again, I didn't reply.

'I wish I could write poems that changed things the way your paintings can,' he said, softly. I thought he might be about to call me *Lee*. He did sometimes. It usually got him a kicking. 'I'm not sure I ought to wish that, though. There's something dangerous between you and Harry. It has to do with your paintings.'

I thought of the spatha in Harry's hand. I smiled.

'You think, just because you're the one who's created the pictures, you're stronger than they are,' he whispered.

'No,' I replied, 'I don't.'

'Those pictures may be stronger than you. They might be coming off the walls already. They might be coming to life.' He paused a little, then, 'They could hurt you.'

'Let them,' the words orgasmed out between my teeth. 'Let them.'

11: Polly Gauvain.

I got out of my car, stepped up the drive to his front door and rang the bell.

But there was no answer.

I waited a bit. I felt sure he was in. Once more, I stared up at the house. It still looked ordinary. Not very old – none of the houses in Barratt Road were very old. But there was something strange about it – something ancient, something fierce. It wasn't my place to understand this – Only to obey. I could not explain. I didn't want to explain. Only to feel, only to obey.

I rang the bell again. I wasn't impatient. Perhaps he'd been in the back garden. It wasn't my place to know. He, not I, was the judge of when it was right to open the door.

Movement, inside. Calm movement, taking its time.

The door was pulled open. He was very still, then he nodded. For a moment, I felt relief. I had been afraid – and I could now admit it – that he would send me away again. But such fear had been foolish; I had trusted my feelings and they had told me, quietly and clearly, that now was the right time for me to come here.

'Come in.'

I sensed the door closing behind me and I was in his home. A tiny part of me was astonished that I was not afraid. But knew I was where I belonged.

There were paintings on the wall. I did not allow myself to look at them, not without his permission.

'Come in the front room.'

I obeyed.

'Sit down.'

I obeyed.

I knew he was looking at me, though my eyes were fixed to the carpet. It was nice carpet, but the chair I sat in was strangely cold, the way chairs get when they haven't been sat in for a long, long time.

'Look up, little one.'

I looked up.

'Look at the paintings. The murals.'

I did so. I had been permitted.

Brave knights. Castles and beautiful women. Dragons and swords and battles and crowns. All things I would have laughed at, before now. But now, I knew there was more here than I was allowed to understand.

'See all this?' he asked. 'King Arthur. Knights of the Round Table. Blokes who did the right thing. Blokes who stood for what was good. That's what I believe in. So you see...' he paused, '...you shouldn't be afraid of me, little one.'

I tried to tell him I was not afraid of him. I could not speak. But it was not 'fear' that I felt for him. It was something else. I was in his power – utterly so – and I neither needed nor desired a will of my own.

'Would you like a cup of tea?' he asked.

I managed to nod, very slightly, and watched him get up. Behind him, a vast black dragon spread its wings and glared out, through the delicate lace curtains, at Kingswinford. People in Kingswinford didn't believe in dragons. That did not seem to bother this dragon. In fact, that was just how this dragon wanted it. For the time being.

Harry noticed my stare and one corner of his mouth turned upward, just a little.

'Looks fierce, doesn't he?' he asked.

Again, I just nodded.

'Lee painted him,' he went on. 'Alice's brother. Lee painted all this lot. Here, get up and have a look at it.'

I did so, as he went into the kitchen and made kettle and teapot clatter.

'You were a friend of Alice's, weren't you?' he asked, returning with a loaded tea tray.

I smiled and nodded again.

'Thought so. Alice was a good girl. She should've been given the chance to be a good woman. Milk and sugar?'

'Just a little milk, please.'

'Mhm. There you go. Let me tell you about Alice…'

I sipped my tea as he spoke. It was strong and bitter; usually I preferred Earl Grey but this was the right tea to drink with Harry.

'It's a few years ago, now, and I'm going through a bit of a rough patch. My wife, Christine, she's just died, you know. A good woman. Never say "boo" to a goose. But she did love her fags, did my Christine. Would not pack 'em in. So I lost her.'

His eyes were fixed on mine as he said this – fixed very strangely. And I felt something happening in my blood. Something I should have been wanting right now… should have been needing right now… I just didn't need it anymore.

He was very quiet. His face did not move. He sipped tea. The taste and the warmth seemed to focus him.

'I lost her, and I nearly lost myself. I'd given the business up. Had to. Had to look after her – didn't want anybody else doing it. No. But when she'd gone – that was it. Nothing left for me to do. Charlotte had gone by then. Off with her own life…' his brow creased for a moment, as if there was something he did not understand. 'Off with her own life, so there's just me. Me with no point. Then, round comes Alice. She's got the touch, has Alice. She's got a way of talking to people – to other people – when they ain't got no point anymore, and making them see why it's worth carrying on. And she spends a lot of time with me. And she talks to me and, funny thing, I can hardly remember a single thing she says but there's something in her voice that brings me out of where I've been. Brings me out of the bad place. And I can ask Lee round to paint this lot.' He waved at the murals. 'And this lot puts me right. Gives me my soul back. It's a good thing to have a soul.'

I nodded, though left to myself I wasn't sure whether I'd have thought having a soul was all that important. But, if this man said it was, then I believed it was too.

'Calls himself "Satansfist", does Lee,' Harry went on, and he looked at his own hand, balled it into a fist and laughed, very softly. '"Satansfist!" Saft sod! There isn't a bit of *him* that's Satan! But he paints like an angel. Look at this stuff! Paints like an angel – and not a fallen one, either!' The last few words were spoken very quietly. I didn't think they were meant for my ears.

I looked up and around me, once again.

'The pair of them, they've saved me from... from nothingness,' Harry explained. 'But what I don't realise, back then, is that Alice only has the gift of helping other people. She can never help herself. I don't understand that. By the time I do, she's dead. I'm grateful to you for trying to help her. You and that other girl.'

'Mary Maitland.'

'Mary Maitland. Hmm. Yes. Not your fault that you couldn't. There's too much bad stuff in Alice's family. Stuff that goes a long way back. Don't really know what it is, myself, but... You know, sometimes you can almost taste it. A bad taste. The taste of somebody who's been hurt.'

Harry's eyes were hazel: soft green at the edges with circles of gleaming copper around the pupils. The copper in them shone, now, shone fiercely.

'I don't like,' he said, in a low whisper, 'anyone to get hurt – anyone who doesn't deserve it.'

I lost track of time in that room. He asked me about my family, my life, my job. Finally, when I stood to go, he came close to me. Reaching out, he took my chin between his thumb and forefinger. The strength I sensed in just those two digits would have frightened me, once. But I knew I did not need to be frightened. Harry Ronsard would never hurt me.

'You're a pretty little thing,' he murmured, 'and you're a good 'un. There's no harm in you.'

I tried very hard to think of another time when a man had said anything so kind to me, anything so loving. I could not. Now I thought about it, I'd only ever had sneers. Harry Ronsard never sneered. He loved, he hated, but he never sneered. Sneering was for lesser men.

Outside, I walked up the street to where I'd parked my car.

'Who are you? What d'you think you're doing here?'

The voice was a cold one. It nearly made me jump. I turned.

Alice's Mum, Shirley Icement.

'Oh. Hello. I'm Polly Gauvain.'

'I don't want to know your name.'

'Er – you did ask me who I was…'

'Don't get gobby with me. What were you doing in Harry Ronsard's?'

She sounded cross – icily cross. But I was too happy to get cross back.

'I was visiting him.'

'Visiting him?'

'Yes.'

'Visiting him?!'

'Visiting him. He's my friend.'

'Friend?'

'Yes. We met at Alice's funeral.'

'Alice?'

'Alice. Your daughter Alice. I used to know her.'

'I don't want to know about that. I want to know what you think you're up to in Harry Ronsard's?'

'I told you. I was visiting him. He's my friend.'

She stood there, silent. There was a look in her eyes I could not understand. She had the same eyes as Lee – the eyes so many of my classmates had sighed for. I could see why. They were very very beautiful eyes. But they were very very unhappy.

'You little fool, what d'you think..?'

'Is there a problem, Shirley?'

Harry had approached silently and, it seemed, invisibly. But he was at our side now. We could hear him and we could see him. It was everything else that had ceased to exist.

Shirley looked at him and their eyes met. There was something between them that I could not understand…

Yes. Yes I could understand it. It was respect. I almost hated her then, almost envied her. I felt my heart quicken, my breath get faster…

Then slow again. Respect was something I did not need from Harry. All I needed from Harry was... was for him to take care of me. Yes. That was it. I needed him to take care of me. It wasn't the same thing at all.

Harry had, very briefly, rested his hand upon my shoulder. His eyes remained fixed on Shirley's, as hers remained fixed on his. And an understanding seemed to grow between all three of us.

'Have you had any more thoughts,' Shirley asked softly, 'about the work experience placements?'

This seemed to be changing the subject completely. But it wasn't.

Harry nodded, very slowly.

'I think I can do what you want,' he said.

She nodded.

'Good,' she said. 'I thought you might be able to help.'

And I knew that, somehow, all three of us had got what we needed here.

The wind blew, hot and urgent from the south, shredding the white clouds and leaving the blue above naked and vulnerable. Over the roof of Shirley's house, the branches of Cally Wood waved their bright springtime leaves and each leaf was a little green sword. Harry looked up at them. And one corner of his mouth twitched upward a little.

As soon as I got home, hardly thinking as I did it, I collected up every fag packet in the place and chucked them all in the bin.

12. Mary Maitland

Hard, bright light shone through the net curtains – June light. The front room of Mrs Atkinson's was very clean. There were photographs of her parents, of her daughter's graduation, of her grandchildren by that daughter and of her son.

Renato Atkinson had never graduated. He'd never had a job to speak of. And, a month before, he'd disappeared.

When, for five weeks, nothing's been heard of a small-time amphetamine dealer... And when he's thought to have been poaching on the territory of those who sell nastier stuff... And when his two known partners have similarly vanished...

Mrs Atkinson wasn't a fool. And I didn't treat her like one. I listened to what she told me and, bit by bit, I began to gain some understanding of her lost son.

I'd been visiting a few pubs and a few cheap bedsits, talking to people who wouldn't have said much to the police. I watched my back but I was known – my dad's name still counted for a lot. Plus, one of his former cell mates, a shaven-headed ex-burglar called Mike Stevenage, was now a trainee minister at a black Baptist chapel in Tividale. People wanted to be your friend if they knew you were a mate of 'Pastor Mike.'

Occasionally, trying to keep the fear out of my voice, I asked people if they'd seen a black Audi anywhere near the lads who'd vanished. Nobody had, but that meant nothing. If Harry Ronsard didn't want to be noticed, he wouldn't be. He was the sort who could do that.

Alice had been into smack, a year or so back, but she'd made an effort to get herself off it. She'd been prone to black moods, though, and it wasn't surprising, when things turned grim, that she'd gone looking for the stuff that she knew could make it all go away. But no one would have thought she'd get it off these three – they were a set of pill-dealing wannabe gangstaz called Peter Thatcher, Russell Holman and Renato Atkinson. Two white, one black. They had not

111

been exactly professional. They'd been flogging pills and dope to fund their own amphetamine dependencies. Recently though, Holman had been mouthing off about having 'nicked' a stash of smack from somewhere. 'Somewhere' necessarily meant one of the bigger operators – quite possibly the mob Sharukh's Abdul had been in with. 'Things', it was darkly suggested, were going to have 'happened'. So far, so grimly probable. Nobody had any idea who had actually done it but, again, that was hardly surprising.

Renato's lot came across as a bit pathetic – three loud, strutting, wretchedly insecure boys who'd made every bad decision possible. Now – let's be honest, because there was no doubt – they were dead.

Pastor Mike introduced me to Mrs Atkinson, a scrupulously proper Afro-Caribbean lady who lived in a primly kept semi overlooking Russells Hall Hospital. She'd never quite given up on the hope of a better life for her family in Britain. Never, despite the asbestosis-related death of her husband at fifty, which could never quite be laid square at the door of the dust-choked factory where he'd worked. Never, despite her son's descent into petty crime and addiction.

She was, it seemed, almost honoured to have me as a guest in her house – as I said, my dad's name still counted for quite a lot in Evangelical circles. She did all those polite things that people aren't supposed to do anymore – made us a pot of tea, turned Radio Four down while Mike and I sat on the sofa. Then she'd told us about Renato.

He'd not been accepted into any of the serious local drugs gangs. Mike had heard that he'd been given a trial, but he hadn't had the *nous* to be useful. Mrs Atkinson knew very little for sure – Renato had been hanging out with Peter Thatcher, white boy and small-time dealer. She'd not thought they'd been peddling heroin.

I told her that I didn't think they had, either – not normally. They just weren't the sort who could get hold of the stuff in wholesale quantities. I'd known plenty of wretched, silly people like Renato. I'd known just as many others who might have been his victims but that didn't take away his humanity – not for me.

So, murdered by one of the bigger operators. Except no one knew which one – or, if they did, they weren't saying.

Was that really it, though?

Polly, I thought, would have gone mental at me for considering it but, as Mike and I left Mrs Atkinson's, my instincts were screaming the name 'Harry Ronsard.'

***

About a week later, I came across him again. It was a Saturday but my elder brother, who taught at Lawnswood Comprehensive, was in work that morning. Extra tuition or leadership meeting – not sure which. Anyway, I was looking after his seven year old, Los, as well as Luke and Mattie, whose mum and dad were in Glasgow, where a family friend had just passed away. Luke was cheesed off at not being allowed to go with them, because this friend had been a famous aircraft designer in the fifties and sixties and apparently had met his share of Apollo astronauts. My sister had been adamant that a drive up there, a funeral and a drive back the next day, was a sure recipe for car sickness so, along with his more willing brother, Luke had got stuck with me and Los.

Los was a bit of a daft monkey. With my brother Paul for a dad, he was bound to be. He sang a lot – he was a good boy soprano – but he hated his own voice; he had his ear on deeper stuff. One of Paul's mates – who our sister continually told us never to trust – had got Los into Wagner. So that's what he wanted to sing.

Anyway, that morning our plan was to have a walk in Cally Wood, which was just over the road from Paul's school, then meet up with Paul himself and go up Merry Hill, the local Mega Mall. Unearthly mystic of the nuttiest sort, Paul wasn't going to approve. The youth vote, though, would swing the result.

It was only about ten, so most kids and teenagers weren't out of bed yet; the wood was quiet...

Except for Los singing, as he explained to me most seriously, edited highlights from *Das Rheingold.* Oh dear.

His voice was a sweet thing, which partly made up for the

awfulness of the music. I mean, I don't hate all opera – quite like a bit of Verdi or Puccini, in fact – but oh dearie me, Wagner..!

The voice echoed around the green trunks as we climbed to the top of the wooded ridge and walked through the leafy tunnel, northward.

The trees to our right turned to conifers, then back to oaks, as we got closer to the ridge's end. Through the leaves above, the sky was a deep June blue, clouds making huge cotton wool castles for brave little Los to conquer.

Luke did not look impressed. Mattie was bemused.

And I was bemused when Los's soprano trill was answered by another voice, from the darkness within the trees: a bass baritone that could have sung any of the horny-helmetted abominations professionally. A voice that knew this music very very well.

A figure emerged from the trees, wearing a brown leather jacket and brown corduroy trousers. Harry Ronsard. And, trotting obediently behind him, at a respectful distance, was Polly Gauvain.

This had just turned into a very bad day.

I didn't think I'd ever been so afraid. Harry's expression though, was polite not derisory. I was afraid of him because I understood him. He would think this was to my credit because, after all, he would know himself to be something worthy of fear.

The boys reacted differently – bizarrely so. Luke didn't care – there was nothing about Harry Ronsard that was the least worthy of his attention. This was mutual – Harry barely noticed him. Los was troubled but, more than that, fascinated. He walked right up to Harry, grinning hugely.

Mattie froze.

It was the second and last time I was to see that look on his face and I shall never forget it – that expression of wide-eyed wonder, now tinged with a sadness utterly wrong in a six-year old. At that moment, I felt something change in the world. The sun was still bright, the blue and white still summer lovely and yet, above us, something felt as if it had closed in the sky, or as if the sky itself had turned to concrete, behind the blue.

I think Luke might have half-sensed it.

And Harry Ronsard seemed to sense it, too. His head snapped upwards and he fixed the clouds with a stare of ferocious defiance. Then, he seemed to realise it was hopeless, and his gaze returned to us.

He looked lost and bereaved, but still driven by an implacable purpose. He looked at Los, levelly, and allowed himself a half smile, his glance flicking over to me.

'Hello!' cried Los, still joyful as birdsong. 'I'm Los Maitland!'

My guts got in the lift and went down thirty floors. I did not want this man – if it was a man – to know anything about my loved ones.

'Harry Ronsard,' Harry replied. 'What's that name again?'

'Los.'

'You look more like a gain to me.'

I blinked. Harry had made a joke. I knew this must be fabulously rare.

'Not *Loss,*' Los explained, *'Los.* One "S." Los is the Zoa who builds!'

My brother's love of mystical poetry had got his son lumbered with a very strange name. Harry, I felt sure, would never have read the poems that name came from. Yet he frowned, very deeply, as if Los's words *did* mean something to him – as if they were connected with memories he was struggling to dig up from a very long time ago.

'Hello, Polly,' I said, turning to her and keeping every shred of terror and criticism out of my voice.

She just nodded, once, and said nothing.

'He yours?' Harry asked, still fixed on Los, expression inexplicably respectful.

'My brother's.'

'Hmm... *The Zoa who builds.* I used to be a builder. You sing good songs, my lad. Wagner.' Then to me, 'Did you teach him?'

'No, one of his dad's friends,' I admitted.

'Then your dad has good friends, my lad. You're lucky. Is it the giants you like best – or the dragons?'

'The dragons,' Los beamed. 'I love dragons!'

'So do I,' Harry nodded. 'A friend of mine painted a lovely big black dragon on my living room wall.'

'Wow! I'd love to see that!'

'Maybe you will,' Harry replied. 'Not today, but maybe you will. Farewell for now.'

There must have been a look of real horror on my face at the idea of little Los marching unafraid into that dragon's lair. Harry wouldn't have missed it – there wasn't much that got past him. He made a harsh barking noise that I realised was meant to be a laugh. Then he disappeared into the trees. Polly nodded and followed.

The birds hadn't stopped twittering. Luke was staring at the sky, still troubled by it. Mattie was kneeling by a patch of wildflowers, eyes wide with love and wonder. Los burst into song again, *'Glad times have come, come to our Rhine, when Hagen, grim Hagen with laughter can shine...'*

I'm pretty sure Harry Ronsard never saw Los or Luke or Mattie again. But the memory sticks because I'm certain that something important happened, that morning, in those woods. And it wasn't spiritual or mystical – though I am a Christian and I think that, yes, such things do take place. But this was something I didn't understand, perhaps couldn't understand, though it was something as much a part of our universe, of our lives, as the big, solid old oaks around us.

13. Harry Ronsard

'These work placements,' Shirley says to me, 'we need to get them organised.'

'We do,' I agree. 'I know you'll send me the right sort. Come on in.'

For the first time, she comes into my hall. She's never shown any interest in doing so before. And she does something else, something very peculiar – something I'd not have thought anyone could ever do: she takes no notice of what's on the walls.

It must take a particular sort of mind to do this. One that's very exclusively focused – on Something. Something that takes away the reality of everything else so that she's only aware of the One Terrible Something. And I know what the Something is. I do. I can see it in Shirley's face and all the beauty in that face and all the strength in that face are just the ways in which the Something is expressed. It is all they are there for. It is all she is there for.

It is Pain, this Something. Pain. Everything else about Shirley Icement fizzed away long ago – fizzed away in the acid of this Pain. Shirley Icement is as purely Pain as I am purely Retribution.

I still try to test her, though. 'You don't seem to have noticed your son's pictures,' I say.

She looks blank.

I have to nod, very deliberately, at the big Sir Lancelot on the wall of the sitting room. At first, she will not see what's there. I nod again. Her eyes follow my direction, but still she will not see.

'Perhaps,' I say, 'you don't notice it because it's Lee's. Too close to being yours for it to make much impression.'

I've trapped her! Now she has to see it! I swear, though, she's made it difficult for me. I've never been up against a human mind so strong, so utterly unbending. In that moment, I realise I love Shirley Icement. I love her more truly than I loved my sweet little Christine and poor little Polly, who dotes on me. But it is a different kind of love – it is a love that is founded upon What Is Right.

Shirley looks at Sir Lancelot and dismisses him. To her, he's unconvincing.

Her gaze turns to the black dragon. That's a different matter. She knows the dragon, alright – sees him in the bathroom mirror first thing every morning. And she looks at me and she sees that I do too.

I push things a little further:

'I owe you a lot, Shirley,' I say, 'for Alice's sake.'

She looks at me and she thinks about sneering. I've said something that, if anybody else had said it, would have been worth a sneer. But she can't sneer at me, though. And she knows it.

'I don't care about Alice,' she says. 'Alice wasn't important.'

'She *was* important,' I insist, 'but she went to a lot of trouble to convince you that she wasn't.'

'Trouble?' Shirley asks. 'Trouble meaning drugging herself to death?'

I think about that. And I feel myself start to look the way I look when there's a problem to be solved. I enjoy problems.

'I think so, yes,' I tell her, finally.

And we're silent for a long time because we realise that Alice has set us a puzzle here, one that we ought to try to work out but, perhaps, one that we never will. Because, if we were the sort of people who could solve puzzles like Alice's, we'd be the sort of people who make a habit of listening to Ozric Tentacles.

'Work placements, then,' I say, finally.

***

Takes about an hour for us to get the paperwork sorted, then she's on her way. Not home, no. She's in the car, off round to see somebody called 'Derek Chiselhurst', one of her deputies or assistants. She's at the job twenty-four, seven. It's clear she expects her subordinates to be the same. She's the right sort, is Shirley, the sort I can work with.

Much to be done, though. Upstairs I go, because there's swords that need cleaning and polishing. After I've done that, I come down for a cup of tea: Typhoo, of course – don't give me any of that trendy

PG Tips muck. Anybody who drinks that kind of muck is a bit suspect, the way I see it. And, give 'em half a chance, they'd be sending us round Waitrose and having us knock back camomile or Lapsang Souchong or who knows what sort of decadent decaffeinated filth. No. Typhoo for me.

After that, I go in the garage. And I open the boot of the car. And there are these two wide eyes staring up out of it. There's a bruised face around these eyes, with a mouth that's got a gag in it. Close at hand, there's wrists tightly bound in white clothes line, held together so that it looks, even though he's got his hands balled into fists, as if he's praying.

There's a look almost of curiosity in those eyes. It's Cooper's ducks for him, he thinks. And he's not wrong. But he's starting to wonder exactly how it's going to be done.

His suit's posh and his skin's white. His accent, when he's not got the gag in, is public school or a very good impersonation of it. I'm going up in the world, me, in terms of the fat wallets of those I'm preying upon and in terms of the amount of harm they do. That is as it should be.

I've got the spatha in my right hand. That is also as it should be. And I let him take a long, careful look at it. And I see him start to sweat and tremble.

'Now, see here, young feller-me-lad,' I tell him. 'You know what one of these is?'

He nods.

'And you don't want it going in you just yet?'

He shakes.

'But, we both know it is going in you, fairly soon. No point trying to pull the wool over your eyes about that, is there?'

He is very very still.

'No. No point at all. All the same, you really want to put it off. If only by a few seconds. Or a few minutes. Well. I'm going to tell you how.'

He's still very still.

'You do it,' I tell him, 'by remembering not to make a noise when I take this here gag out. Reckon you can remember not to do that?'

He nods.

So the gag comes out.

And I start asking him questions. These are mostly about names. Names and addresses. And, for the most part, they get answered fairly satisfyingly. So he gains himself a few minutes. There's not much to get me fired up, though. Nothing to show I'm climbing the ladder much further.

It's not until he gives me an address in Chipping Norton that my ears begin to prick up. I smile at him and stuff the gag back in. He panics, then, and starts to make these pathetic, whimpering noises. I'd been going to let him live a bit longer but, on balance, I decide to put him out of his misery. Needless suffering is not what I'm all about. So the sword goes through him and his eyes go wide and then, very soon after, they go blank and dead.

The inside of the boot has been lined with some of that bright blue damp-proof membrane I got from work – top-quality stuff, so the blood won't go everywhere and make a mess. I don't like mess. Tonight, I'll have him in the hole I've got ready for him in the back garden. Not going to be able to do that many more times because, truth to tell, the place is getting a bit full up. That is a nuisance. Never mind. I've already started dumping a few of them in the cut. And there's plenty of space in the wood, and miles of countryside beyond it, where a hundred bodies might lie for years and, once found, might never be identified. Look what happened to Bella in the Wytch Elm.

Chipping Norton, ay? That gets me thinking. You get newspaper editors and politicians and all that sort living there. And, apparently, you get cocaine importers. Well, one cocaine importer – one particularly important cocaine importer. Can't be co-incidence. He's there because there's something in it for him, hob-nobbing with the big nobs. Doing him in is going to get me noticed by powerful men.

I'm surprised at how little that bothers me. Notice away! All you lot with your eight figure take-home pay, your farm-sized back gardens and your discreet but expensive personal habits! A right load of Jeremiah Topshines, the lot of you! Think you can take me on? You're clueless, clueless and pathetic! Because you have no idea what you're dealing with here.

The spatha is light in my hand. It ought to feel heavy, especially for a man in his sixties. There are going to be a fair old few who will feel its edge before the week's out. A fair old few.

Got to wait till night though, for now. Because there's a body to go in the back garden and blood to get sluiced down the sink. All very discreet, though I've never had enough to do with next door on either side that they're going to take any notice, whatever I get up to. So I sit down with another cup of tea and read the *Daily Mail*. As you do.

And I'm aware that I'm being watched.

The awareness creeps up on me. At first, I don't take much notice of it. Then I go to the window and have a look out. Along the road, about fifty yards farther on from the Icements', is parked a Renault. There's someone in the driver's seat but, at this distance, I can't see who it might be. The car looks familiar, though...

Of course. Polly's friend, the good woman. Who I finally got to meet last week, up in the woods, with that grand young nephew of hers with the funny name that seems to slip from my mind like mercury so that I can't remember it for my life... And those other two nephews, who seem even stranger to me. Her name, Polly has told me, is Mary. Mary Maitland.

The name sounded familiar. Mary's father, Polly explained, is the priest who stabbed that black magic pervert to death seven years or so back. Remember reading about it in the *Daily Mail*.

Mary, though she's not the sort to go stabbing anyone to death, isn't one to miss much. She's taken one good look at me and she's seen I've got Death written all over. That's why she was so scared in the woods – frightened I might hurt her nephews, who she loves. She needn't have worried – I'm only dangerous to those who've done evil. But I respect her fear. Concern for children's safety is a proper feeling – a feeling that it is right for a woman to have.

For a moment, I consider going out and talking to her. I decide against it. *Not yet;* I think to myself, *there needs to be a few more battles won before I can prove to you what war it is that I'm waging. Once I've fought those battles, though, I'm going to change your mind about the sort of bloke I am. Because you're on my side, Mary Maitland, you just don't know it yet.*

14. Mary Maitland

'Are you sure you're alright?'

'Yes, Ryan.'

''Cause you're looking so wound up it's a wonder your spring ain't bust.'

'I'm alright, Ryan.'

'I think you should stay in tonight. We can get the rest of the front room painted.'

'I can't. I've got to go and see somebody. We'll do it at the weekend.'

'You're going to see that bloody Harry Ronsard. The bloke's bad news, love. If you've got nothing against him good enough to take to the coppers, he's best off left alone.'

I deserved that.

'I need to know, love,' I whispered. 'I need to know if he's up to anything.'

Ryan plonked himself down on the sofa and breathed in heavily. To me, he seemed the one wound up with anxiety. I had no right doing this to him. It only made it worse that he never stopped offering help, despite my constant refusals.

If he'd known I was intending to go chasing after Harry when the old sod went on what might turn out to be a murder spree...

I decided not to imagine his reaction.

'I've been asking around about this bloke as well,' Ryan said, softly. 'At work, round the pub – you know, just asking. Nobody's got much to say against him, it's true. But there's people who know him... I don't know – they're frightened. I don't think they're aware of it, but they are frightened. Look, I don't like bringing up what happened eight years ago but, back then, there was nobody...'

'There was somebody to be frightened of,' I cut in. 'There was Dad.'

'Yes, I know there was your dad, but that was... that was family stuff. It was a tragedy, it was a murder, but it was all family stuff. There wasn't any real devilry going on – nothing... supernatural.'

'No. There wasn't.'

'But this time... this Harry bloke... love, this time I think there might be.'

I nodded. 'Yes,' I said, 'I think there might be, too.'

'So can't you..?' He dried up. He knew what my answer would be.

I sat on the sofa next to him and said quietly, 'I'm a Christian, Ryan. It means I have faith. And it's like Dad says – faith is knowing that, if that's what it takes, you'll be prepared to let them bang the nails in.'

I'd needed to be honest with him, because I knew how he felt about me. But I couldn't look at his face because I wouldn't be able to stand seeing him tearful.

***

After all the soul-searching, though, that evening's attempt to keep track of Harry Ronsard was so unsuccessful it was laughable. By seven, I'd got the motor parked up the road from his place. I'd done this a couple of times before, just to get a bit of practice at surveillance.

Sure enough, at about seven twenty, he came out and got in the Audi. I started the Renault. As he pulled out of the drive, he glanced, very briefly, in my direction. He gave no sign that he'd noticed me. He turned away, heading south towards Lawnswood Avenue. There was a little triangle of blue plastic sticking out of the boot of the Audi. It was a second before I recognised it as damp-proof membrane – the sort builders put underneath concrete floors to keep the groundwater safely below. I pulled out and followed him. Cally Wood loomed darkly to our right. Ahead, the Audi turned left into Lawnswood Avenue. By the time I'd made the same turning, he was at the end of the street and I sped up a little as he pulled into Lawnswood Road. He took a left, heading into Wordsley. I kept well back. I didn't think he'd spotted me.

I lost him somewhere in Brockmoor. Which meant I'd been a successful tail for all of two miles. You ever tried anything like that? It's trickier than it looks in the movies.

'Oh, stuff it!' I said to myself, quite a lot, as I pootled fruitlessly round the streets of Pensnett and Brierley Hill, all of them bare of Black Audis.

I had a funny feeling that Harry had been going somewhere quite different from Pensnett.

Eventually, it got dark and I gave up.

Ryan had stayed at my place. He forced the relief from his face so as not to upset me, which meant it upset me all the more. We kissed a bit, cuddled a bit and thought about having sex, without either of us mentioning it. It didn't happen though – not that night. We'd slipped up on the chastity before but, now we'd finally fixed a date for the wedding, we both felt that it would be fairly pathetic to repeat that mistake, though we both had siblings who'd have disagreed. Again, we didn't mention this decision aloud. We didn't have to.

'I don't think I'm going to have much luck keeping tabs on Harry Ronsard,' I said.

'Good,' Ryan said, softly, 'Good.'

***

That did not mean, of course, that I wasn't going to have *a good go* at keeping tabs on Old Harry. A couple of nights later, I was waiting there once more, this time a little bit farther down the road. Harry came out, looked around and, again, did not appear to spot my motor. Then he was in the black Audi and heading off.

This time, he took a right out of Lawnswood Avenue and drove, very sensibly, down to the main Kidderminster Road. Bit of a nightmare at the best of times, that road. Kids use it to show off so you always have to dodge the odd nitwit in something sporty, desperate to imply that the loudness of his engine says something about the size of his willy.

Turning left, heading towards Kidderminster, I still had Harry in sight. That little triangle of blue damp-proof membrane was still sticking out of the boot – a small thing yet, in Harry, it seemed incredible. He just didn't seem the sort who'd allow himself such slovenliness.

I stayed on him. For mile after mile. I hung back; I couldn't be sure but I still didn't think he'd seen me. The road was wide but well used. And my car wasn't the sort that stood out.

Countryside. Big wide early summer fields on either side of the road. The sort of place Elgar wrote music about. And off to the right were the Malvern Hills. Now though, Harry was heading south east and minutes later, we were on the motorway. Soon after, we were in Oxfordshire.

There was a moment when I thought I'd lost him. A couple of big Eddie Stobart trucks overtook me and got between us. When they'd moved on, I was sure the Audi would have disappeared.

But no – there it still was, the little blue triangle of damp-proof plastic marking it out, as if by design.

At that point, I wondered if he knew I was there? If he actually wanted me to be following him? Annoyed with myself, I dismissed the idea, but it wouldn't quite go away.

I wasn't keeping track of the names of places; I did vaguely notice a sign offering me a cool metallic welcome to Chipping Norton. I felt the name ought to mean something.

Then I lost him again.

Not for very long, but long enough to frighten me badly. I felt lonely and exposed and a big part of me wanted to twist the steering wheel through a screeching u turn and head for home. I did not let myself do this. Instead, I drove slowly along the prosperous-looking roads and avenues, until…

There he was.

…Or there was the black Audi, at least. Parked at the top of a long, curving gravel drive, between a Bentley and a Rolls-Royce.

I pulled up on the opposite side of the road.

The house wasn't conspicuously expensive. It was ivy covered,

126

thatched, with small lattice windows. But the expensive isn't always conspicuous, is it? No, this place had big money.

The front door, I could see from here, was open. The gate at the bottom of the gravel drive was open. That was unusual, somewhere like this. In fact, that gate meant business: it was tall and spikey and wired up to an intercom on the brick gatepost. Not the kind of gate that you'd find just 'left open' – ever.

The sun was getting low. It was a fiery and beautiful sunset that glittered off the windows.

I walked up the thick crunching gravel of the drive.

At the door, I barely hesitated.

Inside, the soft ticking of an ancient grandfather clock. Dark wood panelling and the smell of what I thought must be expensive whisky, mixed with something else.

Some kind of kid's toy on the thick stair carpet. I wasn't sure what it was – about the size and shape of a football, but hairy.

I climbed the stairs. Lying at the top was a strange bundle of something, wrapped in expensive material…

It took me a moment to work out that it was a human body. But it was a body that had something wrong with it, something missing…

Spinning away from it, mouth open to scream but some instinct for self-preservation keeping me dead quiet, I looked back down the stairs. I saw that the thing I'd taken for a child's toy had a face.

I did not run. God only knows why not. Instead, I put my head round the doors of all the rooms upstairs. I'm not sure how many bodies were there. I tried to count but my mind was all over the place. And some of them were cut up into such small bits. The man in the bathroom – I think it was a man – he was the one cut up the worst; if it hadn't been for the severed hand holding the gun, I might not have realised he had ever been a man at all.

And there was such a lot of blood – the place reeked of it.

Stepping around the severed head on the stairs, I started to tremble. By the time I got to the bottom, I was could hardly stand. I didn't let that stop me. I checked the downstairs rooms. More dead men, some carrying guns, each one parted from his head. The clock carried on ticking.

A voice, low and soft with politeness but very strong.

'Hello, Miss Maitland.'

Harry Ronsard stepped out of the shadows at the back of the house.

'Sorry it smells a bit. Clearing out the rubbish – always a mucky business.'

There was a strange noise. I'd heard it when we'd met in Cally Wood, but it was still a moment before I recognised it as laughter. Harry Ronsard's laughter was hard to recognise because it was so utterly without humour. It was a laugh that was no laughing matter.

I breathed in. And out. And in. And tried to shape my breath into words. It took a while.

'Killing people,' I gasped at last, 'killing people is wrong!'

He was quiet for a moment. Then he nodded.

'I only do it when it's what's needed,' he said, something like humility in his voice. 'Don't go thinking this lot deserved any sympathy. You have a look at the papers. You have a look at the news in the next few days. You'll hear about them. You'll hear what they were like.'

I did not dare reply. I knew better than to try getting into an argument with this man.

'You just think about what happened to poor little Alice,' he went on, 'what people like this lot did to her. You were her friend. You know what this sort of rubbish deserve.'

Still, I made myself stay quiet. The sunlight gleamed in the deceptive softness of his eyes.

'And there's other little girls like her out there who need to be protected. You've made it your life's work to protect them. I can respect that. Like your father before you. You know stuff like this is necessary.'

Like my father before me, Harry Ronsard? Like my father who has confessed that, even if he had the right to murder anyone – which he had not – he actually went and murdered the wrong man? But I'm not sharing that with you, Harry Ronsard – I'm not sharing any part of my soul with you!

'It's wrong,' I repeated, and I felt the tears on my cheeks.

He didn't argue. He just nodded, quietly.

'Going to be people round here in a bit,' he said, 'lots of people. Don't want you getting seen by them. There's big posh 'uns live round here and they can get a bit funny when there's trouble on their doorstep. They look for people to blame. They won't be so daft as to try any of that rubbish with me but they might try it with you; it's as well for you to be out of their way.'

I stepped past him, out into the sunset. The light shone from the blades of the two swords he was carrying. Swords that dripped blood. How had I failed to notice them? How?

I crunched back down the gravel, my steps weak and uneven. I got in the car and managed to get the keys in the ignition. As I drove away, I was aware of Harry's Audi, pulling out behind me and heading off in the opposite direction.

It was getting dark when I pulled into a service station. I sat in the car park and thought about phoning my family – my dad, my brothers, perhaps even my sister or poor little Mom. But that wouldn't have been a good idea. They'd have wanted to help. And maybe some of them *could* have helped – maybe my big brother Paul could have exorcised Harry or maybe my self-defence sister could have kicked his head in. Maybe. But *maybe* wasn't good enough. I would not put any of them at risk.

I started the car and drove home.

Ryan was still there. I told him nothing – I begged him not to ask where I'd been, what I'd seen. He did not ask, but he would not leave; he insisted on sleeping on the sofa. I could not shift the daft sausage.

15: Dave Calper

''Ello, Dave.'

Ryan Sheepshanks' voice sounded worried. He filled the shop doorway about as completely as an actual door. I'd not seen someone do a better physical impersonation of a Sherman tank since the Wolf himself. This wasn't a bloke who'd get worried over nothing.

'I'd like you to go round Mary's,' he said, straight to the point before I'd even offered him a cup of tea. 'She's not happy about something and not keen to talk to me about it. I think she might talk to you.'

'Alright,' I said. 'She going to be in tonight?'

'Should be.'

'Any idea what it's all to do with?'

'That bloody Harry Ronsard.'

'Oh. Dear. Right. I'll get round soon as I can.'

He looked at me. His face was calm but his eyes were afraid. I didn't blame him.

'Cheers, Dave,' he said. 'That's a big help.'

So I knocked on Mary's door about six in the evening, unannounced. She smiled at me but, yes, 'not happy about something' was a fair description. Her face was pale and there were bags under her eyes.

'Ryan thought you could do with a chat,' I said.

She smiled a bit more.

'I thought he might,' she said, quietly, sitting down in the back room.

The CD player was on and, to my surprise, it was one of ours, made a couple of years before. Quite a funky little number, to be honest. Around then, la Keyboard had been having her thing with Charlotte Ronsard but I wasn't going to mention that.

'So what's been the bother?'

She stared at the carpet for a bit.

130

'The Chartington murder,' she said. 'I was there.'

I was silent. I'd never met the bastard but I knew him by reputation.

I sighed.

'Look, love, don't shed no tears for *him*.'

'I wasn't about to.'

'The bloke was a coke dealer.'

'Thought it might be something like that.'

'Ay?'

'The men he had with him. They had guns. They've not said much about that... on the news.'

'Well, no, they're not going to. There's a lot of people going to want it hushed up.'

'Hushed up?'

'He was one of the biggest, love. What I hear, he's been the one keeping Tory Party conferences in Columbian marching powder since Thatcher was in. They're going to be trying their damnedest to stop that getting all over the papers.'

She nodded, understanding.

'Respectable house in Chipping Norton!' I said. 'Just bloody shows, don't it?'

Mary started trembling. I leaned over and took her hand.

'You want to tell me about it?'

She breathed in, then said, 'Harry Ronsard killed them.'

I was still. Then I nodded and said, 'Oh.'

Then I paused.

'Oh,' I said again.

'I'd been following him,' she went on. 'Stupid thing to do but I had to know. I had to see for myself. He shouldn't have been able to do it. They had guns and there were... I don't know how many of them. All he had were a couple of swords.'

'Swords?'

'That's all I could see.'

She was quiet again for a bit.

'By the time I got there, he'd killed the lot of them. Bodies all over

131

the shop.' She was quiet for a moment, then said, 'I think he's... the Devil... possessed by the Devil... I don't know but it's got something to do with the Devil...'

I struggled to find an answer.

'I can see how... I can see how... you might think that. And I can see how it sort of might be true... Careful, though: it's going to be more complicated –'

'Dave,' she cut me off, 'I don't usually preach at you, do I?'

'No,' I admitted, 'you don't.'

'And, given what my dad and my brothers are like, that's pretty amazing, isn't it?'

'Yes. Yes it is.'

'Okay, then. So shut up a bit because I'm going to preach at you now. What I saw Harry Ronsard do was impossible. But he did it. Now, if something is not possible, but it is happening, then it can only be God or Satan. And this must be Satan. Because God doesn't murder people. He has to let them murder each other because to prevent them would be to do their thinking for them. And that would be to destroy them. But, no matter what the... misconceptions of the... well-meaning people who wrote the Old Testament, God doesn't murder people. Not even the most evil. Never. Ever. Fact. End of Story. Get Used to It.'

She wasn't about to be argued with. I didn't try.

'You going to go seeing him again?' I asked.

'I don't know.'

'Try not to. Having people around him who believe he's the Devil will make him more powerful. Make the Devil in him more powerful. We don't want that.'

'We don't. No. We definitely don't.'

'And, Mary...'

'Yes.'

'You need to take a breather. You saw what he's like. It's a bloody wonder you've stood up to him so far. Dunno – must be something to do with what you've picked up from your sister, what you've picked up from your dad. And from work, one way or another. But

132

this has taken it out of you, love. Next time you see him, you're not going to be able to cope so well...'

She nodded, to my relief.

'I ought to go to the police,' she said, softly.

I knew that would be a very bad idea. 'Don't,' I said. 'Coppers, judges, MPs, people like that, they're trained to follow the rules – to follow instructions. And from what you've said, Harry's marvellous at dishing out the instructions. If you've got someone like him, they're always going to act like sheep. They're going to be halfway in love with him before long, the bloody lot of 'em. Try accusing Harry of anything, you're the one who'll get banged up in the nick. Give yourself a break, Mary, please!'

She looked horrified.

'Mary,' I said, 'you remember what people used to be like around your dad.'

Her face froze, along with any attempt to argue with me; she remembered alright. I knew I'd sown a bit of doubt in her mind. Enough doubt to keep her out the bloody cop shop? Christ, I hoped so.

'Dave.' A soft, broken little voice.

'Yeah?'

'Don't tell Ryan anything about this, will you? I want him to know as little as possible about it.'

'Why? You trust each other.'

'We do. But I need him to be someone... to be somewhere in my life that's got nothing to do with Harry Ronsard.'

'I see,' I said, 'I see.'

16: Polly Gauvain

'Hello, Polly.'

Harry's voice was gentle. He was always like that with me – gentle. And he took my chin between his thumb and forefinger and tipped my head so that I had to look up at him and he said, 'Pretty little thing you are.'

I felt my cheeks go warm. I loved it when he said that to me. It made me feel as if I was his pet guinea pig or hamster.

He let go his hold of me and I came into his house. It was a warm evening. I wanted to stay with him tonight. But I knew that wouldn't happen. At about ten or eleven, he'd take my hand and lead me to my car, hold the door open for me as I got in and he'd say goodbye. And nothing I could do would change that, even if I had the power – which I didn't – to do something crazy like tear my clothes off for him and beg him to give me a child. A boy child like the men in the paintings on his wall.

That was what I wanted. And it was not my place to ask why I wanted it. Nor to ask why Harry would not yet satisfy me. Laws had been made by Harry and by my own body, and I had no right to question those laws.

As he let me in, something caught his eye over my shoulder. His gaze narrowed.

'Back again, is he?' he whispered and, moving past me, walked out into the evening light.

A few yards up the road was a metallic grey Mercedes. Someone was in the driver's seat, watching us.

I followed Harry as he strode over, unconcerned, and tapped the tinted window. It purred as it came down.

And behind it was a face I knew, though I did not know from where.

'Yes?' asked the face, in a voice I'd not expected. It was a posh voice, not from round here – the kind of voice that was used to getting its own way, used to feeling confident.

But after he'd looked at Harry for a moment, all that confidence went away.

'Yes... sir?' he corrected himself.

'That's better,' Harry replied. 'You're usually here to take a look at Shirley, aren't you?'

The man nodded, wordlessly.

'But right now, you're here to have a look at me.'

Another nod.

'So – what have you got to offer me?' Harry paused, taking his time. Then, one corner of his mouth went up a little. 'You really think you've got anything I could possibly want?'

The man struggled to answer. There was sweat on his brow. Then he managed to squeeze out a half-strangled little 'Yes'.

Harry folded his arms and looked at him, mercilessly.

'I don't think you're someone I can respect,' he said at last.

The man said nothing. His eyes narrowed a little, then widened, never leaving Harry's face.

Harry stared back at him, considering him carefully.

'You related to Shirley?' he asked, at last.

The man nodded.

'Oh aye? How?'

'Nephew,' the man croaked.

'What's your name?' Harry asked.

The man did not reply. It was the first time I'd ever thought anyone was standing up to Harry, even a little bit. But the man seemed to get away with it by glancing, very quickly, in the direction of Shirley's house.

'Ah!' said Harry, 'I see! You don't want to tell me without Aunt Shirley's say so, that right?'

The man nodded.

The corner of Harry's mouth twitched and he stepped back a pace. The man inhaled, sharply, three or four times.

Harry nodded once more, dismissively. Relief on his face, the man twisted the keys in his ignition and a moment later, the car was gliding off.

Harry looked after him, curious.

'Didn't seem at all keen to let us know his name,' he said.

I didn't reply.

'Come to think of it, Shirley's never mentioned her maiden name to me, either.' He frowned. 'That ain't going to be a coincidence.'

I almost remarked that round here, not knowing your neighbour's maiden name was hardly unusual. But no. If Harry had smelt a rat, there was a rat.

Shirley had appeared, like a ghost, outside her house. Her eyes met Harry's.

'Why has that revolting abortion been bothering you?' she asked.

'He hasn't said.'

'Hasn't said? Evasive little twerp!'

'I think I can trust him to get back to me.'

Shirley grimaced. 'I'm sorry. You really shouldn't have to put up with horrible little creatures like that.'

Harry looked at her. 'What exactly makes him so horrible, Shirley?'

Shirley stared at him, without fear or self-doubt. Then she glanced at me.

'I'd rather not say. Not here.'

'You can trust Polly, Shirley. She's the most trustworthy little thing I've ever met.'

Shirley glanced at me – briefly. She clearly didn't think glancing at me was worth the bother.

'He didn't seem all that keen to tell us his name,' Harry added.

Shirley scowled. 'Good,' she said. 'It's not a name I'd want your ears to be polluted with.'

'It was your name, once, though, wasn't it?' I said.

Harry turned to me and I saw delight in his eyes.

Shirley turned to me and I saw astonishment in hers; I don't think she could quite accept that I knew how to talk, not really. And she certainly sounded like she'd rather I shut up.

'It was,' she said and her voice came from a very dark and very cold place, far far away. 'It was, once. A long time ago.'

Harry stretched out his arm and patted her on the shoulder. I was amazed that anyone could do this – even Harry. Shirley accepted his touch without a tremble. 'No,' she said, looking at Harry, then at me, 'I really wouldn't want your ears to be polluted with it.'

So we left her. Harry led the way back inside. I followed. Harry went to put the kettle on.

'I wish you'd let me do that,' I said.

Harry looked puzzled.

'Making the tea and stuff,' I explained. 'Kitchen things. Things for a woman.'

Harry still didn't get it. 'I don't mind the kitchen,' he said.

I laughed at him, then. In some ways he was really easy to laugh at, because he was a big man and he had no understanding of little things.

'I'm not saying you should mind it but if you've got a woman to do that sort of thing for you, then she *should* be doing that sort of thing for you. It's how things ought to be.'

'Got a woman?'

'Yes.'

'*Got* a woman?'

'Yes.'

'Have I got you, Polly?'

I looked into his eyes. There was amazement in them.

'Of course you have,' I told him.

'Well…' he said.

Then he paused. And he was obviously having to think very long and hard about what to say next.

'Well…' he said again. And paused again.

'*Well…*' he said for a third time. Then, finally, 'If it's The Right Thing to Do. We must always do The Right Thing to Do. Do you think it's the right thing to do?'

I laughed at him again. When it came to little things, he was so clueless.

'That's not for me to say!' I said. 'Deciding what to do! Right and wrong! Thinking! That's all man's stuff.' I looked up at him from

137

under eyelashes that I could feel delicately fluttering. 'I'm a woman, Harry.'

Harry looked down on me and, again, took my chin between thumb and forefinger.

'Hmm. A woman. Hmm. Yes. S'pose you're right. Well. If you want someone to do all the thinking and all the deciding what's right and wrong for you…'

I realised I'd waited my whole life to hear someone say those words. Had they been worth waiting for? Yes! Oh yes!

'I do!'

'Hmm. Well then. I suppose I'd better ought to, then…'

My arms went around him and I buried my face in him. I felt a deep, booming yet soft laugh, through his clothes.

'Oh my little bunny rabbit! Oh my little hamster!'

And I could feel all the things that had ever hurt me, all the things that had ever given me pain – mind, memory, personality – being washed away, as was only right. I had always hated them. They had done nothing for me. Now, I had only what I wanted – I had feeling; I had my love for Harry and that was everything.

The kettle started to boil and I broke away from him to make the tea.

But I didn't know where he kept the tea bags, so, as it happened, he had to do it after all.

17: Satansfist

The Cunt had been about to start snivelling, and his snivellings could be relied upon to become unbearable very quickly. Had that not been the case, I would never have agreed to this.

Thankfully, it was sunny; I'd checked the weather forecast to make sure, because there was no point starting such a job if it was going to piss down. And the platform was safe enough; it was a neat device used by window cleaners to raise themselves up and down while scrubbing the glass of tower blocks; I was using it to paint a mural on the end of a row of terraces.

One of The Cunt's mates – the pretentious tart who'd organised that wretched 'poetry night' – had come up with the idea. The event had, since her departure, been taken over by a bunch of EDL saddoes who'd very quickly got themselves raided by the boys in blue; the whole place had been mercifully shut down and boarded up.

It seemed, though, that said tart's mummy and daddy were fucking loaded and they'd bought her a house here in fragrant Tipton, where she dreamed of setting up an *'independent alternative arts space'*. I wondered how soon it'd be before, in the breathless pages of the *Express and Star,* somebody's willy was revealed to have been whipped out in the name of 'Art' and the outraged Tipton Taliban firebombed the shithole. Frankly, if those dozy fucking towelheads didn't do the job soon, I'd think about mixing the molotovs myself.

I'd been given the brief to 'express myself freely' by the presiding tart. Like everything she came out with, this was bullshit – she had something very specific in mind but, as is the manner of tarty mediocrities, she expected me to put a lot of effort into working out what she wanted without going to the trouble of telling me.

Bollocks to that.

I chose to ask for the money – including expenses – up front. I waited until she was away for the week at some appropriately wanky festival. Then I got round there quick, meaning to get the job done while she wasn't there to express her predictable reservations.

Okay. Put it out of your mind that this is anything to do with The Cunt's posey wanker friends, and go with the flow...

Something that captured the spirit of the place... Hmm... Have you ever been to Tipton? No, don't laugh; it's no joke. Go back a hundred and fifty years, the average age of death there was fucking terrifying – seventeen, I think. Only neighbouring Dudley's was worse. Nearby was Walsall, which had leather goods. And Stourbridge, which had glass. And Wolverhampton and Birmingham, which, between them, had every skilled trade on the planet. But, in Tipton as in Dudley, the only skill required was the ability to *'lomp it wi' 'ommer.'* Wages and living conditions befitted such employment and, for a century or more, anyone who *could* get out of the place, *did* get out of the place. If you said that those who remained were resentful, you hadn't even got started and, when the immigrants began to show up after the War, those remainders' responses were predictable. I remembered Granddad, poor old sod, while embittered at being 'driven out' to Pensnett, had been relieved that the lot of us weren't stuck in Tipton as the house prices plummeted and the place began to stink of curried goat.

A bunch of pretentious hippies were going to be as welcome, in this resentment-filled warren of Victorian terraces and sixties tat, as the NSPCC dropping in on the Vatican.

Somehow, as I brooded on these matters, the whole wall had got painted black – good start.

Okay, down to ground level and let's give it just a touch of sophistication. Bring in a bit of pale grey at the bottom, like a dismal battlefield dawn, the sort of breaking light that bodes no good to anyone.

Then, hanging in mid-air, a door. A bit Dali-esque, this, and I usually tried to avoid all the obvious Dali-isms but in this instance it seemed right. Off to the right of the image, this door opened into... somewhere else: a nasty sort of Narnia, where a knot of brown and black took shape, seething with vengefulness. What was this thing? From our point of view, it seemed unutterably hideous, yet I sensed there was something more to it. I decided it had a name. Perhaps many names. I plucked out 'Hastur' as the one I liked best. I decided, though he didn't look too chummy from this angle, I sort of quite liked Hastur, though there was no denying he'd be a dangerous bugger to get on the wrong side of.

Right side of the image sorted and, by now, it was near enough close of play. The sun was getting low and even in July, it didn't pay to keep at it past about eight pm.

It was only on the way home, stuck behind a smash-up on the Wolverhampton Road, that I realised Hastur, in some peculiar way, was Harry.

The following morning, the left side – blank grey rising into dead blackness – beckoned me. Much fun to be had here, I felt: something worse than Hastur, something to really make the buggers shit themselves.

Oddly, the image that began to take shape didn't seem to be too frightening. Just a face. Male. Middle aged. Grey haired and heavily lined. And the eyes... Blue. A very cold blue. A blue that told of death. And they were wide, these eyes. Somehow they were wide, despite the heaviness of the brow. And they were frightening.

It took a while for me to recognise these eyes as my own. Mine and my mother's.

Little by little, I created this face. This face out of nowhere. This face that I had never seen but which seemed so hellishly familiar.

The more I created, the more I saw of myself in it, the more I saw of my mother. It was neither of our faces, yet it was both. And it was something else. Something unspeakable.

End of Day Two. Things had gone more slowly this time. I was pissed off about that, but being pissed off never had to be a problem for me – if I was pissed off, I just slapped the shit out of The Cunt; that was what he was there for.

And, indeed –

'Cunt! Slag! Piece of shit!'

– he copped it that night – my word, something chronic. Which he seemed to accept, which was rather frustrating: I'd kind of hoped he'd beg for mercy as I got the belt to him but he took his thrashing with an almost Zen-like resignation. Awkward little shit!

Feeling rather narked, I began Day Three. The face began to emerge into three dimensions. Its skin was greyish and stone-like, its hair greyer still. It was a bitterly cynical face that denied the possibility of any relationship not based on aggression and the gratification of immediate pleasures. The ideas of soul, spirit, mind – even of awareness itself – all disintegrated under that wide blue stare. Nobody could survive that gaze. I approved of what I had done; I felt I had told the truth.

Getting towards the end of the day, I was interrupted by the squealing of tyres on tarmac, followed by a loud metallic crunch. I put down the aerosol I'd been using and turned round; somebody had crashed into a streetlamp. What made it funny was that he'd been driving a very posh car indeed...

A metallic grey Mercedes that I recognised from Barratt Road.

A bloke in his thirties got out, apparently unharmed. He was the sort who doesn't get harmed – not by anything less than a terrorist bomb and even then only rarely. He wasn't too bothered by the state of his car, which showed he wasn't short of a bob or two. He stared, wide eyed, at the face on the wall.

'Why are you painting him?' he asked.

'Who?'

'Arthur Tolland! Why are you painting him? The bastard's been dead thirty five years, for Christ's sake!'

I stepped down from the platform, which at that moment was only about three feet off the ground, and strode up to the car-crasher. His voice was shiny with generations of public school polish – very weird to hear such an accent in Tipton.

'I made this face up,' I told him. 'It doesn't belong to anyone. It's not real. If you fancy taking me to court or something for copyright theft, go ahead. Otherwise, fuck off.'

And he looked at me. And I looked at him. And the more I looked, the more I saw that his face looked like the face I'd painted, which meant it looked like my mother's. And like what I saw in the mirror.

The same thoughts must have crossed his mind, because his brow

142

creased and he asked:

'Are you Lee Icement?'

'Who wants to fucking know?'

'I'm Graham Tolland.'

'Meaning?'

There was a pause. Then, 'Do you not know who Arthur Tolland was?'

'No I fucking well do not. And I don't know who you are either. What's going on, here?'

He stared at me and, after a moment, I realised the look on his face was horrorstruck; he really didn't know how to handle this. And that, for him, was a very very rare situation to be in.

'I'm... I'm Graham Tolland.'

'You've said.'

'I'm... your mother's nephew.'

I went numb, the way you do when someone says something that makes no bloody sense whatsoever. He pointed up to the mural.

'That's our grandfather, for Heaven's sake. That's Arthur Tolland.'

The name still meant nothing to me. That was finally beginning to sink in with him.

'I just came here to look at your mother's school,' he attempted to explain. 'I had no idea you were doing this. Your mother's not going to be happy...'

'The frigid fucking retard can piss off then, can't she?'

He stared at me, looking perhaps a bit nervous. But though the picture had shaken him, he was getting his self-possession back.

'I see...' he murmured.

I didn't, and I told him as much.

Finally, he backed away.

'I... I'm going to get back to you on this,' he stammered. 'We're going to have to talk very soon.'

He passed me the plainest of white business cards, with just his name and mobile number, then got back into his Merc. He tried to get it started – and succeeded. That's the thing with Mercs: you can get away with that sort of shit. Couldn't do it with a Nissan.

So off he went, leaving me standing at the foot of the portrait I'd painted. My grandfather? It was a big face, filling most of the left side of the wall. Now, I wished I'd made it smaller. It dwarfed me and I didn't like the look of it. It wasn't looking down on me, though. It was staring off into some unseen distance, with an implacable steadiness and certainty. What it wanted, it would get. I, along with most other people, was irrelevant to its desires. I felt small and helpless and...

I felt like The Cunt.

Not very reassuring, that. I finished painting early and headed off home. The Cunt was at some writers' group in Oldbury – bunch of wankers, no doubt – so I decided I'd head into town and hit Hurst Street.

I pulled an ageing muscle mary at the Loft Lounge and wound up back at his place for predictable but adequate rumpy pumpy. Scrupulously safe, of course. All the while, brooding on the bizarre concept of my mother having a family. It had never occurred to me that she, like the rest of the human race, must have sprung from the usual mess of relationship and bodily fluid.

No, that wasn't quite true – and Big Dez's enthusiastic attentions to my rear end were doing wonders to bring my mind into focus, here – it wasn't that it hadn't occurred to me, it was that my mind had, covertly but very effectively, been steered away from the thought.

I came, at the exact moment when that troubling light bulb flashed on above my head. No coincidence: such revelations are what sex – when it's any good – is for.

Leaving Dez's place in the very small hours, I went home to find The Cunt back and, predictably, full of accusations at being thus shabbily cheated upon. Oh dear. All a part of the deal, of course, but at that moment I could have done without the histrionics. I was glad to get out of there and over to Tipton.

I stood at the foot of the mural and my eyes looked up at his.

Granddad, then, is it? Hello. I'm... Well, the name on my birth certificate says 'Lee Gordon Icement'. But everybody calls me 'Satansfist.' Due to certain amusing sexual habits of mine. And I've

144

never actually heard of you. Never knew you existed. Which, I'm beginning to realise, is a bit bloody peculiar.

I'd accepted, the way kids do accept, that I'd only ever had the one grandparent: Dad's dad. Seemed like enough. It had never occurred to me that Mother must have come from somewhere. And it had never occurred to me because Mother seemed so fleshless – sometimes abstract and disengaged, sometimes fierce and metallic – but always relentlessly non-biological; it was easy to assume she'd just sprung into existence as a result of random probability, like the Big Bang. And this had been an assumption encouraged by her very metallic brittleness. The people she worked with saw her as something implacable and indestructible but to me and to Alice and even, I think, to Dad, she was like cast iron – easily provoked into breaking and showing her sharp edges. You took care not to stray into areas where this was likely to happen.

I felt no anger, no annoyance even, at finding my consciousness had been manipulated. Even though I had little time for her, I had never really supposed Mother was in charge of her own behaviour. Something had prevented her from saying anything about this man, her father. I supposed he'd been a shit.

That would go a long way to explaining her. Granddad was a vicious, persecuting psycho, probably a kiddie-fiddler. Somebody with a dad like that could easily have turned out... well, pretty much like Mother.

'About time you got over it, though, you silly cow,' I grated, under my breath. I try not to do sympathy because it's a load of wank.

Another day's painting brought the old bastard's head a little further into to the three dimensional and allowed me to put a spot of ethereal glitter around Hastur. Close to finished now – just a few secondary details to get right.

Getting home and finding The Cunt in a close-to-catatonic sulk, I got the computer fired up and Googled 'Arthur Tolland.'

Bingo.

Bin-fucking-go.

Wikipedia:

145

'Arthur Maurice deGrieves-Tolland (12th February 1910 – 15th August 1975) was an English writer, British Conservative Party politician and journalist. He is best remembered for his suicide, subsequent to his abrupt resignation from the shadow cabinet of Edward Heath in late 1974.'

There wasn't much more; the brevity of the piece betrayed a measure of embarrassment on the part of its contributors.

'Tolland was the eldest son of Miles Henderson deGrieves-Tolland and Violetta Blanche deGrieves-Tolland, née Culpepper-Sidmouth. He was educated at Harrow and at Magdalen College, Oxford. He served in the Eighth Army, in North Africa 1942-3 and in Italy 1943-4. Tolland's record was exemplary, being decorated for bravery in respect of his conduct during the siege of Monte Casino. After the war, he was a journalist for the Daily Telegraph, *1946-58, Member of Parliament for Belbroughton, 1964-74, and a junior minister in the Heath Cabinet, 1970-73. As a journalist, his writing has been judged to be competent, if unspectacular. Similar assessments have been made of his political career...'*

There followed a quote from the obit. page of his former employer, the *Telegraph.*

'"It is sad that he will be remembered chiefly as a celebrity suicide and a child molester of the worst sort..."'

Another quote, from elsewhere:

'"There can be no doubt that Tolland's experiences in Italy were highly traumatic and, though they do not excuse, they might go some way to explaining his decline into the sadistic child abuser whose actions did much to break up the Lucas Group in 1970..."'

'The Lucas Group', it turned out, was a gang of hippie mystics who'd hung out in Halesowen in the 1960s. Toddler tupper and Black Magician! And a Tory MP! It was beginning to be obvious why Mother preferred to avoid the subject of 'Granddad'.

Looking again at that last quote, I spotted it was from a book called *Langdon Tremayne and his Disciples* by none other than old David Calper!

Alice used to love Dave's band, partly, I thought, because she had a crush on the flautist. Not that I supposed for one minute he ever knew this. Most of Alice's crushes were hopeless. She could be hopeless about anything.

Should I saunter over to Dave's shop sometime soon and pick his brains? Sounded like a good idea. Saunter over to the Bell shortly thereafter and pick up something of a different nature? Also not a bad idea.

The following weekend, round to Mother and Dad's. Dad out the back in his bloody shed, as ever. I'd say I sometimes wondered what he got up to in that place, but I'd be lying. It never occurred to me that I should be remotely interested.

I'd disturbed Mother halfway through a pile of pre-Ofsted huggerybuggery so she wasn't pleased to see me.

'Been over your way,' I began, 'working on a mural.'

No response. Either she'd not driven past it (possible), she'd not noticed it (more likely) or she'd seen it, recognised both her father and her son, but refused to give me the satisfaction of seeing her upset by the thing (more likely still).

I resorted to cruder methods.

'While I was at it, I bumped into my cousin,' – nice dramatic pause – 'Graham Tolland.'

Slowly, she turned to face me.

'He has no right calling you his cousin,' she said, flatly. 'None of that lot have any right to say they're family. When they were needed, they made themselves very scarce. I don't want to talk about them.'

No hysterics, no screaming, all very English, all very Kingswinford.

The fact that she'd avoided talking about 'that lot' for the whole of my life – that itself was unmentionable. In Kingswinford, it's the silences that are the real weird shit. The huge, jagged edged silences, the sizes and shapes of whatever's unbearable.

I could have gone along with those silences, then; standing up to them seemed a lot of effort with little good likely to come of it. But I couldn't resist needling them a bit more.

'I think he's been keeping an eye on you,' I drawled. 'He seemed to imply as much.'

'If he comes snooping round my school,' she whispered, 'I'll make sure what happens to him will be what happened to his bloody grandfather.'

'His grandfather' meaning her father. 'What happened' meaning suicide. She was threatening to drive Graham Tolland to suicide. Hmmm... Yes, she was capable of it.

'If I bump into him again,' I said, 'I'll let him know.'

'You do that,' she grated. 'You do that for his sake.'

I hung around for lunch, then buzzed off, realising I could drop into Dave's bookshop now; it was only a mile or two away.

Bowing my head, I went in through the low front door. I'd not seen anything of the dear old suburban Gandalf since Alice had died.

There was something like shock in his face when he saw me. He was going to ask me about something, then changed his mind and began:

'I heard about Alice. I'm sorry. I met her a few times. She liked our band.'

'You probably saw more of her than I did, the past few years,' I told him. 'She tended to... keep to herself a lot.'

The shop was empty but his voice went very quiet when he said, 'Yeah, well, the smack does that to people, doesn't it?' Nice knack of telling it like it is, had Dave. Uncommon in suburban Gandalfs.

'I bet,' I suggested, 'that you know who my grandfather was.'

'No, actually, I don't.'

'Arthur Tolland. He was my mother's father.'

'*Tolland?!* Bloody Hell! You drew the short straw with that one,

148

mate; I'm sorry. For you and poor Octavia.'

'Octavia?'

'Yer mum.'

'Her name's Shirley.'

'Shirley? She must have done the deed poll, mate, before you were born. You can't really blame her for that.'

'No,' I agreed, 'not for that. So was Granddad bad as he's supposed to have been?'

'As far as I can work out, yeah. The official story is he did himself in. That might be true. All the same, having a nonce turn up in his cabinet was pretty embarrassing for old Ted Heath. There was a shedload of that sort of stuff going on back then, I reckon, and it was mostly swept under the carpet. But, ah, one way or another, your granddad's messing about got in the papers. The Tories had just been booted out after the miners' strike, so they were in no mood to forgive anyone who'd caused 'em any more bother. If you ask me, at the very least, somebody leaned pretty hard on him to "do the decent thing", as they'd have put it. One of the cabinet hard cases, I bet – Keith Joseph or Thatcher.'

'Good for bloody Maggie, then.'

'Yeah. Never thought about it that way but I see your point.'

'Was he ever done for anything?'

'Nah. By the time it was ready to go to court, he was dead. He had a partner, though, John Mervyn, who got brought to trial. There were quite a few who'd survived the pair of 'em. And, those poor bleedin' kids, they got right in there and dished the dirt – you can hardly blame 'em. Mervyn died in jail.'

'I think I heard about that.'

'Yeah. Here's a coincidence, though. Somebody cocked up pretty badly and banged Mervyn up with the adoptive father of a friend of mine – a girl Mervyn and your granddad both had in their sights, back when she was eight or nine. This adoptive father was in for murder, but he was also a priest and he hit Mervyn with the old *if thine eye offend thee* routine. Mervyn took him at his word, repented sincerely, and hacked his own bollocks off with a woodwork file.

149

Bled to death.'

'I think I like this priest! But how's that a coincidence?'

'Well, he also has a natural daughter. Mary Maitland. She works with addicts. She was a good mate to your sister.'

I doubted that. I mean – how possible can it ever be, to be a 'good mate' of a smackhead?

Dave sensed my doubt.

'I know. She couldn't save her. But she tried... Here, sit down a bit.'

I did so. Dave went to put the kettle on.

'This Mary, she's been keeping an eye on your mum and dad's neighbour.'

'Who? Harry?'

'Yeah, Harry. Have you noticed anything funny about him, lately?'

'No more than usual. Though he has been looking a bit knackered. His daughter's noticed it, too.'

'Right... Hmm...'

Dave was silent, then he went to get the kettle. Tea poured, he was still silent.

'Look,' he said, very quietly. 'Keep this under your hat but Mary reckons it's Harry who's been bumping off all these dealers that have been seen to lately.'

'What? Chartington and that lot?'

'Not just that lot. Mary's been putting herself under a lot of pressure. Alice was more than just a client. She wouldn't be the first to start imagining things when she's stressed out but... She reckons she saw Chartington get topped.'

I thought about this for a bit.

'You know,' I said, 'there are friends of mine who swear that coke's getting wickedly pricey. Smack too, the past month or so. And these friends would know.'

I looked at Dave. He looked back at me.

'He can't be bumping that many dealers off,' I said, 'can he?'

'Mary reckons it was like he had them hypnotised.'

Hypnotised? How could he..?

I was silent. The images in my mind were those I had painted on Harry Ronsard's wall. Belief in something can be powerful enough to be infectious. And I'd painted belief on Harry's wall – belief that he was a mythical avenger. Harry had been soaking it up for years and it was very powerful belief because I was a very good painter.

'There's a book of mine you should read,' Dave said, softly.

'*Langdon Tremayne and his Disciples.* I know. It's quoted on Wikipedia.'

'It is. £12.50. I'd give it you, because you need to know some of that stuff. About your granddad. But you've never struck me as the sort who takes kindly to being offered stuff for free.'

I stared at him. I really did like this guy. Then I reached for my wallet.

Leafing through the bulky paperback, I saw that, indeed, there was quite a bit about Arthur Tolland in the last third of it.

Deciding to give the Bell a miss, I got home in a very weird mood and tried to find some reason to take it out on The Cunt – but the uncooperative little cock tease failed to provide one. I hid behind Dave's book and made it clear I did not wish to be disturbed.

18: Dave Calper

'Mary?'

'Hello, Dave,' she croaked down the phone line.

'God, love, you sound rough!'

'I feel it.'

'Been off work?'

'No. Ought to have been. But there's nobody else to do what needs doing.'

Silly cow, I thought to myself. That was the thing with Mary: you could muck her about as badly as you wanted, just as long as you never came between her and whatever she'd decided was the Right Thing to Do.

'How can I help?' she asked, still croaking. Her function was always to 'help', whatever state she was in.

I hummed and hurred a bit. She'd still not got over whatever had gone down at Chartington's and I didn't want to add to her worries. All the same, she wasn't going to let me off the phone until I'd levelled with her about why I'd called.

'Alice's brother's been round to see me,' I confessed.

'The painter?' Over the phone, I could sense her pulling herself together. Her voice got sharper and stronger. But she still didn't sound well.

'Yeah. Lee.'

'What's going on? Did he say anything about Harry Ronsard?'

'Not much. Not directly. Thing is…'

A pause. To tell her or not? But there was no way out, now.

'He… Well… Lee and Alice are Arthur Tolland's grandchildren.'

Mary was very quiet, then she tutted to herself, softly. 'Him and his mother… I was sure I knew that face from somewhere. Hmm… Dave?'

'Yes.'

'I don't want you mentioning this to my sister.'

'Nah, love. I wasn't going to. I'd kinda sussed… that wouldn't be

152

a good idea.'

'It wouldn't.'

Then there was a silence. And then I heard a soft, funny noise down the phone line and I realised that Mary was crying.

'Jeez, love, don't get upset...'

'Harry Ronsard acted as if he was on my side,' she breathed, 'at the Chartington house. And look what he's been doing! He's been avenging someone... avenging Alice Icement... Shirley and Alice... He's been avenging people who've been hurt by the bastard who... well, you know what Tolland was going to do to my sister...' She was afraid, now. Really sick with terror. *'It's me Harry Ronsard's after!* He wants my soul – he wants my approval. And he's getting it! He's getting it by standing up for the people I love. He even took to Los when we met him in the woods...'

'He wants everybody's soul, Mary. He's the Devil.' *Dave, you twat, what a stupid thing to say!* It had come out me bleedin' gob before I could stop it. Quickly, I tried to change the subject.

'I want you to come and meet Satansfist.'

'Ey?'

'Lee. I mean Lee. Alice's brother. You need to talk to each other. I'm gonna have him round one evening in the week. You need to be here, too.'

'Well I can try...'

'Do it, Mary. You need to talk to each other. Both of you. And not just about Harry. You need to talk about Alice.'

'Alice... Yes... You're right. Alice. I'll be round, then. Just let me know what night.'

I was shaking as I put the phone down. To listen to Mary's voice, you'd have thought she'd landed herself with some stinking fluey cold. Her sense of right and wrong had got physical on her. Harry – The Devil Himself – seemed to have taken her side against all the stuff that had put her family through the shredder. However much she might want to fight him, he'd got under her skin.

I rang Lee and asked him if he'd drop round later on in the week. I didn't try hiding anything from him – that would have been pointless.

'I've been thinking you should have a get-together with Mary Maitland,' I said, not very confident it was the right thing to suggest.

I heard him suck air in through his teeth. 'You think that's a good idea? I am a screaming shitstabber, after all, and I'm assuming she's as much of a holy-knickers as you tell me her dad is.'

'She is. But her adoptive sister's AC-DC. She's learned to look for the good in people, has Mary.'

'Well this sounds like a recipe for disaster.'

'It might be. Or it might be the least worst option.'

'Okay, then,' he said. 'Ask her if she's free tomorrow.'

***

Back when I'd first met her, Mary had been a big nineteen-stoner – not someone who'd been taking care of herself at all. Now she looked worse but this time it was nothing physical. It was in her eyes. Harry had gone barging his way into her head and had smashed things up in there. She was spending her days looking after other people's problems, hoping that this would mend what he'd done. Which, I thought, it might – given time. But it would have to be a long time.

'Sit down, love...'

She smiled, wanly, came into the shop and did so.

'I've invited Lee round,' I said.

'Yes... What did he call himself again?'

'Satansfist.'

'Satansfist...'

'Yeah... Er...' I must have looked a bit embarrassed.

'My sister used to shag your keyboard player, Dave. I have been told what "fisting" means.'

'Er... yeah... er...'

I was almost relieved to see Lee Icement's silhouette in the doorway. He was done out in his full goth cyberpunk kit. Including a pair of black leather gloves. With fearsome chrome spikes.

154

Mary and I looked at those gloves. Then we looked at each other. She shook her head, sadly amused.

Lee caught the expression. I was surprised he didn't turn on his heels and march out in a huff. Instead, he looked at her curiously as he came inside.

'Mary Maitland?'

'Lee Icement.'

A few seconds' pause. Lee finally chipped in with, 'Hear you've been having problems with Harry Ronsard.'

'Yes,' said Mary, 'he's been killing people.'

'Smack dealers.'

'Yes.'

'Coke dealers.'

'Yes.'

'Lots of them.'

'It… seems like it.'

Lee wandered over to the bookcase where I kept the art stuff. He picked out a catalogue for a big Van Gogh exhibition from a few years back and leafed through it quietly.

'Does that bother you?' he asked at last, eyes flashing up from the catalogue and walloping Mary with a hard, cold stare.

Mary looked at his stare, evaluating it coolly without cringing or blinking. That unnerved him a bit.

'Killing people is wrong,' she said.

Lee smiled. But his smile did not last long.

'I created Harry Ronsard,' he said, matter-of-factly.

'What, with the murals?' I butted in, failing to sound incredulous.

'I'm a bloody good artist.'

Mary must have decided Lee's arrogance could do with a dent or two, so she tried to find a bit of common ground.

'I know about your grandfather: my sister narrowly escaped getting damaged by him when she was nine.'

Lee nodded. He didn't need her to be any more specific. 'Sounds about right,' he said. 'The old turd seems to have gone in for a fair bit of that sort of shit.' He nodded at me. 'You read Dave's book?'

155

'Yes,' Mary whispered.

'And your dad…'

'He used to be a pastor – a priest. Now he's doing life for murder.'

She gave that time to sink in.

If ever there was a moment when Lee Icement could have accepted sympathy, this was it. Someone had equalled him in the dysfunctional family stakes. And, to give him credit, I think he tried. A lifetime of keeping yourself so nailed down, though – that wasn't going to get solved in an instant. I could sense his armour going up again, behind his eyes.

'Tell me about your paintings,' Mary asked, softly. 'The ones on Harry's wall.'

'King Arthur stuff,' he replied. 'I was into Burne-Jones.' Then his eyes lit up. 'Still am, actually. I like the power. I like the directness. You can take the piss if you want, but the guy wasn't the sort who'd care. He'd paint what he wanted to paint. Fuck the consequences.'

I could see Mary coming back to life, just a little bit. She was rising to Lee's challenge.

'King Arthur,' she said.

'I know. Not fashionable. So what?'

'King Arthur worried about consequences.'

Lee uncomfortable again. His mouth twisted a little bit.

'He remade his world in his own image. That's what I do. Every time I pick up a paintbrush.'

'And he punished the guilty. And he protected the weak.'

Lee didn't like where this was going. But he didn't want to look like he was backing out of a scrap. 'Okay,' he said at last, 'you win. I wanted revenge.'

'Because you loved your sister.'

That was too much.

'I don't do love,' he said, stiffly. 'It's for wankers.'

Then he was gone. And Mary was drained.

'He doesn't realise,' she sighed. Then she was in tears: 'He doesn't realise how… how like Alice he is…'

***

A few days later, I began to see how things could be getting still worse. I'd just sold twenty quid's worth of James Herbert to a once-beautiful woman of fifty-five who'd never have admitted she liked to imagine her husband was getting eaten by rats. But I knew the git – he'd bought the entire *Tarnsman of Gor* series off me – so I wasn't fooled for a minute.

After she left, the place went quiet. Then there was a shadow in the doorway. It was cast by a lad in black trousers and a grey shirt, who stood, straight and unmoving, about as lively and responsive as the old Kraftwerk promo poster he so closely resembled. Sixteen, seventeen, I'd have guessed. Bleedin' Hell, that was one sinister haircut he had going on!

'Can I help you?'

Showroom Dummy took his time answering. This was meant to give me the willies. It did, but not in the way he intended.

'Is there something wrong?' I made my voice a bit harder, which I don't like doing.

He looked at me directly, surprised.

'That's what I'm here to find out,' he said and stepped inside.

Cool as custard, he checked out what was on the shelves. He took his time.

'Everything seems fine,' he said finally, his disappointment clear.

'Fine?' I asked, incredulous, 'How could it not be fine? This is a bookshop. There's books on the shelves.'

'Ye-es,' Showroom Dummy grated, robotically, 'Bu-ut we need to make sure they're suitable books.'

Well – I saw bleeding red, there, didn't I? I had to remind myself I'm getting on a bit and really shouldn't be mixing it up with no teenybopper KGB, however obnoxious.

'I think,' I grated back, even more robotically, 'that you had better leave. Now.'

He glared at me. If I'd wanted to look, I could probably have seen the scared kid behind those eyes, blue as the sleeve of *Autobahn*.

But, at that moment, I didn't want to look.

'Be careful,' he said, softly. 'You've done nothing wrong. But it would be a mistake to upset us.'

Us: there had to be an *us*. It's never a *me* with bumholes like that, is it? It's always an *us*.

'Us?' I scoffed, 'Who do you think you bleedin' well work for then?' Then I took a leap in the dark. That, or my subconscious decided to hit little Showroom Dummy here, with a bit of the ol' Dave Calper telepathy. Either way, the name was out of my mouth before it came into my head: *'Harry Ronsard?'*

His head jerked back. I suddenly noticed that he was a bit spotty. And he had a slight twitch in his left eye.

Without another word and quick as the Trans-Europe Express, he turned and shot out the place.

I sat down. Because my legs wouldn't hold me. Say what you like about my old chair, it was comfy. And I needed it to be. My hands were trembling horribly and – God – I felt old. It was the first time in my life I'd ever felt old. Dammit, I was in a bloody rock band, wasn't I? I wasn't supposed to feel old! And anyway, as feelings went, I didn't like it much.

19: Harry Ronsard

My brave young lads! And a few lasses, too. Well, mine and Shirley's. Proud of them, she is. And so am I.

Clean grey shirts, the lot of 'em. The sort they've worn all through school so I don't see no reason for 'em to change now. Suits – neat but not too pricey – not all that different from their school uniforms. So they'll definitely know where they stand. And haircuts – not too long, none of this patterned rubbish. Practical.

Yes, that's it, my lads! Now you look the part!

Starts off, I have a few of them in up at our place for work experience. Best part of anybody's schooldays, that – there wants to be a lot more of it.

And as they get settled in, I begin to realise, if you want to get a good bunch of people round you, you need to get hold of them young. And you need to have been straight with them from the word 'go'. Which is what Shirley has been. And now, she's sitting on a goldmine – a moral goldmine of good people waiting to be put to good use.

Problem is, of course, they're not going to stay good for long. There aren't enough Shirley Icements in the world – not nearly enough. Most of the gaffers you get these days are rubbish. Shirley's lads and lasses will lose it once they've not got her to tell them what to do. People need to be told what to do. So here I am, ready to do just that.

The gaffers are impressed, of course – none of the usual bone-idle whiners, Shirley's lot. And one way or another, we fix it up that, strictly on the QT, any vacancies we get are going to be filled with fresh faces from round hers. Can't go wrong there! Pretty quick, I've given the existing workforce a look over and found good reasons to sack half a dozen. I say 'good reasons,' not 'excuses' – no need to cook up excuses, what with some of the rubbish you get. And their places are filled with good stuff from Shirley's who'll get the job done. They've just finished their 'O' levels or whatever tripe they do these days. Some of them haven't been sure what they were going to do with themselves. Others have been about to start on some poncey 'A' level course or other. In either case, I'm offering them something a lot better.

Come September, when I have a day off, I drive past Shirley's and take a look at what's there. A careful look. I'm impressed. Rough 'uns, but she's got them knocked into shape. Nobody putting a foot wrong, nobody leaving a hair out of place. Different races, but no signs of scrappings on that score. That doesn't mean they can't handle the aggro. They've got it about 'em, you can tell – they've got it about 'em but they're saving it up for something special. And, when that something special arrives, there'll be blood in the gutters – a good few gallons of it.

I like these kids.

In the streets round by our place, things are getting a lot better. It's up Dudley, of course, which means there's a good few hard knocks – some of 'em plain bad, some just needing a firm hand. So we've had the odd spot of vandalism and there's been grumbling off the gaffers about how best to deal with it. One evening, early August, I'm up the road to Shirley's and I'm asking her, who's the biggest, scariest young so-and-sos she's let go from her place over the past three years?

She reels off the names and the addresses without having to look them up. Like I say, she's good, is Shirley. Inside a week, all but one of them is working up ours. Security. The last one I have to hang on a couple of weeks for. But then, I'm waiting for him, when the doors open and he walks out of Winson Green Prison. I'm the only one waiting for him.

And with all of them, all I need to do is have a word. And give 'em the look. And, when I give 'em the look, the look I get back tells me they've been waiting all their lives for me. Or someone like me.

They're a keen lot, now someone's taken them in hand. The vandalism stops overnight. More than that, inside a week, one of them – big Mohammed, the very one who'd got himself banged up – comes up to me and he says 'Mr Ronsard, me an' the lads have been wondering. We're keeping an eye on the place, right, and there ai' no bother on site no more but, y'know, it's a bit rough round here, ayitt? And we've been seein' stuff kickin' off over the road and, like, it does give round here a bad name and it might put customers off...'

I wonder about this for a moment. I decide to be careful. No need to rush things.

'Any serious trouble,' I tell him, 'and you call me. Not the gaffers, but me. Any time – day or night. If it's just some prat being a nuisance, grab him and call the coppers. Then call me. But remember, we've got the CCTV in, so be gentle with him. We don't want to give no *Guardian*-reading human rights rubbish any reason to take an interest in us...'

'I hate all that fucking human rights shit.'

'So do I but, Mohammed...'

'Yes Mr Ronsard?'

'Don't swear, Mohammed. It's disgusting'

'Sorry, Mr Ronsard.'

Inside another week, I've had this lad's granddad on the phone to me, speaking through one of his younger grandkids because his own English isn't up to much. And he turns out to be a very devout old gentleman, very right and proper – just the sort of bloke I can respect. And he's telling me how grateful the family are, because they were despairing of the kid, they'd just about given up on him – how he'd been drinking and nicking stuff and hanging round with bad women. Now that he's working for me, he's turned himself right around and he's speaking to the family with respect and he's even started going to mosque again. And they invite me round for tea. And I go.

I sit, very politely, even though the tea I have to drink is most peculiar. And the food they keep waving under my nose... not my sort of thing at all. Have you ever eaten *samosas?* What the bloody heck do they put in those things? I've found chopping up a dead body more digestible! Doesn't matter, though, I make myself eat the lot. As is only proper. And I listen to what the granddad has to say –

161

again, through one of his younger grandkids. And I find we've got a lot more in common than you might expect.

While this is going on, of course, Lee's doing my walls, as he always does in the summer. One day, he turns and says, 'By the way, I hear one of your teenage fan club has been putting the wind up poor old Dave Calper. I wish he wouldn't.'

I don't know what he means, and I tell him so.

'One of those lads you've got on work experience or something. Went round Dave's shop in Amblecote and tried to check it out for subversive material. Which is odd because this lad didn't sound like the sort who'd go in for – *ahem* – reading, very much.'

And I think a bit and I remember. Little Danny Cosgrove who we've just taken on has moved down to Amblecote. He's a very keen lad – wants to do the right thing.

But, as Lee suggests, he's probably not the brightest.

So, the following day, I have a word with him. Because we don't want to get the reputation as a bunch of people who go throwing their weight around.

Not yet, anyway.

By the second week in September, we've got a dozen more from Shirley's round at our place – ones who've taken a look at what the colleges are offering and have decided they prefer a drop of the Real World. And they're all bright eyed and ready to go. It's them as puts the last few of the Darren Hatch mob to flight – good riddance! *Zombies*, the little Darrenistas call them. Fine, lads, call them Zombies! Then go back to your piss-stained pubs and turn yourselves into the real walking dead with ten pints of Carling Black Label!

No, this new lot are the good stuff: they put the hours in, get the jobs done and go out there and get us the customers. They've got that look – they've learned it from Shirley and they learn it some more from me – that look that people can't argue with. They're more than just salesmen or buyers – they're leaders in the making.

There's other stuff I've been up to, of course. Quite a bit of it. And I've been almost wondering how I've been able to get so much done.

162

Then I remember the look in the eyes of the men I have killed. Nobody has got it about them to stop me. The only one even to try has been that friend of Polly's – Mary Maitland, the good woman.

Nobody's stopped me, but somebody's noticed me. 'Somebody' being Shirley's nephew.

The gaffers have been talking about opening a new warehouse in Kidderminster. They'll been needing to take on staff and, of course, there'll be a bunch ready for them. I nip over to Shirley's school to talk to her about who she has in mind; we're in her office and she's got the names and addresses ready but, this time, takes it upon herself to get in touch with them. Breaking a few rules there, I've no doubt, but I don't suppose you'll find a school inspector breathing who she can't sort out in half a minute. Like I say, she's like me: she knows how to give them the look.

We've sorted out everything and I'm thinking of leaving when she goes to the window and looks out. And she notices something. When she turns back to me, there's a funny look about her. One I've never seen on her face before.

'I suppose I should tell you about my nephew.'

'You don't have to. Your business.'

'Not just mine. I've noticed him around, lately – more than I might have expected. Normally, it's me he's concerned with. But I'm afraid he may have taken an interest in you.'

'Why's he interested in either of us?'

She laughs, which I've never heard her do before, and it's a bleak sort of laugh.

'Why's he interested in us? Oh dear, why indeed?'

She's quiet for a long time and, in the silence, I begin to wonder about her voice. Now it's a funny thing, is Shirley Icement's voice. Over the years, she's said the odd thing that's made me think she's got roots round here, but her accent is odd. It's not the sort of accent as you'd say goes with a load of money. In her mouth, spectacle-wearers have glasses, not glarses. But there are things about it that suggest she's gone to a lot of trouble to get it sounding the way it does. She's started off with a lot of posh BBC vowels but she's given most of them a scrub down with the Black Country wire brush. Some of them are still there, all the same. Voices like hers usually get to that state from the opposite direction – Coseley to Birmingham Uni, say. Her voice has gone – from some posh public school or other – to a place not far from Tipton.

'Where'd you go to school?' I ask her, suddenly.

'Roedean,' she answers. When I look blank, she adds, 'You've not heard of it?'

I shake my head. She looks out the window.

'Independent school. Girls. Just outside Brighton.' She pauses again. 'Some people like it,' she says at last. Then she turns back to me. 'My nephew's name is Graham Tolland. He works for the Conservative Party.'

Now, truth be told, I haven't been paying a heck of a lot of attention to the cup of tea in front of me – I think it's that Earl Grey muck – but now Shirley's said something that's surprised me and I find myself necking it in one.

'He works for the Conservative Party – not for the government, for the party. Not in any honourable capacity: he keeps an eye on people who might be sources of embarrassment. Buying them off or threatening them, whichever works better. All political parties employ dung beetles of his sort.'

'How could we ever be sources of embarrassment?'

'Not us – me. Old… family issues. I've no interest in digging them up after all this time and, in all honesty, everything worth telling came out years ago. Anyway, it's my nephew's job to keep an eye on me and to dissuade me from publishing my memoirs or anything else conspicuous. It was also his job keep an eye on that coke dealing party hack you bumped off.'

'Ey?'

She leans forward and looks, very levelly, into my eyes.

'Harry,' she says, 'I'm not stupid.'

Most people in Kingswinford keep themselves to themselves. Most people in Kingswinford won't notice if, every morning when there's news of another massacre of drug dealers, you've been out –

somewhere – the night before. Most people in in Kingswinford. But Shirley Icement is not 'most people'.

'No,' I say, 'you're not stupid.'

'Somebody like Chartington, who did a marvellous job of keeping the entire British Government coked off their heads throughout the Eighties – well, maybe not Geoffrey Howe – somebody with that on their CV is a major source of potential embarrassment. When his CCTV got looked at, after you did him in, my nephew will have recognised you as my neighbour.'

'So why haven't they tried to arrest me or something – or do me in?'

She laughs.

'Arrest you? Do you in? Oh, Harry, you've lot to learn!'

'Hmm?'

'They're not going to do you in! If I know my nephew – and he shows every sign of being an action replay of his revolting little worm of a dad – he'll have been checking up on you very thoroughly. And, having done that, he'll have been trying very hard to market you to the grandees as MP material.'

This comes as an even bigger surprise. I try to think of possible objections.

'I'm getting a bit old for that, Shirley.'

She smiles. 'Doesn't matter. Not while they're as desperate as they are. But be careful. I don't want you appropriated by the likes of Graham Tolland. The Tory Party isn't what it was – it's gone soft. You don't get the Thatchers anymore. Or the Tebbitts. The ones now are weak. Tolland knows that – so do all the other little creeps like him. They're desperate to sniff out the sort of people the base wants: people who won't muck about.'

'And they'll cover up all that business in Chipping Norton?'

'Of course they will. As I said, Chartington was a potential embarrassment – so you've done them an awfully big favour, already. And you are what their support base wants. Two big big plusses. What's more, since poor old Gordon Brown handed them the poison chalice, they've been finding the brew far stronger than they expected. They need people with the stomach for it.'

We stand. And look long and hard at each others' faces. And like what we see.

It's four o'clock and the kids, very quietly, troop out. Shirley's taken me down into the main hall and I look at their eyes, which are bright as laser beams. We follow them.

A gang of about twenty sixteen-year olds – lads, mostly, though two or three of the bigger, stockier girls accompany them – head out the front, turn left and walk, slowly and purposefully, towards a brand new navy blue Merc.

Shirley and I are both aware that it's got Graham Tolland in it.

An enemy. They've sniffed him. And, if we let them, they're going to do him over. No ordinary way of knowing this, of course. No ordinary way of having any clue to what's going on inside those intense young heads. But it's the truth. I just look into the kids' eyes and I know it's the truth. I love these kids.

They gather around the car; he can't drive off without knocking some of them over. He's smart enough not do that; instead, he gets out the Merc and starts shouting at them. Not so smart. Even from here, I can hear his voice – public school, Oxbridge, used to getting its own way. Only now, a gang of Tipton oiks are stopping that from happening and his red-faced bawling shows he's lost his knack of keeping his class prejudice under wraps.

They really will have him, if we don't do something about it. I look out the corner of my eye at Shirley and she's very very calm. She knows how to handle this lot and posh little Tolland doesn't. And that is driving him nuts.

'Kraygon,' says Shirley, in a very soft voice, but one that carries.

The biggest, meanest, ugliest of the lads looks round at her and is quiet. And because Kraygon does, all the others do, too.

'Yes, Mrs Icement?' Kraygon rumbles. But it's a very sheepish rumble.

'Step away from the car, Kraygon.'

'Yes, Mrs Icement.'

And they all do, with a bit of sheepish shuffling.

Everything's really quiet. Posh Tolland is sweating.

'This,' Shirley declares, 'is my nephew, Graham Tolland.'

Takes them half a second to work out how to respond. Then, in unison, like a bunch ten years younger than they actually are:

'Good afternoon, Mr Tol-land.'

Y'know, for a bunch of Tipton kids, their accents are turning out quite a bit like Shirley's.

Posh Tolland really bricking it by now. Still not sure he's going to get out of this one without his guts ripped out and tied round his neck.

'He believes it's his job to keep an eye on me,' Shirley explains. Kraygon and mates look back at posh Tolland and the look they give him is enough to tell him one thing – being nice to Mrs Icement is, right now, a very very sound investment indeed.

Shirley herself is smiling but it's a chilly smile. 'The people he works for think I might say or do something to embarrass them. He's here to threaten me, or to bribe me into not doing that. Do you think I'm likely to let him tell me what to do, Year Eleven?'

'No Mrs Icement,' and there's an edge of chuckling in their voices. And in it, I can hear that they love her; I can hear that she makes them feel powerful.

'Do you think I care enough about people like him to be bothered to embarrass them?'

'No, Mrs Icement.' Laughter, now, and a frosty sort of laughter it is, too.

'No. And it seems silly that they've started to take an interest in what I might say, so long after all the things they've got to be embarrassed about. But these are very very silly people.'

Teen laughter tinkles like the sort of huge icicles that fall off glaciers and impale the unwary.

'So I've decided, I don't want silly Graham Tolland keeping an eye on me, anymore. And, if he has any sense, he'll remember that.'

Kids turn back to little trembling Posh. He realises he is being given a break here, and the look on his face is rapturous.

Kraygon can't resist stressing the point.

'You remember,' he rumbles.

'Thank you, Kraygon,' Shirley concludes, and Kraygon withdraws immediately. And so do his mates.

Posh Tolland, still terrified, steps backwards to his car. In a shot, he's inside and – vroom – he's out of there. Merc noise fading round the corner of the Tipton street as he heads for the safety of the M6 and sunny Westminster.

I've seen plenty of buggers like him on the telly and I reckon it must be easy to smell them coming. They have a certain stink – arrogance, grace, the assumption that they're born to rule, all undercut by the reek of fear. If one of 'em's heading your way, you can whiff him miles off. Never mind, diddums – go and buy another thousand quid suit to cheer yourself up.

But I know he'll be back.

I turn to the backs of the kids, slouching away up the street.

'That Kraygon,' I tell Shirley, 'could turn out to be a real baddun, if somebody's not very careful.'

'Somebody is going to be very careful,' she says. 'I'm sending him to your place.'

And I feel a warm sense of rightness and I smile and I'm thinking, there's only so much you can do on your own – King Arthur needed his noble knights; Robin Hood needed his Merry Men. However good you are, you need good blokes around you – blokes who see what you mean when you tell 'em it's all about doing the Right Thing.

Takes me another couple of days before I remember the name 'Tolland': that bloody nonce who was in the Heath Government and who topped himself. I remember hearing about it on the BBC (funny the *Daily Mail* never mentioned it). And Shirley's his daughter. Therefore, she must be his most wretched victim. But now, she's ready for her vengeance. Now, she's recruited her army. Now, she's recruited me to be their general. And they and I will rise up and put a stop to what wants stopping.

***

Getting them to see things from this point of view at work is going to be a bit tricky – you'd think. Most of the blokes, though, just need a good talking to and they come round. Even the gaffers, more and more, are coming to me for advice on any number of things. And they're doing well. Doing well in hard times, too. Hard times! Obviously the Conservatives have just got in but that hasn't made much difference – not like it would've done if they still had Thatcher. In fact, the simpering little fool they're calling 'Prime Minister' strikes me as no better than that bloody Tony Blair.

So there are loads of firms round our way going to the wall, but not us. We can be trusted to come up with the goods and people know it.

I feel all this most strongly when I've been for a walk or a run, up in Cally Wood. In the evening or first thing in the morning, it makes me feel ready for anything. The way those pines clatter together in the wind like the swords of a thousand men. The way that wind roars like a war horn: this is one of those places where the Saxons and the Welsh fought it out after the Romans had gone and you can feel it. More and more, I'm unwilling – unable even – to stop feeling it.

It's no surprise when posh little Tolland shows up again, this time at work.

'Mr Slocum's asked you to come to the office,' says Big Mohammed, one morning late in September.

Slocum's the oldest of the gaffers. He's coming up to retirement and is all for anything that doesn't rock the boat.

'Mr Slocum, Mr Tolland,' I say to them, as I swan into old Slocum's office.

Slocum smiles, indulgently. Graham Tolland looks about ready to make a mess in his trousers. He'll have guessed I've had a whiff of his family's dirty laundry. I don't suppose the idea reassures him one bit.

'I'll leave you two gentlemen to discuss what you need to,' Slocum bows, wisely making himself scarce.

I turn back to Tolland and give him a big smile. Smiles, as I've said, are expressions I don't much go in for and I suspect I don't do them all that well. Still – well enough for this little prat.

'You've been wanting to have a word with me, I think.'

'You've not been very willing to talk.'

'I have a sense of the proper time and the proper place for things,' I tell him. 'And now is the right time for the talk we've been going to have.'

He nods.

Then he tells me what's going on.

No surprises. Pretty much what Shirley assumed. There's a local MP – safe Labour seat, up to now – with cancer. Poor bloke, nasty way to go. Not a winnable seat by any means for Tolland's lot. But he's suggested me as a long shot candidate. Slocum's in the local Cons Club and has filled him in on where I stand on most things. So am I interested, asks Tolland? He knows I will be – he is good at his job, I'll say that much for him. Am I sympathetic? Well, maybe not exactly, but that doesn't have to matter: he's got an idea I'm the sort the base will take to. He's not wrong there. So he, and a couple of others he's spoken to, are all for giving me a shot. Because it's not a winnable seat.

Except he knows and I know that it *is* a winnable seat. Because an electorate is just another one of those things that always – *always* – falls into line. You just have to give it the right look. And I know exactly the right look for the electorate of Kates Hill and Tividale.

Two hours later, I'm back home.

Having said 'yes'.

A good strong pot of Typhoo and a bit of gardening out the front are just about getting my head straight when I hear Shirley's sensible, low-heeled shoes clacking up the pavement.

'My ex-students doing alright?' she asks.

'You in any doubt of that?' I half-smile at her. She gives a terse, but equally satisfied smile back.

'Thought they would be. Keep me posted on how they're getting on.'

'I will. Had a bit of a surprise, today. Graham Tolland's been to see me. He said what you expected him to say.'

'I hear Bruce Freeman's not long for this world.'

'Bowel cancer. Safe Labour seat, though.'

'Not safe from you.'

'Not a lot of people realise that.'

'They will. Little Tolland thinks he's got the measure of you. He hasn't; it'll be an awful shock for him when he begins to realise as much.'

'A lot of people will be in for some awful shocks by the time I've finished with them.'

There's a silence between us but it's the sort of silence that has a lot to say for itself, and what it says is very very good. We're a day or two from the end of September now, and the light's going. I won't be doing any more gardening today.

Behind my house, the wind hisses and roars in the trees of Cally Wood.

Shirley and me and the wind - we three are One.

20: Polly Gauvain

'That man,' my mom said, 'has been round again.'

I didn't know who she meant.

There was a lot of traffic noise outside. I got up and went into the kitchen.

My mom hadn't done the washing up. There was a plate, a saucepan and some cutlery next to the sink. She'd definitely not washed them: I could see that she'd had baked beans on toast. It was four or five hours since lunchtime, and I'd never ever known her leave washing up so long. Who could 'that man' have been? It must have been someone quite unusual to make her so forgetful. I went back into the lounge.

'He was round on Tuesday,' she continued, 'that man.'

'That man?'

'Yes. You know. That man.'

'What man?'

My mom looked up from her knitting. She'd always liked knitting – which I'd often wondered about. She'd been young, back in the sixties, and knitting can't have been very fashionable then. Everybody was supposed to wear nylon, weren't they? Or cheesecloth? People must have taken the micky out of her for it.

'You know,' she said. 'That man.' She paused. 'Your father.'

'Oh. *That* that man.'

'Yes.'

There was still a lot of traffic noise. People were getting home from work. I'd had the afternoon off. I'd always tended to build up a lot of flexitime. Not so much now I was with Harry, but I still had some to use up. Harry had told me to spend an afternoon with my mom – that was the right thing to do. So here I was.

'What does he want?'

'He thinks we've got something of his.'

I frowned. 'After all this time?'

'He thinks we've still got it.'

I'd always thought my dad had taken everything he wanted when he left. I tried to imagine what was still here that he might have a claim on. I couldn't think of a single thing.

'How long has he been over from Texas?'

'A few months. I think it must be a few months. I think things are over with him and Michelle. He said she was still over there. He didn't sound very happy about it.'

'What about his job?'

'I think that's over, too. He was talking as if he was back here for good. As if he had some... debts.'

My dad's money had run out. My dad's wife had run out. The two were probably connected, but I didn't really want to know. I was curious, though, about why he'd come back here.

'What was the thing he was looking for?'

'I don't know. Some sort of book, I think. He said it might be up in the loft. I said I'd send you up there. To look for it.'

I didn't mind going up into the loft. I'd thought there might be a few bits of housework to do here, so I'd put some jeans and a sweatshirt on before coming round. It was one of my old Take That sweatshirts – with a big picture of Jason Orange on the back. Harry said it made me look daft, but I told him I didn't mind that.

I went upstairs and searched around for the stick with the hook on the end that undid the hatch into the loft. I found it under my old bed and stretched up, hooking it on to the hatch fastener... With a crash, the thing fell open and the aluminium stepladder inside swung out and down, narrowly missing my head and landing on my right foot.

'Aww-woo!'

'You alright, up there?' My mom sounded concerned.

'Okay. Just... stubbed me toe... sort of...'

'Well you be careful.'

'I will.'

Switching on a torch, I limped up the stepladder and shone the light around.

There wasn't much up there – fluffy yellow loft lagging, a big cardboard box which I knew contained only Christmas decorations

173

and... Oh... wait a minute... There were a couple of other, smaller cardboard boxes, one on top of the other. I was scared that if I tried to reach them, I'd end up putting my toes through the bedroom ceiling. They were still throbbing as it was.

I stretched across. I was just able to grab the lower box and I dragged them both over. Then I started sneezing with the dust I'd disturbed. By the time I'd got the two boxes to the bottom of the stepladder, my eyes were streaming and the sneezing fit was making my sides ache. I went into the bathroom to splash some water on my face.

Downstairs, I took the boxes into the dining room and put them on the big table. Then my mom came in and we both opened them.

The first had a lot of my mom's old things in it. There were postcards from school friends she'd long lost touch with, bits and bobs of jewellery that she tried on, giggling, and photos of her posing with some mates. This must have been during the sixties and she'd been dead good looking, back then. Loads nicer than I'd ever been.

The other box was a bit more surprising. Again, bits and bobs of jewellery, though none of it was stuff my mom remembered. It all looked quite a lot older, to tell the truth. There were some spring-hinged, leather-covered cases with serious-looking medals inside.

And there was a book.

It was leather-bound and really old. Taking it out very carefully and opening it, we found it wasn't printed inside but had a lot of very neat, very small handwriting. There were dates, lots of dates – all of them from the 1790s – and it was in French. Flicking through, I could see the family name mentioned quite a lot, so it seemed like it did belong to my dad as much as it belonged to anyone. When we looked towards the back, we found it was about three quarters full but the last few pages that had been used were in a different handwriting – bigger, messier and generally looking like someone who, in all honesty, wasn't that bright. The last four words were: *'Radoub. Liberté, Egalité, Fraternité!'* I knew what three of these were: the motto of the French Revolution. The word *'Radoub,'* I thought, might be a signature.

It had been nine years or so since I'd last read any French, but I remembered, all of a sudden, that a lot of my school books were still stashed away in my old wardrobe. I nipped upstairs and had a look – sure enough, there was my battered little French Dictionary.

Nipping back down, I looked at the start of the old book again, with the dictionary's help.

It was the diary of somebody called Cimourdain. Just 'Cimourdain' – it looked to me like a surname, but there wasn't a first name anywhere. The bloke with the small neat handwriting. There were other names I half remembered, perhaps from school history lessons – Robespierre, Danton, Marat, Lantenac. And my own name – Gauvain – over and over and over again.

But it was the name 'Cimourdain' that I came back to, because it made me feel funny. It made me feel loved, and it made me feel very very afraid.

And angry.

'He's not having this,' I heard myself say. 'The fucker's not having this!'

'Polly!'

My mom was shocked at me. I was shocked at me. Harry would have been shocked at me. I'd hardly sworn for years – not since my schooldays, when everybody swears. But now, I looked up from the old book and I looked into my mom's eyes and I said, very quietly, 'He's not having it, Mom.'

I closed the book. There'd be time to work out what it had to say once I made sure I kept it.

'It's something from your father's family,' my mom whispered. 'It belongs to him, really.'

I wasn't sure about that, but it didn't matter because I wasn't going to try to handle this on my own. It wasn't a woman's place to do so. I was glad of that, partly because it saved me a lot of bother. I got on the phone to Harry's work and when they realised who I was, I was put straight through to him.

'Hello, my little hamster. How you doing?' Harry's voice was warm and it warmed me, too.

I explained the problem to him.

'Hmm. So it's your mom as has been looking after this book, all these years?'

'Yes,' I replied.

'And he's taken no notice of it until now, when he's fallen on hard times?'

'Well... we're not sure of that.'

'Hmph! I'm sure! Come across his sort many, many times, little hamster. He wants it so he can flog it. Two hundred years old, you say?'

'1793.'

'And there's some famous people in it?'

'I think so. Robespierre? Danton? Weren't they pretty important in France, back then?'

'Hmm... Know what, little hamster? I think you're right. If it's handwritten and there's stuff about them in it, the thing could be worth a fair old bit. And I bet your father knows as much. Yeah, he wants to flog it, alright.'

'I'm not going to let him.'

'No reason why you should. Here, when did he say he was coming round to pick it up?'

I wasn't sure of this, so I asked my mom.

'Tomorrow evening, about seven. He told my mom she had to have it ready for him by then.'

'Oh he did, did he?' I could hear something in Harry's voice and it made me feel very very safe. 'Well I'm sure we'll have *something* ready for him by then!'

***

Six fifty-five, the following evening. The noise of a car pulling up and its door being slammed. A knock at my mom's front door, which she went to answer.

'Where is it?' I didn't recognise the man's voice: his accent hadn't turned American in all the years he'd been over there but, some time since he'd gone, without realising, I'd forgotten what it sounded like. Forgotten so completely that hearing it again now didn't bring back the memory. There was nothing in this voice that I could connect with any recollection of the person I'd once called 'dad.'

'You'd better come in,' my mom murmured.

'I haven't got time. Just give it to me.'

'Polly's here.'

'I said I haven't got time to piss about; just give me the fucking thing…'

'Polly wants to have a word with you.'

I heard a noise of casual irritation and disgust, then a slight shuffling – he'd shoved her to one side as he came in. From the sound of it, he'd shoved her quite roughly too, had this person – who I'd once called 'dad.'

'Look, I haven't got time for this shit…'

And his voice left him, when he saw me, because he'd expected me to be afraid of him, or in awe of him, or something… I wasn't. I looked at him, and I saw a bloke ten, fifteen years older than my mom. He looked a lot like me but – not long ago, I reckoned – he'd have passed for handsome. He made the mistake of dressing as if he could still pass for handsome. The brown leather car coat, in particular, looked really silly on such an old – on such a *little* old man. It was true – he was hardly taller than I was. And grey hair should never be worn *that* long.

'Do you want this?'

Cimourdain's diary lay on the dining room table, where we'd eaten not long before. There was still a half-full teapot, with salt, pepper and bottles of brown sauce and tomato ketchup.

'Because you're not getting it,' I told the little man.

And there was something in my voice that scared him. It would have scared me too, I think. My mom's eyes, sneaking a look from out in the hall, were very wide and blinky.

My eyes did not blink at all.

It must have been a very nasty moment for the little man, when he became aware of Big Mohammed and Kraygon. They'd been in the kitchen, having coffee, but now they were at his shoulders.

I don't think he said anything as they dragged him into the kitchen. He certainly didn't say anything once they started kicking him. He did make a funny noise, though; after a moment, I realised that, when they kicked him – over and over again – he was accidentally whimpering the tune the saxophone plays in that George Michael song, 'Careless Whisper'.

'This,' Big Mohammed explained, pointing at me as I came to the doorway, 'is the Gaffer's Woman.'

'And this,' Kraygon continued, 'is what happens to them as don' show the Gaffer's Woman no respect.'

They kicked him a bit more.

Once they'd finished and dragged him to his feet, his little face was bloody. Before the night was out, at least one of his eyes would have puffed up too badly to see out of. Looking at him, it seemed strange to admit that his disappearance had once left a hole in my life and it had seemed like a big hole. Yet it couldn't have been a big hole – not when he was such a little man.

'Okay, get out,' I told him, and he did.

I rang Harry.

'Everything go alright, then?' he asked.

'Everything. Yes.'

'The lads do okay?'

'You'd've been proud of them.'

'Good, good. Didn't think they'd let me down. You not feeling distressed at all?'

'No. Not at all. We'll get no more trouble off that one.'

'That's my brave little hamster! See you tomorrow evening, then!'

I smiled and felt curiously aware of my teeth as I did so. They felt sharper than usual.

I told Kraygon and Big Mohammed what a good job they'd done and they were really grateful. Kraygon called me 'Mrs Ronsard' by mistake. I could have kissed him.

After they'd gone, I found my mom had disappeared. I looked for her and found her upstairs, sat on her bed and crying. I could understand her doing that. I sat next to her and put my arm around her. She trembled and for a second I thought she was going to push me away. I knew, very suddenly, that she was afraid of me. That upset me a bit, because I didn't want her to be afraid of me. Not her. But the feeling didn't last long and she leant against me and, a bit at a time, her tears went away.

***

A little bit of shopping, because I needed it. I'd got some money to spare and I wanted to look good for Harry. So up the mall at Merry Hill I went and, after two hours and three hundred quid, I reckoned I looked a good deal less of a div.

Harry looked pleased when he saw me. He nodded and his eyes narrowed, appraising me, it seemed, and finding me satisfactory.

'You've made a lady of yourself,' he said, softly.

'Thank you,' I replied, softer still, as I stepped into his house. I put my handbag on the coffee table and took out the leather-bound diary.

'This it?' asked Harry.

'Yes.'

He picked it up, opened it with something like reverence and turned over the pages, delicately.

'Don't know much French,' he murmured. 'Granddad spoke French. He was French, of course. That's me mom's dad. Came over before the First War. I've got French on both sides of the family, as it happens, but it's going back fair old bit on Dad's side... Hang on! Here's Granddad's name – *Lantenac!*'

'Do you suppose this means we've got ancestors who knew each other?' I asked.

'Hmm. Maybe. Wonder how well they got on? I wish I could read this...'

'I know,' I said. 'Have you looked at the other names in it?'

'Hmm... *"Robespierre."* Here...' Harry stared hard at one of the pages. ' *"Robespierre m'a dit..?"'*

' *"Robespierre said to me."'* I translated.

'Well then! This bloke was either a conman or he knew some of the bigwigs back then pretty well. In which case...'

'It's worth a lot.'

'Could be worth thousands.' Harry looked hard at me. 'I'm afraid your dad was out to swindle you out of a lot of money, my little hamster.'

I sighed.

'It's alright,' I said. 'He doesn't matter to me anymore.' We sat on the sofa together and I put my arm around him. He made a surprised sort of noise, but didn't move away. As so often before, I had the wild and crazy notion that I should get up, stand in front of him and take my clothes off. I wanted to be naked for my master. There were voices inside me telling me that that was a daft idea. I couldn't be so stupid as to think..?

Couldn't be so stupid? But why not?

'Kraygon called me "Mrs Ronsard" this evening,' I said.

Harry's head shifted and I felt him turning to look down at me.

'Did he now?'

'Yes.'

'How did you feel about that?'

I thought about it for a bit.

'Warm,' I said at last.

'Warm?'

'Yes.'

'What sort of "warm"?'

I considered, carefully.

'Warm all over,' I said. 'Warm, but not burning warm. Warm as if...' and I hesitated then and, for some reason, I felt a tiny, sharp point of fear. The little man's bloody face flickered briefly in my mind. I ignored the memory. 'Warm,' I said, 'as if warm were the right way to feel.'

Harry's thumb and forefinger took my chin and raised my face to face his face.

We kissed, very softly, but for a long time.

Drawing apart, at last, we looked at each other.

'You know, my little hamster, there are things about me you don't want to know.'

'I know. I don't care.'

'You don't care?'

'It's not my place to care about such things.'

He looked down on me and nodded. Then, together, we stood.

'You'd better be on your way, now,' he said. 'We've got a lot of things to sort out.'

I smiled up at him. 'We have,' I said.

'But we will sort them,' he promised.

'We will,' I agreed.

He kissed the top of my head.

Outside, I turned left and walked up the road. Shirley Icement had brought home a couple of big document cases in the boot of her car. She came out to get them, just as I was passing.

Her eyes fixed me with a fierce expression and it was all I could do not to tell her how much it made her look like the black dragon on Harry's wall.

'I don't know what Harry sees in you,' she sighed.

I was silent.

'You're such a silly little girl,' she explained, 'such a silly, silly little girl. It's ridiculous! A sensible man like Harry. And he goes falling for a silly little girl like you!'

At her front door, there was a nervous, shuffling movement. I turned my head and there was her husband, tottering out on to the drive.

He looked terrible. I wasn't sure if he knew where he was. He stared up into the evening sky and it stared, blue and blank and indifferent, down at him. His eyes fell to the hard grey concrete slabs of the driveway and he got no more sympathy there. Finally he tried looking at his wife, but one glance at her and he saw how things stood. His eyes collapsed into themselves and his mouth made funny, indistinct murmurings.

'Was a great...' he murmured.

Shirley Icement spun round on him. Making a quiet, disciplined and ferocious noise of disgust, she closed and locked the boot of her car.

'What are you doing out here?' she snapped.

'Great laugh, was Mick...' her husband mumbled.

I couldn't help myself. 'Are you sure your husband is all right, Mrs Icement?' I asked. 'Because he doesn't look too well to me...'

Shirley Icement took no notice. 'Just a silly little man! A silly silly little man! It's ridiculous! You...' And then she heard herself. And listened to what she'd been saying. And the look on her face was the look you'd get if somebody had stuck a knife or something into your back. And she looked back at me and, when she saw that I had seen and that I had understood, she looked terrified, as well as shocked.

By now, she had steered her husband through their front door.

'Blind, steaming drunk...' he rambled.

The door crashed shut.

21: Mary Maitland

I knocked quietly on Sharukh's door. Across the landing, there was a baby's cry. It wasn't loud, but it soaked through the door that had been Alice's like pee through a nappy. I smiled – some silences are better broken. Sharukh opened up and nodded, tersely.

'Been alright?' he asked.

'Okay, thanks,' I said, not too convincingly. 'Getting married in April. This anything to do with Abdul?'

Sharukh frowned as we went into the lounge. He nipped from there into the kitchen and came out with a full teapot. He waved me to sit.

'Dunno. Partly. Abdul's still not well. There's been this funny business though. I've got a cousin – my mum's sister's son. He runs a newsie's in Dudley.'

'Thankless task.'

'Can be. Things have been quite well behaved lately. Which I'd thought was too good to be true. But apparently, it's all down to these young guys doing this neighbourhood watch stuff. Seen 'em round? They like to wear grey shirts and suits. Some of 'em wear brown leather jackets. And there's getting to be a heck of a lot of 'em.'

I nodded. I'd noticed them, too, though I'd not been feeling well enough to be out and about very much, apart from work. They looked, for the most part, like sweet, well-intentioned kids.

'Nobody really minded,' Sharukh went on, 'because they were doing a good job with the drug dealers...'

I looked up. Suddenly I knew where this was leading. And to whom.

'Now, though,' Sharukh said, 'they're starting to throw their weight around. You've got gangs of them, hanging around Hasan's shop, and anyone buys a packet of fags, they've been giving 'em a hard time! And the way he tells it, they've started telling people they shouldn't go buying them lads' mags. I mean, don't get me wrong – Hasan's a good bloke, good Muslim. Better than me, to be honest.

183

He don't like selling that stuff – *Nuts* and *Loaded* and that. Or them papers with the topless women in. Sell that stuff, y'know, and one day it's gonna be your sister's photo in there, y'know, bringing the shame on the family...'

'I *know,*' I said, wincing.

'...and he wouldn't have that stuff on the shelves if the supplier gave him any choice. That's all bad enough. But, y'know, what these young lads are doing, it don't seem right, either...'

'What makes you think they've got anything to do with what happened to Abdul?'

'Well, we thought he was getting better. His mum took him out last week. They bump into a few of these lads in the grey shirts and they don't get no aggro off them but Abdul, he goes to pieces, like. Starts screaming these are the Devil's kids, like, and they're gonna drag him to Hell. She has to phone me and some others to help get him back home. He's not been so bad since, as long as he stays in, but there was something about them that sent him right off the deep end...'

I breathed in and wanted to cry. Abdul had smelt Harry Ronsard on those kids. I was a fool not to have recognised the stench myself.

If a big part of your job is trying to sweep up the mess persistent drug users make of their lives, you'll not usually find the work drying up. Over the past couple of months, though, it *had* come close to drying up. And the reason was very straightforward – all the major suppliers were dead. So having accomplished that, what would Satan's next move be? He would begin gathering his disciples.

Maybe Harry Ronsard would wind up saving some people from horrible deaths, but there'd be a price to pay. There always is, with Satan. And these poor kids in their grey shirts would be the first to pay it.

'Sharukh, I think I know who's in charge of these lads.'

'Oh, everyone knows that! They ain't keeping it a secret! Bloke from Kingswinford called Harry Ronsard. You alright?'

I'd felt the most revolting twitch spasm through me – repulsion at the name.

'I know this man,' I whispered, pulling myself together. 'I think he's the one... Abdul saw before. And, for whatever reason, you won't find the police and the courts and the solicitors will be ready to help you when it comes to anything he's done. In God's name, please keep away from him.'

Sharukh looked at me, hard.

'This sounds bad,' he said.

I nodded.

'Is he really... what Abdul thinks he is?'

I struggled to find the words:

'I think he... I'm sorry – it doesn't fit with anything I've been taught, but... I think he might be... becoming it, yes...'

Sharukh paused for a moment, then he started to pray – in Arabic, maybe. I waited a moment longer before I started to pray in English.

When I left his place, the baby across the landing had quietened off. Sharukh had told me that a single mother lived in Alice's old place, lying low from the little 'un's dad, who'd been kicking the living daylights out of her up in Stoke-on-Trent. God bless them both, mother and child. And keep them safe.

***

'Been anywhere good, love?' Ryan asked me, looking up from *Steam Classics Magazine* as I came in.

'Dropped in on the bloke who used to be Alice's neighbour,' I explained. 'What's that?'

Ryan's picture was in the mag, alongside his dad's. They were both grinning manically and pointing to a large plan of an ocean liner. 'REBUILD THE *TITANIC?* IT'S POSSIBLE, SAYS FATHER AND SON TEAM' – announced the headline.

'Oi, you!' I was stern. Sternness was needed.

'Yes, love?'

'Not in my bloody back garden, it isn't!'

'Oh no!' – his voice all mock innocence.

'So put it right out of your mind!'

'Oh, of course!' – still full of cod *'not-me-governor.'*

'I know you!'

'No, no, not a problem...'

I eyed him suspiciously. He smiled.

'But now we've got *Excalibur* up and chuffing...'

'It's just a traction engine, Ryan. It has nothing to do with King Arthur and it's not going to confer any engineering super-powers on you...'

Relaxing into Ryan's well-meaning daftness was everything I needed. Inside ten minutes, I'd agreed to go for a ride on the chuffing great monstrosity at the weekend. He'd've had me up on that footplate the same evening, except the nights were drawing in.

Then my phone went.

'Hi Mary. Dave Calper. How's it going?'

Voice as enthusiastic as usual – no doubt itching for my thunderous drummer of a brother-in-law to return from his trip to London so The Death of Wallenstein could get making their barmy racket again. But there was an edge to it. Dave was spooked.

'Alright, Dave. How can I help you?'

He took a deep breath. 'I've had the weirdest invitation,' he said, 'off Lee Icement. He wants me to come to Kates Hill Conservative Club in three weeks' time –'

'That really doesn't sound like anywhere I'd expect him to be.'

'– to hear Harry Ronsard make a speech.'

I was silent.

'They reckon Harry's MP material, apparently.' Dave added, apologetically.

'Oh,' I said, horrified.

'And he's asked me to ask you to come, too. Apparently, Harry would like you to hear what he's got to say.'

'Oh,' I said, surprised and bewildered now, as well as horrified.

'Mary?'

'I'm going to come, Dave. But, Dave?'

'Yeah?'

'Could I bring Ryan along? I need the moral support.'

'That's no problem. Lee said everyone could bring a guest.'

'Then we'll be there. Tell Lee.'

'I will.'

'Dave. Stay calm. If you hear any more, give me a ring. Otherwise, I'll see you at the weekend.'

'Cheers, beautiful. I'll have the kettle on.'

'You always do, Dave. It's one of the laws of the universe.'

I put my phone away and noticed Ryan was gaping.

'You're telling Dave Calper to calm down.'

'I am.'

'Dave Calper is so calm he's horizontal.'

'Usually.'

'What's happened? God forbid somebody's put six million volts through him.'

'God forbade it indeed but Harry Ronsard hath done it,' I semi-quoted.

'Oh no! Thought we'd heard the last of that bugger!'

Despite his words, there was a note of relief in Ryan's voice and I knew why. Lately, I'd made sure I'd not mentioned the name 'Harry Ronsard' in front of him; I'd wanted him to be my place of refuge from all that. But it had been obvious I was still brooding over something, so he'd known the matter was far from sorted. Yet my lovely bloke hadn't asked me a thing – he'd trusted me to tell him as soon as I felt up to it. I was so grateful.

'Have you seen those lads and lasses hanging round? In the grey shirts? Like a load of trainee bouncers?' I asked.

'What? Them? They anything to with Harry Ronsard?'

'They're his teenage fan club.'

'Oh bugger.'

'It gets better, love. He's making a speech at Kates Hill Cons Club in three weeks' time and we've got an invite.'

'Bastard buggerin' 'ell!'

'Ryan?'

'Yes, love?'

'Please don't swear so much; my nerves are shredded enough as it is.'

'Sorry, love, but...'

'I know, Ryan.'

'A Conservative Club, love!   You're asking... *me*... to go... *inside*... a Conservative Club?!'

'Yes, Ryan.'

'Me dad'll go mental!'

'Perhaps you'd better not tell him.'

'He'll smell it on me, love. You know what he's like!'

He had a point there.

'Well tell him it's a matter of knowing your enemy. Harry Ronsard can wrap people round his little finger, and if he's getting into politics I want to know as much as I can about what he's up to.'

While I was talking, I'd got up and gone over to the computer, which was logged on to a website featuring a big picture of the predictable steam-powered chuffer. I opened another window and typed in 'Harry Ronsard' on YouTube. Quite a bit of stuff there – all of it very enthusiastic. Harry turning up on *Midlands Today,* talking about how the building trade was 'turning a corner'. Harry on a similar TV show, introducing a huge lad called Mohammed who, having done time for assault, was now a part of something Harry described as a 'neighbourhood watch' scheme.

'If those two are running a neighbourhood watch scheme,' Ryan chuntered over my shoulder, 'then Genghis Khan was in charge of a community outreach programme.'

Worse than all that, though, was the confirmation that Harry was to have a shot at Parliament. The member for Kates Hill and Tividale hadn't been looking well for some time and, now in his mid-seventies, he'd learned he'd got cancer. He'd been an MP for forty years, a shop steward before that, and a soldier before that – proper Old Labour. His party thought they'd got a 'safe seat' on their hands so they were putting up some anaemic little Tony Blair clone – of whom, it was clear to me, Harry would make mincemeat. The election was due early in the new year.

The comments under each of the YouTube clips were uniformly ecstatic:

'The sort of bloke as the country needs a lot more of.'

'At last! A bugger as sounds like he knows what he's talking about!'

'Well I'd vote for him.'

That last one posted by somebody in Alabama.

I turned back to Ryan.

'See? Everybody loves him.'

'You reckon he's that bad do you?'

'Ryan...'

I took a deep breath, because this was the last thing I'd wanted to tell him. I'd wanted him to be completely apart from the knowledge. But...

'He's killing people, Ryan.'

And I told him everything.

He was very very quiet.

'Don't,' he said, finally, 'you go near that bloody Kates Hill place without me.'

'I won't,' I said.

***

The day after, I spotted some of the grey shirt kids in Dudley town centre, outside the shop that had once been Beattie's department store. I took a deep breath and sauntered up.

'Hello,' I said, smiling.

There were three of them: they were all in their late teens and all lads. Two white, one Asian.

'Hello,' they mumbled back, polite and shy. From then on, the bigger of the white lads did pretty much all the talking. No surprise that any organisation Harry had dreamt up was so hierarchical.

'I'm interested in the work you're doing,' I said, matter-of-factly. 'How's it organised?'

'Oh, we just keep an eye on things,' said the leader – eighteen, I guessed and still very spotty. 'It can get a bit rough, round here.'

'Oh, I know!' I replied, with every appearance of profound agreement. 'So what happens if you see something kicking off?'

'Any serious trouble,' he said, 'and we call the Gaffer. Any time – day or night. If it's just some prat being a nuisance, we grab him and call the coppers. Then we call the Gaffer.'

'The Gaffer?'

'You know, the Gaffer. You'll've sid him on telly.'

'Do you mean Mr Ronsard?' I said, adding a touch of awed respect to my voice.

They all nodded seriously, and the leader replied, 'That's right. Been on *Midlands Today*, ain't he?'

I put on an impressed expression.

'Have you had much serious trouble?'

'Nah. Word's got out, if it gets bad, we call the Gaffer. Any prats think the Gaffer's gonna show, they chill their beans fast.'

'Well, they would do...'

''Sright. Everybody knows, you don' muck the Gaffer about.'

'Which towns are you keeping an eye on?'

'Oh, we got boots on the ground in Dudley, Netherton, pretty much the whole of Sandwell. Brierley Hill – down to about Silver End. We're getting things started in Wolverhampton, Walsall, Perry Barr, Handsworth...'

A worrying thought crossed my mind. 'But not Stourbridge?'

'Nah, not Stourbridge. Thing is, we don' have nothin' to do with them but, what we hear, them wenches have got things sussed out down there... Stourbridge Women's Self Defence Unit...'

'Oh, I know the Unit – my sister was the one who put it together.'

Murmurs of 'Respect' from all three.

'You can tell her,' the leader said, with deep seriousness, 'the Gaffer's got a lot of respect for her. Really appreciates what she's doing.'

This, at least, came as a relief. If Harry had decided to put 'boots on the ground' in Stourbridge, things might have kicked off all over the shop – my sis and her kung-fu ninjababes on one side and Old

Harry's Teenreich on the other. Somebody – lots of somebodies – would have got hurt.

'Do the police mind you being here?' I nodded at a couple of luminous yellow officers standing nearby.

'Coppers know we're never the ones to start anything.'

Never the ones to start it, I was sure, but always the ones to finish it. This, despite the grey shirt and sensible suit that could, on someone as young as him, be mistaken for a school uniform and a haircut just as conservative.

What a good lad he was! His mom must have thought the world of him! She must have blessed Harry Ronsard's brimstone-scented cotton socks for turning her little lad into such a fine little gentleman! How sweet, how eager to do the right thing – how bloody terrifying.

I wandered over to the luminous coppers. Who, if anything, turned out to be bigger fanboys of Old Harry than the greyshirts. Wonderful, the work he'd been doing with local communities, with local youth groups, with local gang members, with local Uncle Tom Cobbley and all...

And with local schools.

Oh dear.

This meant Shirley Icement was in on it too, and that frightened me all the more.

***

The southbound road out of Dudley forked, just past the top of Kates Hill. Left took you over Rowley to Blackheath. Right took you down into Netherton. The Conservative Club was on your right, just before the fork. It had apparently been put up at the end of the fifties after the previous one had been petrol-bombed by a drunken mob who'd just been kicked out the Gypsies' Tent Inn. It was an uninspiring building – yellow brickwork long faded to ochre, flat roof of the sort that always leaked.

We were early but the car park was rammed. We found a space a few hundred yards down the road. We were assured, by a grey-

191

shirted lad of about fifteen, that everything would be fine. 'I'm keeping an eye on the motors, this end, and nobody's gonna nick nothing with the Gaffer just up the road.'

On Ryan, a formal suit looked a bit awkward. On Dave Calper, it looked an outright abomination. He told me he'd last worn it sometime in the 1970s when such clobber was still required for old-fashioned jazz gigs. He had his hair washed, combed and ponytailed, and he was more recently-shaved than I'd seen him for quite a while. I felt it was my duty to straighten both their collars and ties, and to pick off certain bits of stray fluff that had got randomly attached to their jackets.

Ryan put his hand on my arm and we walked, with apparent calm, back to the car park. There were two more lads in grey shirts at the entrance, telling drivers it was full but assuring them that their vehicles would get 'kept an eye on', if left on the streets.

One of them noticed me. He smiled, which was an expression he didn't do terribly well; you sensed he was much more used to snarling. He had a little badge on his grey shirt, announcing 'My name is Kraygon' and he recognised me.

'Hello Miss Maitland.'

'Hello – er – Kraygon. How have we met?'

'You came to our school, Miss. Talked about drugs.'

'Ah. Was your head teacher Mrs Icement?'

'Yes, Miss. She's here, tonight. We're very pleased you've made it. Gaffer reckons as you talk a lot of sense about drugs.'

'Thank you, Kraygon.'

On the way towards the butter-yellow light of the club entrance, I saw Lee Icement get out of a parked car – on the passenger side. With easy, confident ferocity, he headed for the entrance, not noticing us. The driver of the car did not get out, but he didn't drive away. Lee disappeared into the club, acknowledging no one.

'Give me a few minutes,' I said to Ryan and Dave. 'If Lee or Harry ask, I've had to nip to the loo. There's somebody I want a word with.'

'Okay,' said Ryan, trusting me, and they moved towards the light.

I made my way to the car Lee had left and tapped on the driver's side window. With a quiet buzz, it wound itself down.

'Hello?' I whispered.

The face stayed in the shadows, but there was a soft noise and I knew he'd turned and was looking up at me. I leaned closer to him.

'I know you,' he said. There was a broken gentleness about the voice.

'Oh.'

'I used to go to your father's church.'

'Ah. I see.'

'With my family. My whole family. We all used to go. Don't you remember us? The Gladrells?'

I tried and failed.

'It's all right,' he went on and I could hear a sad little smile in the voice. 'You won't have noticed us. We never had much to say for ourselves.'

'There were a lot of people like that,' I admitted, 'in Dad's church.'

'There were. There were.'

'Things went wrong for you there?'

'They did. They went wrong for us. Same sort of thing as happened to you. Only not as bad. Nobody got killed. And you won't have seen it in all the papers.'

'All about you and Lee?'

'Partly. Me and... Lee.'

Something changed about the voice, then. It didn't just sound broken anymore; it sounded broken and angry. The gentleness had gone.

'You sound like you don't like saying his name.'

'I'm not... allowed.'

Something darker than abjection and enslavement in the voice – a kind of deep fury that didn't know of its own existence and was all the more dangerous for that.

'What's your name?'

He paused, then said, 'Lewis.'

'Lewis Gladrell.'

'Yes.' He spoke as if the name was strange to him.

'Does he call you Lewis?'

'No.'

'What does he call you?'

No answer.

'What does he call you, Lewis?'

'He calls me... The Cunt.'

I think he expected me to be shocked. But I'd known how bad things were just from the sound of his voice.

'Does he slap you around for saying his name?'

'Yes. I'm permitted to call him... Satansfist.'

'I know he uses that name. He's not really very Satanic, you know.'

'Isn't he?'

'Not compared to Harry Ronsard, no.'

'I've only met Harry a couple of times.'

'Do you want to meet him now?'

A long pause.

'No,' he replied, finally. 'No I don't.' He made a soft little noise that I realised was a laugh. 'But Satansfist created him.'

'I know. That's what he told me, too. With the paintings, apparently.'

'With the paintings, yes. On Harry's wall. I've never been allowed to see them. But he'll let you. Look at them and you'll see. You'll see why I'm in love with him, too – with Lee...' The last few words sounded desolate as a suicide note, the name 'Lee' most desolate of all.

'Why does he slap you around?' I asked.

'It's what I want.'

'Really?'

'Yes. Really.'

My dad would need to know about this. He wasn't one to be spared the details of his own sins and betrayals; he would see this as one of them.

But I was most worried about something more immediate – the

194

sharp-edged anger I could hear, rising slowly but steadily through Lewis. Getting very near the surface.

'If Lee doesn't stop this soon,' I warned, 'you're going to turn on him. I think you might kill him.'

There was a silence.

'I know you can't believe it at the moment,' I added, 'but I can hear it in your voice. This time next year, he'll be as dead as his sister. That's what he thinks he wants, and he's just like her – she used heroin; he's using you. You need to get away from him.'

'I can't.'

'You must.'

Silence again.

'Can I look at you?' I asked.

He didn't reply. But three cars came through the front entrance as I asked. Lewis's face was briefly lit up. There was an obscene purple and green bruise under his right eye and his mouth was horribly cut and swollen.

I nodded to myself and said nothing.

The three cars drove up to the front door of the club, which I saw was guarded by six or seven short-haired blokes in heavy Crombie coats – older, bigger and meaner looking than Harry's greyshirts.

Pulling up, the cars spilled a few neat little men, all with the same frightened little way of walking. They were inside the club and out of sight in three seconds flat. I thought I recognised one of them. Some cabinet minister or chancellor or something – I don't know.

'I think you should go and listen to Harry,' whispered Lewis.

'Are you sure you're not coming?'

'I'm sure.'

'I think you and I need to talk,' I said.

'Perhaps.'

'No. For certain.'

'That'd be nice.' The voice was flat and empty. I straightened up and turned from him, feeling as if I ought not to, feeling like a failure.

I headed up to the club entrance and was let in by the short-haired men with the thin lips – the men who did not think they were Harry's creatures, not yet.

22: Satansfist

'Lewis,' croaked the deathshead, 'is just what you need.'

I gaped at her.

There had really been no point in going there, that drab afternoon, the previous November.

I hadn't known that she'd be dead within six months, but it wouldn't have taken much to work it out. The state she was in was pitiful, pathetic. She'd gone the whole hog: croaky voice, skull face, flat that stank like a cat's arse. If there'd been an award for best smackhead in Sandwell, she'd have won it. And, believe me, there was competition.

'He's right for you,' the deathshead croaked again. 'You should be good to him.'

'Assuming he wants me to be good. You don't know him very well, if...'

'I don't have to know him. I know you. He's what you need and you should be good to him. He loves you...'

'Assuming I need to be loved...'

The deathshead turned to me abruptly, and the bloodshot orbs tried to focus on me from somewhere far back in that blasted skull. They didn't have much luck.

'You and Mum,' she croaked, 'two for a pair...'

'Don't compare me to that frigid fucking retard.'

'Two for a pair.'

Drifting in and out of consciousness, the hideous rattlebag wrenched herself to her feet and shambled over to where she kept a collection of three CDs. She picked one out.

'Dad used to be in this band,' she croaked, waving it at me, unsteadily.

I looked at it. I'd seen a copy before – in Dave's shop. I nodded.

'I heard as much. He was never on any of the records.'

'Tha's a shame...' she sighed, 'Tha's a shame...'

She was looking around, even more confused than usual.

'You sold it,' I reminded her. 'Your CD player.'

She turned back to me and the papery flesh on her forehead wrinkled a little.

'Oh yeah…' Then, even more confused, 'How did you know?'

I didn't reply.

The CD slipped from her fingers and bounced on the floor. I picked it up and for no reason, checked it wasn't scratched. Then I clicked it back into its digipak, which I put back with the others. I'm not sure why I went to the trouble. Her mind was so out of focus that she'd not have noticed if I hadn't. Loyalty to Dave, maybe? Seemed a shame that, of the three albums she'd not been able to flog for smack, one was his. Still, life was a bastard, wasn't it?

Oddly enough, I stayed round there for quite a bit longer than I'd intended. I think the whole thing appealed to my sense of humour. I'd always been ready to strangle her for all that Ozric Tentacles bollocks. Now she was admitting with every shrivelled cell of her soon-to-be-corpse, that I was right. About everything.

A year later, when the stories were coming in of all the smackheads topping themselves because they couldn't get the gear, I thought about how she'd been, that afternoon. I knew who was responsible for the current chemical drought and I asked him, when he rang me, how he felt about it?

'The good 'uns'll get over it,' he said, 'those as have got anything about them. The others. Well. *Hmph!*'

'Hmph!' – what a novel way of saying *I do condemn ye all unto the fiery pit of Hell*! Then again, Harry was full of surprises. With this in mind, I asked him why he'd called?

'Inviting you to the Conservative Club,' he said, 'up Kates Hill'

'?!!!!!' I thought. Full of surprises was one thing but this went a bit beyond that.

'I'm giving a speech,' he continued, 'about Things.'

'I see,' I said.

'Having you over. And I'd like you to have a word with that Dave Calper. Get him over too. If you know how to get hold of that Mary Maitland…'

'Dave does. He knows her quite well... But doesn't..?'

I was sure that ridiculous Polly Gauvain knew the Maitland woman's number. Then again, Polly seemed such a twerp that Harry probably didn't trust her to convey a message, or to do anything but sit in a corner and simper. Nonetheless, a speech from Harry ought to present us all with a point of view that was... interestingly unusual, to say the least. I was up for it.

'Well, this ought to...'

'Never you mind what it ought to do. It'll wind up Doing the Right Thing. That's what it'll wind up doing.'

'I see.'

'You will see. And you'll hear. I'm not going to muck about, I'm telling you that.'

I'd got the idea of Harry 'mucking about' filed away in my back brain, somewhere between 'Harry standing in for Ken Dodd' and 'Harry dancing in *Swan Lake*' – but I didn't say as much.

This was going to be entertaining. But there was one loose cannon I had to get bolted down. I clicked my iPhone off and looked around the flat.

The Cunt rose from his chair and stared at me.

He'd noticed something unusual. There was wide-eyed curiosity in his face. And something else. He reached out a hand as if to touch me, perhaps on the shoulder or the top of my head.

I felt breaking tooth enamel slice into my knuckles as I smashed my fist into his mouth.

***

As October grew darkeningly into another November, I'd spotted more and more of Harry's little soldiers hanging around Birmingham and Wolverhampton. There were, no doubt, just as many up Merry Hill but, now I'd completed and been paid for the murals, I kept away from that shithole as much as I could.

These fresh-faced vigilantes started to get mentioned in the local papers. With glowing approval. Then, bliss for Harry, in the *Daily*

Mail itself – three of them had come upon a smackhead mugging an old lady in Netherton. The BBC had sent a news team along but, the way I heard it from an occasional shag who worked in the Mailbox, nothing broadcastable had been put together: they'd wanted a story of vigilante lynch mobs and Hitler Youth psychopathy. Nobody round here was prepared to give them such a story – everybody loved Harry.

In a year's time, he'd be Tory MP for a big chunk of Sandwell and Dudley. That was inevitable, given the flaccidity of the Blairoid abortion that the other side were fielding. What a laugh!

Shortly thereafter, he'd be Secretary of State for Education. Yeah, Education... that'd be it. He'd be coming to Mother Dearest for all his notions of what constituted 'best practice.' Fucking hilarious!

After that – but let's not get ahead of ourselves.

So was I really going to the torchlit rally up Kates Hill? Of course I fucking well was! If for no other reason than, if Harry's little darlings did wind up running the show, I wanted to be prominent in his circle, and prominently gay, just in case they wondered if it might be a good idea to whip the old pink triangles out of mothballs. That really wasn't the way I wanted to go.

The big night came round quicker than I expected. Thankfully, The Cunt was still looking like shit from the slapping I'd given him, so there was no danger he'd want to come in and spoil the effect. Another fortunate by-product of said slapping was that he'd had to cancel three or four appearances at his wanky friends' 'Alternative Arts Space' over in Tipton, where Granddad still glowered ghoulishly down from the side wall. The Cunt did give me a lift to Kates Hill, though. I told him to make sure he was there when I got out or he'd be saying 'Ta-ra' to a tooth or two more.

The place was packed – three or four hundred. There was the local Tory equivalent of frenzied excitement in the air – for the most part, this meant they'd all got their hearing aids turned up full blast. Rock-and Roll!

Mother was sitting at the end of the front row, facing away from me. I didn't try to attract her attention. Keeping as far away from her and as far away from me as he could, Graham Tolland sweet-talked a couple of self-important local nonentities.

I'd wondered if I was going to feel at home but, counting the number of blokes under forty... Let's see... Twenty three... four... five... twenty six! And no fewer than eighteen of 'em cringed with embarrassment when I attempted eye contact – so everything was cool. In fact, I had a dim recollection of number nineteen but he didn't seem too bothered. Anyway, I'd been at the absinthe the night it happened and, in all honesty, I didn't recall him having been much good.

Vodka and lime in hand, I perched at the bar and decided to find out how uncomfortable I could make the lot of 'em. The one with the most insipid and virginal-looking girlfriend was always the right place to start, and indeed my knowing smile soon had him squirming almost as much as my dick had the year before.

Which was when Dave Calper walked in, alongside a broad-shouldered thug who I wished I'd had as a model when I was putting Sir Percival on the ceiling of Harry's landing.

Dave's hair: ponytailed. Dave's suit: purple. Dave's tie: kipper. Dave's shoes: platform. How long had this getup been in... mothballs? Cryogenic suspension, more like!

The pair of them came over, not as nervously as might have been expected.

'You met Ryan?' Dave asked.

'No.'

'Mary Maitland's fiancé.'

Regrettably straight. Well, no surprises there. Of all the blokes in the room, Ryan would have been the one I'd have filed most quickly under *'All-fucking-RIGHT-but-I'm-not-even-going-to-bother.'*

'You're the painter,' Ryan rumbled.

'Ye-es...'

'You paint King Arthur stuff.'

'Er... yes...'

'You into all that King Arthur stuff?'

I hesitated, because there was an undertone in his voice that indicated, very clearly, he had a Big Surprise he wanted to spring on me, and I was far from sure I fancied having it thus sprung.

'Errr...' was the best I managed, not very satisfactorily.

'I'll take that as a yes,' he commanded. And I really don't like being commanded.

Not much I could do about it, though, because things began to happen. There was a bit of bustling and murmuring as some weedy little turd of a cabinet minister was ushered in, at which we were all supposed to be most impressed. Graham Tolland and two or three of the local big nobs smarmed him to the front row and he smarmed himself into a seat. He'd brought a bunch of heavies in Crombies with him. They dispersed themselves evenly around the walls and looked tooled-up.

Mary Maitland came in shortly after. She was very calm. She came up to us, took Ryan's arm and looked at me, levelly. This was a woman who, one way or another, was going to make life difficult. I sighed inwardly and looked away.

A lavender-scented old ponce infested our space for a few moments and told us where we were supposed to be sitting. Mary thanked him and led us to the places he'd pointed out.

I looked up at the stage – plush blue curtains. Very nice.

Harry came out from behind them and everybody shut up.

He looked at the crowd in front of him, noticed Mother, noticed us, then fixed his gaze on one of the Crombied heavies who'd come in with the minister.

The heavy's Crombie seemed to wilt. Everything about him seemed to wilt. Everything about him seemed to recognise its master.

Harry shifted his eyes to another heavy. One by one, he looked at each of the minister's bodyguards. And, one by one, he broke each one of them, snapped each one's soul, made each one his creature.

I don't know how he did it, and I certainly don't know how I knew he did it, but he did it. I sensed it, as clearly as if what I was seeing had been one of my own paintings. Perhaps it was. I thought Dave sensed it, as well. Perhaps even Ryan did. I knew Mary Maitland did. She knew what was going on as well as Harry or I.

The room was silent, the way I imagined one of Mother's assemblies got to be silent. Everybody else knew something was happening. They didn't know what, but they knew it was important.

Finally, Harry glanced, very briefly, at the little minister, but saw immediately that there was nothing there to break. He stepped up to the front of the stage. There was a mic there but it had been turned off – he didn't need it.

'Good evening, ladies and gentlemen,' he began. 'This is an important night. Not just for me, not just for us, but for everything that all of us believe is Right.

'A few months ago, Shirley Icement approached me, looking for a place where her boys and girls could come and learn how to do a good job well. Fortunately, I was able to offer a number of her pupils the training they needed...'

I was disappointed. I'd been expecting *Rivers of Blood* at the very least, if not *Virgins, ye labour in vain to prevent...* This was tame stuff! But looking around the place, I could see what he was up to. He'd said nothing that would sound outrageous in the ears of the old flowerpots listening. He was the ordinary bloke, doing his ordinary job in ordinary Dudley. And he was helping out a few ordinary kids. Nothing to object to there, was there? No, he'd got them well and truly lulled and thinking he was on their side. When he started on about his grey-shirted little fanboys, it sounded just as reasonable.

'You must by now be aware that, from a core of those young people who've been learning trades and skills at my place of work, I've helped to organise a group of volunteers who've been keeping an eye on the area. Spotting undesirables and anti-social behaviour. Working with the police, of course, and existing neighbourhood watch schemes.'

Still sounding oh-so-fucking-innocuous! Come on, Harry! I'm gagging for some red meat here!

'I'm pleased to be able to tell you that, according to my friends at Brierley Hill Police Station –' here he nodded at a grey haired senior copper who smiled and nodded back – 'the figures for street crime, in the areas of the Black Country and Birmingham where we have been active, have fallen by eighty-five per cent, compared to this time last year.'

He'd got them now and, I must admit, I was beginning to be a little impressed. The audience was 'oohing' and 'aahing' and clearly having a good time.

'The question is, what are we to do next?'

That was, indeed, the question. Let's leave aside the fact that if Mary Maitland and Dave were right, Harry'd been doing in more than his fair share of dealers – some quite big names, too, by the sound of it. Let that go. Let's focus on *What's Next?*

Not one to get the old feathers too ruffled at once, Harry kicked off with more platitudes.

'It is in all our interests that bonds are forged between those who value Duty, Tradition and a sense of Right and Wrong. And here, I'm afraid, I have to get a bit... I think the word is *philosophical*.'

Think the word?! Pull the other one, Harry! You know exactly what it means! Better than this lot do, including the ex-Eton turd on the front row!

'Because the world is not a good place. It's time we faced up to that. There've been too many people, over the past two or three hundred years, who've been trying to tell us that Evil is just an accident, that Mankind is basically good. I don't know where they got this idea from. I don't particularly want to know, because I don't see the need to waste my time finding out. But if you look at the world in the hardest, coldest light of science, we arrived here by accident through a process of kill or be killed. Good will and benevolence are not in our nature. They have to be taught. Then again, if you turn to our religions, to our traditions, whether of Judaism, of Christianity or of Islam – all religions I respect – you learn that we are living in a fallen world. A world ruined through our own self-indulgence. A world in which the first begotten son of the human race murdered the second – murdered his brother. A world in which the first parents learned to loathe their firstborn utterly. What must the expression on Adam's face have been, on discovering

Abel's body? We cannot imagine. Nobody could ever imagine the loathing that there must have been! Such an absolute extinction of all possibility of love! No other response is conceivable! That is the kind of species we are. That is the kind of species we have been from the Word Go. I do not propose to let us forget it.'

Some of the dodderers were impressed by this. The rest started to glaze over – it was getting a bit airy-fairy.

'It is a grim world we live in and it is a grim world because we are grim people. We restrain our grimness by acknowledging it, not by pretending we are anything better than the bloody animals we all, in our hearts, know ourselves to be.

'Yet in this grimness lies our hope of salvation. For it is in horror alone that we attain some measure of dignity. It is on the Cross alone that we can offer forgiveness and mean it. It is through loss and pain and bereavement, where lies our sole path to a measure of worthiness.

'A lot of people don't seem to like the Jews. They like knocking the Yiddoes. Me, I've got a lot of time for the Yiddoes. And yet, strangely, you might think, I reckon they've got a lot to thank Hitler for.'

Oh! Nice one, Harry! That had got their attention! Some of the oldest were visibly pissed off, of course – 'Hitler' was a Big Red Button Word and, in pressing it, Harry had got the only response you ever would. On the other hand, those who couldn't actually remember bits of dead bodies in the streets of Birmingham were more curious. Harry, quite obviously, had jumped down a really really deep hole and they were wondering how he was going to dig his way out.

'Nobody's ever going to convince me that Hitler was a good man. Nobody sitting in his little bunker, signing the documents to get the cattle trucks moving while, somewhere a long way east, his minions are doing their mucky cowardly business with the machine gun towers and the Zyklon B, nobody like that can ever be anything better than a coward! When odds are as loaded in your favour as that, it's only ever cowardice!

'But the Jews, they saw how they were treated – by an enemy so much less than themselves – and they said "Enough!" And they made up their minds that, from then on, they were going to be a mob you didn't mess with! So they made something of themselves and they got right on over to Israel and they gave the Arabs a taste of the old aggro! And, I'm happy to say, they took no bloody notice at all of those la-di-da Daniel Deronda types who were telling them that wasn't what Israel was supposed to be there for! Because that's the way it's got to be! Everywhere! That's the kind of world we live in!'

Most of the dodderers, if not won round, were at least kind of enjoying this – it was rousing, red-blooded stuff, they thought. And this bloke, if a bit peculiar, certainly had his heart in the right place.

'It's time we took a lot more notice of the Yiddoes and a lot less notice of all this United Nations rubbish and all this European Court of Human Rights rubbish!'

Cheers now, and a smattering of applause. Harry had now pressed quite a few Big Green Button Words and the response was as primevally predictable as if he'd thrown a bleeding seal pup into a tank of great white sharks. Harry really had got these buggers sussed out.

'So far,' he went on, 'it's been easy for me. So far, there's been no rough stuff.'

He wasn't even trying to fool them with that one! They could sense the blood on him now and, like the sharks, they were seduced by it. I noticed a few of my former shags were recording him on their mobiles. Within seconds of the speech finishing, it would all be up on YouTube. Next time, he'd be doing it in front of a way bigger audience.

The little minister whispered something in Tolland's ear. Tolland nodded eagerly – they were clearly trying to kid themselves that they had something they could use here. But perhaps there was a touch of doubt on Tolland's face. Perhaps it was dawning on him that Harry wasn't a man who could be controlled. Perhaps it was also dawning on him that now it was far too late for him to do anything about it.

'But,' Harry went on, 'there are dangerous times coming and we're not going to get through them without becoming dangerous people. These ideas of Rights and Justice and Benevolence are going to have to wait their turn, until we've made sure of something far more important!

'And now, I'm going to have to ask for your patience for a few moments. Because, just a very few years ago, I wouldn't have been able to tell you what that *something* was. I wouldn't have been able to tell you what anything was. I'd lost my wife, you see, and I'd lost my job. Nobody's fault, of course; just one of those things... that happens. I could see the way things were going to go for me: I'd soon wind up having a spot too much beer, which would turn into a spot too much whisky, which would turn into a spot too much... despair. I wasn't complaining. Just the way it was going to happen. Only things didn't go that way. Somebody came along and... talked me out of it. I don't know how she did it. Something about what she said... or just the way she was. She wasn't somebody I'd have expected to make a difference – just a kid in her twenties. But she did make it, and I wish I could tell her how grateful I am.

'But I can't tell her. I can't tell her anything.

'Because she's dead: somebody killed her.

'Some worthless, depraved scum sold her some heroin and it killed her.'

The room had shut up. It wasn't just a matter of nobody talking: there was a silence that had soaked into the floor, the walls and the ceiling. No one had the option of breaking it.

'And now, I'm going to ask you to decide what we ought to do about people like that – people like the people who killed her?

'And about people who say we should be more understanding of people like the people who killed her?

'What ought we to do about people like that, hey? Anybody got any ideas?

'Hmm... I can see there's a few in here who *have* got some ideas. And I can see that those ideas are the *right* ideas!

'Now let me tell you what I will be doing about people like the people who killed the girl who saved my life. And I'm glad there's a tidy few of the young'uns here tonight taping this on their mobile phone whatchamacallits! 'Cause come tomorrow, there's going to be quite a few of those people like the people who killed her, looking at this on their Facebooky-YouTubey thingies.

'Won't you?

'Ye-es! I'm talking to you, now. *You!*

'Been doing stuff as you shouldn't have been doing?

'Been up to stuff as you shouldn't have been up to?

'You know the sort of stuff I mean!

'Well have you?

'HAVE YOU?!

'Got news for the likes of you.

'Harry's got his eye on you.

'Make no mistake about it.

'If I were you, I'd be thinking about getting out of the Black Country.

'I'd be thinking about getting out of the Black Country – sharpish.

'I'd be thinking about getting out of the Black Country – before it's Cooper's ducks!

'And what about you other lot, hey?

'What about you lot who think we ought to be more *understanding?* Understanding of the worthless? Understanding of the depraved? Understanding of the scum?

'Well, let me tell you something: I *understand* them very well! Only, to my mind, *understanding* does not mean the same as *letting them get away with it!*

'So, don't worry. You just keep on writing your little letters to the *Guardian* and your little emails to the *Today* programme. Only don't you try getting in the way of those of us who are going to do the stuff as wants doing! Don't you even think about trying to do that!

'Because when the girl who saved my life was murdered, it was a whetstone. It was a rough old whetstone and a harsh old whetstone but my knowledge of what it was as wanted doing came up from that whetstone sharp: sharp like Excalibur!'

208

Ryan made a curious noise.

'And,' Harry concluded, 'come the new year, there won't be much stopping me using that Excalibur to clear out the rubbish, chop up the rubbish and send the rubbish down to where it belongs!'

With that, Loge piled into Wotan's funeral pyre and the whole of Valhalla went Boom-Bang-a-Bang-Bang. Quite how Harry had managed to provoke such cacophonic enthusiasm in such a pile of arthritic cag-mag, none of them understood but they didn't care. Harry had truly swept them away – off to fabled Avalon, off to the far times and far places I'd painted on his walls. And out of every plastic-hipped dodderer and closet pooftah in the room, he had made a shining knight.

As the applause thundered away, I stood and noticed Mother in the front row, clapping politely. She turned and our gazes met. I think it was the only time we ever smiled at each other.

'Poor bastard,' Ryan rumbled, softly, behind me. 'Poor, poor bastard.'

I turned. Mary Maitland was looking every bit as astonished as I.

'He was never meant to be the Devil,' Ryan explained, softer still. 'He's just in the wrong place at the wrong time. Wish I could... Hmm...' He was silent.

At the side of the stage, Harry was having a conversation with Graham Tolland and the little minister. Whatever they were saying, body language told me everything about who was giving the orders. Tolland's shoulders, previously full of squash-player confidence, were sagging a bit.

At Harry's elbow was his ridiculous frizzy-haired little Polly. She'd been in awe of Alice, for Christ's sake, so it wasn't surprising that her reverence for Harry reached well into the realms of religious transport. And yet, in Polly's very littleness, I could see a ruthlessness I'd not spotted before – the ferocity of a hamster. Because hamsters look all small and fluffy – but make the mistake of sticking your hand in its cage and any one of 'em'll rip a bastard great chunk out of you.

Outside, it was getting quite cold. As I was looking around for the car, someone plucked at my elbow.

'I want to see those murals,' said Mary Maitland. 'The ones you painted on Harry's walls.'

This was no problem at all. Harry would want her to see. I wanted her to see. I wanted her to get a bloody good look.

'Fine,' I told her, and gave her my phone number.

The night was getting colder still.

***

Two days later, I decided to have another look at the mural I'd painted in Tipton.

I was staring up at the two unsympathetic presences, still pretty satisfied with the job I'd made of them, when my mobile went. I took it out but didn't recognise the number, so I ignored it.

It was getting very cold. December, and the weather forecast was for grim stuff: snow before Christmas – unheard of in recent years. Clouds hung low and grey and heavily laden. The Black Country beneath was similarly dismal; however virginally shaggable they were, having all these young Harryoid Stormtroopers around in their grey shirts and humourlessness was beginning to put a dampener on the whole place.

I wondered if Mother had seen her father's malevolence glowering down on Tipton. Three or four months before, I'd hoped she had; now I hoped she hadn't. But I didn't want to change it.

The bloody phone went again. Annoyed, I answered.

'Hello, Lee. It's Neil Haines from The Death of Wallenstein. I got your number off Dave. I'm calling about Martin. I saw him a couple of days ago and he's really not well. I thought I'd better let you know.'

'Not well?'

'I think he's dying.'

Odd thing to be told.

'Oh,' I said.

'Sorry to put it so bluntly. I really hope I'm wrong. But I don't think I am.'

'I see,' I said. 'Thank you.'

And I hung up.

I carried on staring at the mural – my grandfather's face on the left, that seething mess of hate and violence I'd called 'Hastur' on the right.

But soon, it was dark and the sodium orange took away that wonderful three (at least!) dimensionality I'd been so glad to evoke, leaving flat, two-tone abstractions.

A fleck of snow corkscrewed down out of the orange black above, settled on my cheek and melted. I ignored it.

I didn't go round, of course. Dad had never given any indication that it would make much difference to him so, frankly, what was the fucking point?

Then, a few days later, a similar call, this time from my mother:

'Could you come round tonight and keep an eye on your father?'

Astonishment numbing my capacity to tell her to fuck off, I tried to imagine why she wanted me to do this. True, the last time I'd seen him, Dad had been away with the fairies but, for fuck's sake, what was new in that? And the idea that she'd taken enough notice of him to form an opinion on the subject was a bit weird. I realised I was actually curious to find out what was going on.

'He's been acting very stupidly. He went up into the loft and he brought some cassette tapes down. Horrible things! Dusty! And he's been playing them, but they don't have anything on them. Stupid!'

Stranger and stranger.

'Okay,' I agreed.

So, that night, round I went. She wasn't in herself, but this didn't bother me. Probably out at some meeting with local politicians; there'd been quite a few of these, lately, and she'd be bound to come back radiant with vindication. Or perhaps it was the job – the last week before Christmas hols, she'd be frantic at work, making Derek Chiselhurst and all his colleagues lives... no, not a misery: a misery has a kind of glorious intensity you can thrive on, the sort of thing Mother cooked up would only grind you down.

Dad in the back. He'd've been out in his shed if it hadn't been so bloody cold. But he'd got some boggy old cassette recorder on the dining room table and he was talking into the microphone, or trying to.

Christ, Neil had been right – he looked fucking awful! His face was candlewax-grey and his eyes had drawn back into his skull... He looked like Alice – he looked like Alice the last time I had seen her alive.

Hands trembling, he'd press the play and record buttons, very deliberately. Then he'd line the mic up in front of his face and try to think of something to say.

Then there'd be a few minutes silence.

Then he'd press stop, press rewind and repeat the process.

And, once more, he'd try to think of something to say.

At about the third or fourth try, he made a nervous little noise, then managed, 'He was a great laugh, was Mick...' Then his voice trailed off. Even he knew that he'd said that before – many many times.

He looked at the closed curtains – dark brown. Through them, both of us could hear the wind in the branches of Cally Wood. It was a soft sound, merciful.

He took no notice of me coming in and, though he'd looked in my direction a couple of times, I wasn't sure he knew I was there. It occurred to me then, that it had been quite a few years since he had known I was there.

'It's cold out tonight, Dad,' I whispered, 'It's dark.'

His eyes moved a little, as if trying to find where I was. They failed.

'I like the dark,' I added.

He turned the cassette recorder on again, brows furrowing as he tried to say what he wanted to.

'Great laugh...' he murmured, once more.

I sat at the dining table, in the place I'd sat when Alice and I were kids. Looking across, I registered that, in Alice's place, was a little pile of cassettes, in boxes marked with Dad's neat capital letters. I reached across and picked one up.

FIELD RECORDINGS: OCT 1971: RUGELEY POWER STATION, SEVERN VALLEY RAILWAY, HINKSFORD, QUINTON.

I'd never seen these tapes before. If they'd been in the loft all this time they'd surely be pretty knackered by now. Then again, maybe not – tapes are bloody unpredictable things.

'Dad?'

There was quiet, except for the soft squeaking of the spindles of the tape deck.

'Dad?'

More quiet.

'What went wrong, Dad?'

More quiet.

'I mean, I know what happened with Mum. I know why she is the way she is.'

Dad raised his finger and pointed.

A little apart from the other cassettes was one that looked a bit newer. Were they still making the things? It had no markings on it.

'And they were blue and they were wide and they were frightening,' he whispered, almost too quiet to hear.

'You want me to have this?'

He didn't nod. But he gave no sign of distress when I picked the cassette up and put it in my pocket.

Quiet again.

'I've never found out what it was with you, Dad. Don't suppose you can tell me, now. But it must have been something.'

'Great laugh…'

'No. Not that. It must have been before that. Before all that stupid pointless drinking. Must have been. And we know about the drinking. You've kept on telling us about it. Again and again and again and a-*FUCKING-GAIN!*'

Quiet – again.

And I tried to get some quiet back into me.

'What happened, Dad?'

Quiet. Quiet. Quiet.

Who else, I wondered, still used a cassette recorder, for Christ's sake?

Dad fell from the dining room chair, hit the floor with a hollow wooden bump and curled up on the carpet like a sleeping cat. I waited a minute or two. Then I turned off the cassette player.

I found myself kneeling next to him. My hand was outstretched and it was stroking the back of his hand.

Little by little, the colour of his face turned from pale grey to a light, waxy gold.

It was a while before I heard my mother's key in the front door.

She sensed my presence and came into the dining room.

'When did this happen?' she asked me. Her voice showed all the grief you'd expect from a sheet of aluminium.

'A while ago,' I answered, in the same tone.

I could feel her desire to question me, to ask why I'd not done more? She made a grab for the phone – not that she wanted to help him, but for the sake of propriety.

'No,' I whispered, ripping the receiver out of her hand. 'Let him go.'

She took no more convincing than that. I realised, then, perhaps for the first time, that it had never been her intention to be a cruel person.

When I was sure Dad had escaped Kingswinford, I let her telephone the ambulance. After she'd done that she took an interest in the cassettes.

'I want them in the bin, now.'

'They were Dad's.'

'I want them in the bin, now.'

'He did them for the band he was in.'

'I want them in the bin, now.'

'The band's still going.'

'I want them in the bin, now.'

'I'll give them to the band.'

'I want them in the bin, now.'

'I know what you want, Mother, but these tapes belong to The

Death of Wallenstein.'

Not a name she wanted to hear. She considered picking up something and lobbing it at me. Well, I assume she did; that's what I would have done, in her position. I took the tapes out to my car and put them on the back seat, wondering, again, if there was any point because after forty years in the loft, they'd surely be fucked.

We looked at each other as I came back in. I saw again how we had the same face. That face looked at itself and neither pitied the other, for to do so would have been self-pity and we did not go in for that.

The ambulance arrived after an indeterminate, silent interval. The paramedics made polite noises and there was a bit more medical coming and going. At about three in the morning, I left the place; no question of Mother and me sleeping under the same roof: we knew each other too well for that to be possible.

I drove aimlessly through Stourbridge, Halesowen, Quinton, then into Birmingham city centre, feeling at home in all those curving *Blade Runner* tunnels and among all that Gerry Anderson architecture (Launch 'Stingray' into the cut at Brindley Place, why don't you? And don't take the piss because this time next year, you'll all be playing Kyrano and it'll be Harry pulling your strings).

Sky above the sodium light impossibly heavy with snow now. Maybe today, maybe tomorrow, we were really going to cop it.

Midweek, but signs of life visible even at this hour. Some of the clubs – casinos, I guess – still on the go.

Must have been about half four, I headed up the Aston Expressway to Spaghetti Junction, then found my way on to the M6.

A good bit of money had come my way for doing a film poster, so I had this crazy idea of flooring it down to London, getting hold of a stupid amount of coke and not coming down until I dropped fucking dead.

Then I remembered – there was no coke to be had for love or money. Not round here, certainly, and – from what I'd heard – there was a lot less than usual down there.

Harry's doing. Naturally.

Was this inconvenience my fault? Probably: I mean, pour enough

King Arthur into anybody and you can expect him to be Excaliburing your friendly neighbourhood coke dealer – sooner rather than later.

So, perhaps, I should give it a rest with the murals... Perhaps... Perhaps a lot of things.

Just past Watford Gap Services I came off the motorway and turned back. Took me the best part of two hours to get home. The sky was turning from black to grey and the roads were busy. Early morning, the week before the holiday – quite a lot of driving was already compromised by office party hangovers so you had to watch it.

Pulling the car into a space recently left by some off-to-work neighbour or other, I reached into my coat pocket for a packet of B & H. I'd started again. The Cunt had quit, a year or so back – self-righteous ponce! I took my time over a fag and watched my hands. No sign of trembling. Well – not much sign of trembling. Then the interior of the car began to feel cold.

A day or two before, The Cunt had annoyed me again and I'd given him another slapping. This time, he'd actually gone back to his mummy and daddy – the tiresome holy-knickered twats – so the flat would be empty. It would be bare of Christmas decorations. He would have made that concession to convention if I'd let him but, as it was, there were only a few discreet cards from exes – mostly mine, a couple his – plus the usual scattering from faghags and poets, all lining two or three bookshelves.

'I like the dark,' I heard myself whisper.

But it was light, now – cold, unforgiving December morning light.

I turned and looked at the pile of cassettes on the back seat.

23: Mary Maitland

'But then, we had the sad stuff. Which was to be expected, really. The sad stuff always comes along, sooner or later. Can't not have the sad stuff. Things had been alright for a while, so we had to expect the sad stuff. Thought we'd got over it, really. You know, sad stuff will happen so, shoulder to the wheel, nose to the grindstone, get back on with things...

'But then...

'Then...

'He was a great laugh, was Mick.'

The tape hissed. Dave Calper's shoulders shook with grief. Neil wasn't doing much better.

'Mick Anderson,' Neil grunted, '– a right twat. 'Scuse my French – I shouldn't say that. He's dead now.'

'Oh,' I said.

Neil reached out and clicked the 'off' switch. Then he looked up at me. 'Martin's funeral's first week in January,' he said. 'We're going.'

'I don't think Shirley's going to like you being there.'

'Well she can go and fuck herself. Sorry, but... you know...'

'I know,' I said.

Dave reached out and squeezed my hand.

'Did Lee bring these tapes round?' I asked.

Dave nodded.

'What kind of a state was he in?

'Like a zombie,' Dave said, softly, 'but I suppose that's not too bad, considering...'

'Martin says he just did those tapes for himself,' I said, 'but you said you had something to do with them?'

'He's lying,' said Dave. 'He did them to be heard. We were talking about using that stuff...'

'He doesn't sound like he had much to do with the band...'

'He's lying. Or he's just trying to...'

217

'Blank it out?'

Dave was still and quiet. Then he nodded.

'Pity it never happened,' I sighed.

'It *will* happen.' – Dave and Neil together.

'After forty years? There won't be anything left on them...'

'I've played a couple,' Dave insisted. 'Some bits are knackered but others are retrievable. Gonna get them restored. Reformatted to digital, so Madame can use 'em on her sampling keyboard. Gonna get Viv Jones to do it – so it gets done right.'

'What sort of stuff are they?'

'Field recordings – power stations, railways, birdsong. Just wind, one of 'em, wind in the trees. Don't matter – we're using them.'

I could see what they were up to: I can recognise a prayer; sometimes, I can recognise a prayer, even when the people praying can't.

***

'Hello.'

'Hello? Who's this?'

'Lee Icement.'

At least he wasn't trying to call himself 'Satansfist' with me.

'You wanted to see the murals at Harry's?' I could hear the kiddish pride behind the sneer – and, more distantly, I could hear the voice of Alice.

'I do,' I said, 'very much.'

'Saturday do?'

'Saturday would be fine.'

'About midday?'

'Lovely.'

'Okay. See you then.'

End of conversation. Lee kept things very brusque over the phone.

'I'm going over Kingswinford, day after tomorrow,' I told Ryan.

He frowned. 'If you make it over there. Weather says we're all gonna get snowed in.'

I thought about that.

'I really think I ought to.'

'Where exactly in Kingswinford are you going?' he asked, very evenly.

'Lee Icement's going to show me the paintings in Harry's place. I'll be okay. Lee's going to be there, and Polly. I need to see what's going on in their heads. See it for myself...'

There was a very long silence. Ryan looked into my eyes and saw something in them that, he was sure, might take me away from him. But it was a part of me, so he couldn't make himself want to change it.

In spite of how I knew that made him feel, I could sense an idea forming in his mind. There was a certain clever little glint in his eye.

'I won't be far away,' he said, 'and I want you to make sure that bastard knows as much. And I'm gonna be coming over on my prize chuffer. Don't argue! The weather we're gonna be havin', that little motor of yours might get stuck. Traction engine won't. Traction engine'll get through anything, 'specially with me new snow-plough attachment.' (A flicker of pride broke through the misery in his voice as he said that; it was a lovely thing.) 'I'll take it for a ride round Kingswinford, just in case you need me.'

That thought was all he had to lessen the fear, so I didn't argue too much.

'Safest thing to put on the road if it really comes belting down,' he stressed.

We drank tea and looked again at Harry Ronsard's YouTube appearances. There were getting to be quite a few of them – he was on the way to being a star of the Net. And they were getting many more 'likes' than 'dislikes'. Comments of the *what this country needs more of*' sort were the norm.

'You watch yourself with that bugger, darling,' Ryan said, earnestly, as he wrapped his big arms round me. 'You watch yourself.'

***

Saturday – it was awful, as expected. Clouds low, wind in your face and snow very nearly horizontal. First thing – long before it was light – Ryan went off down his yard to get his beloved metal chuffer fired up.

'I'll be round Kingswinford by early afternoon,' he said, 'and don't you get turning up there any sooner. Call me straight away if there's any kind of bother.'

As he'd predicted, the Renault got me as far as the end of Lawnswood Avenue, then made it clear it wasn't budging through the slush. I'd started out at ten in the morning and now it was close to midday.

The snow wasn't bucketing it down anymore, but there was a lot on the ground and we were getting some generous flurries still. Trudge trudge trudge through the slush slush slush until I'd got to the corner of Barratt Road.

Harry's black Audi was outside his place but when I rang, Polly answered. She gestured me inside with the softest of *Hellos.*

We went into the front room.

Harry had lace curtains up, which was unusual in this road, but Lee's murals certainly weren't the sort of thing you wanted people to know you'd got on your walls – not in Kingswinford.

At first, I didn't notice Harry wasn't there, because all I could take in were the pictures, the murals, the power of them.

They covered every inch of the walls and the ceiling in the hall – Ancient Britons, Romans, Saxon Invaders. All stunningly handsome men. And they stretched upwards; I saw an especially beautiful knight on the landing ceiling. This one was different to the others – his expression held the compassion Lee wanted to believe did not exist anywhere in the real world. But he had still painted it.

In one of the spare bedrooms, things got a bit more science-fictionish. There were frightening silver war machines floating above battlefields like metal dragons, and fierce but doomed barbarians who were burned by those machines in the thousands. Then, in a picture perhaps meant to show a later scene, the barbarians

220

seemed to have got hold of flying machines of their own – sleeker, faster-looking and more graceful – and were avenging themselves on those who had destroyed their comrades.

In the main bedroom, I saw the sight that met Harry's eyes first thing every morning. It was not the functional earthworks that the historians tell us Arthur ruled, but the Camelot that dreamers like Ryan and Dave Calper and my brother Paul imagined – the place where evil was opposed and where all that was right was seen to be done.

And, on the wall that met Harry's eyes as he rose from his bed, I saw the stern and armoured figure who he must imagine was his commander: the fifth century warlord transfigured by myth into something timeless. A soldier, but one whose sword was made to protect the weak, to strike only at the cruel and the wrathful. There was command in his stare, but kindness too. Kindness, wisdom and Christianity – what *I* meant when I said 'Christianity'. A Christianity that was everything Harry and Lee lacked.

Only the bathroom walls were bare – tricky to paint because of the condensation, I supposed. But in a funny sort of way, their plainness looked expectant; they were only empty for the time being. Soon, Lee would have something for them.

In the front room, Polly sat on a sofa and looked up at me, silently content. A very slight smile on Lee Icement's face betrayed a pride that was not slight at all. And behind him, most astonishing of all to me…

'Good grief!'

'Seen something you like?' he smirked.

'That… that knight…'

'Yes?'

'Looks just like my brother Paul…'

'Well, he's actually Sir Lancelot. He's supposed to be very holy. But he slips up a bit, with his boss's missus.'

'And… this dragon… the black one…'

'Yes?'

'It's your mother, Lee.'

For a moment, his expression was still. Then it cracked. He was laughing and his laughter was a cold and evil thing. The name 'Satansfist:' didn't seem wrong for him anymore.

'Where's Harry?' I asked, finally.

'He's gone for a walk in the woods,' said Lee. 'He's always liked it up there.'

'But it's diabolical out!'

'That's how he prefers it.' Lee's expression softened, became tinged with curiosity. 'Y'know, he thinks the world of you.'

'Of me?'

'He reckons you're on his side. That's how he puts it.'

'I know. I've got to put a stop to that.'

'To change Harry's mind about something? Not possible.'

'I don't expect it to be easy.'

I looked at the pair of them. Lee – Satansfist – leant against a doorframe and smirked. Polly hadn't moved from the sofa. Each stank of his or her own particular sort of arrogance. Sooner or later, I knew, they'd both find that this arrogance had rotted them away from the inside, but I couldn't talk to either one – they had their shields up. They were still people, though. In spite of everything, they were still people.

It was Harry I needed to see now – and he wasn't a person anymore. Not simply, and not exactly. I'd been reading and hearing about what he was since I was a tiny tot. I had never thought I'd have to face him – not like this, not alone. But it had turned out that way because I was the only person who stood a chance of talking him out of being the Devil.

'Want to come up the road and meet my dear Mother?' Lee asked. 'Most of the teenyboppers in Harry's barmy army are from her place. One way or another, he's found a way of giving her the sort of kids she's always wanted...'

His face froze. He'd let something slip there and he knew it. He was going to have to offload the self-loathing in that admission before tonight was out. If he was still around, the hapless Lewis Gladrell would be having a rough time of it.

Polly looked at me, and there was a terrible pity in her eyes. She was Harry's – to her, all other women were pitiable.

'I'd... better go and see Harry first,' I whispered, 'but is she coping alright with..?' my voice faded.

'With Dad pegging out? She's not bothered. Don't think they'd had a word to say to each other for years.'

'Ah... I see.'

'Dad had hardly spoken at all since God knows when. And when he did speak, all he used to talk about was some bunch of pissheads he used to hang around with in the 70s. All a "great laugh", apparently.'

'I heard... on the tape...'

'The tape. Yes. Full of wit and wisdom that one, I'm sure.'

I was getting nowhere. But I had one last go – 'You know he might kill you, don't you? Lewis, I mean. If you carry on the way you're going. It might be too late already. You've poured a lot of killing into him.'

'Of course I know that,' he replied, eyebrows raised in surprise. I understood him. In his mind, such a death was *predestined*. He was astonished that anyone could question it.

'I'll go and talk to Harry,' I said, softly. Then I walked to the front door and let myself out.

At first, the cold fresh air sobered me up. I realised then, how overwhelmed, how crushed I'd been by all that imagery, all those visions of Arthurian otherworldliness. I paused and glanced in the direction of the Icements' house. I'd never be able to prove anything, but I felt that there'd been some horrible bond between Martin Icement and Harry Ronsard. Their faults complemented each other so perfectly. It almost seemed that a soul meant for one person had somehow got cut in two. I couldn't square that with any belief I'd ever held but there was too much about those two that I knew I would never be able to square with anything.

I got my phone out.

'Ryan?'

Loud chuffing almost drowning out his voice, I could still make out a cheery 'Alright, love?'

'Yes. I've been round Harry's. He's gone for a walk in the wood. Going to see if I can find him.'

'Leave it a bit! Wait till I'm with you!'

'He won't hurt me. He thinks I'm on his side...'

'It's not just that! It's this wind! It's going to fetch a tidy few trees down! If one of 'em winds up bonking him on the noddle that's his flamin' lookout but I don't want him taking you with him! Please, love, wait till I get there! I'd've been with you by now but it took me a flippin' age to get the coal cart hooked up and the snow chains on! I'm just on the way through Pensnett, so I should be there in fifteen or twenty...'

'I'll come and meet you in Lodge Lane, then, by Summerhill School. Give me a ring when you're there.'

'I'll give you a sound of my whistle, love. You'll know I'm there...'

'That'll do.'

I cut the connection and pulled myself together, then marched up Barratt Road to the gap between houses that led into the wood.

The Summerhill School end of the wood was where I expected Harry Ronsard to be – in the place I'd met him with Los and the twins. Why was I so sure? Something Dave Calper had said? Maybe. But I trudged up between the conifers to the top of the ridge. Less snow in my face here, but Ryan had been right: I had to dodge a few heavy branches that came crashing from way way up, any one of which might easily have bashed my brains out.

Turning right, I headed in among the old oaks.

I was remembering the self-defence classes I'd had off my sister. I breathed deeply, exhaling the fear, sending my pulse rate down... I made myself ready to send a boot into Harry Ronsard's bollocks if necessary.

When I finally saw him, I abandoned all hope of being able to do that...

At the north end of the ridge he stood, a tall figure in a long brown leather coat. He was facing away from me. Around him, branches

224

writhed in the wind like multiple arms of something vast, dark and ferocious. For a moment, the wind blew his coat aside and I saw that, from a sturdy brown leather belt around his waist, hung the two swords...

The cold was different, up here. It had a thicker, heavier quality. The noise in the trees was deafening, the sky above was dead grey and concrete-like. The world felt like a prison cell.

Harry Ronsard's face remained fixed on the icy north.

Mary, why are you still here? This cold is doing your head in! Remember what Ryan said. Get out of it! Get down the ridge and wait by the school! Do it now, Mary!

No. No. There was something here I had to put my finger on, had to understand...

This cold is no normal cold, Mary. It's freezing your mind as well as your body. It's freezing your soul...

Then the wind seemed to die down; the cold seemed to lose its thick oppressiveness. And Harry Ronsard turned to face me.

I was something special for Harry – I was opposition. His self-belief had ensured that such a thing had not been an issue until he'd met me. His will had twisted reality to suit his needs. If he wanted something to be, then it was so. He won fights with grinding inevitability, because of his absolute faith in his own victory. His opponents lacked that faith and so they died, without really having fought him at all.

There was a silence and a stillness between us. The hissing and the clattering of the treetops seemed very far away.

'You are a good woman, Mary Maitland.'

The respect was alarming because it was genuine. It did not sound like a voice of temptation – though I knew it couldn't be anything else.

'You want to save lives. To save souls. I've no quarrel with that. I've no wish to change your mind about anything. It's not you I've

been sent to punish.'

The Devil himself had just told me he wasn't after my soul. At that moment, I was sure, he was telling what he genuinely thought was the truth. That did not mean I could trust it.

He smiled and his smile was frightening.

He was about to lose the last of himself. The name 'Harry Ronsard' was less and less convincing. It would soon be time to call him by another.

'I'm here to make sure everyone knows what's what. No mucking about. Toe the line or it's Cooper's ducks. You believe in Heaven, Mary Maitland. You want to see Heaven properly protected. To see no rubbish gets in. That's what I'm here for: to keep the rubbish out...'

And suddenly, I understood something about the Devil – about how he sees himself. And it was so, so like the way my father had once seen him.

And then my soul shouted back –

'That's not how it works! In your unfallen state, Lucifer Seventheye, you understand that!'

His pupils were widening wells of blackness, staring into mine. The name I'd called out plunged down into him, down into those dark wells of past – millions, billions of years deep. Down to a time before time. Down to a time when he had been called by that name.

There was a stillness, then the cold came back. It was worse than before, ferocious at having been recognised. I felt my knees tremble, and I thought they'd give way. My eyelids grew horribly heavy and I staggered...

Then there was the most joyful noise.

It was a shriek of brightness, echoing up into the trees from the road, a noise of absolute innocence, a cry of childhood and of happiness that believed itself indestructible.

Harry turned to face it.

Then he was running, faster than I'd have thought a man his age could possibly run, dashing down the steep and forested slope, the long brown leather coat streaming behind him like a banner, towards the edge of the wood and the white-covered ploughed field beyond it.

By the time I'd staggered down the hill, Harry was most of the way across the field to the road beyond, to the thing he sought.

Its big plume of steam whipped away by the snowy wind, the brightly painted traction engine my love had rebuilt came chuffing along the road from Kingswinford.

Harry reached the roadside and was still. I caught up with him just as the colossal iron boiler-on-wheels drew near. Ryan was spinning the steering wheel, a huge grin on his face along with all the coal muck.

'Oh my love, – yer daft sausage!' I didn't know if I'd shouted those words or just thought them; either way, I knew Ryan had heard them. The engine slowed and halted. I could feel the warmth from it and sense its immense weight through the ground and the soles of my feet.

Ryan jumped down and bounded up. I held out my hand, stopping him from giving me the hug that'd have ruined my cream-coloured coat with all the soot. This gave him enough time to notice the state Harry was in.

'You alright mate?' he asked. ''Cause you don't look it.'

Never one for euphemism, was Ryan. Couldn't take him anywhere, of course, but it did mean he got to the point.

It was true – Harry Ronsard did not look at all well. For the first time, you could see he was a man who'd passed sixty. And, for one moment, his image seemed to turn completely black and white, even two-dimensional and transparent. When I say 'black and white,' I mean just that – there was no trace of grey about Harry Ronsard. But the sight of the traction engine sustained him, he drew substance from it, came back to the real world.

He still looked rough, though. His breath sounded like an old

Woodbine smoker's and his eyes were watering. Behind them, I could still see that terrible cold I'd felt on top of the ridge.

Then I heard Ryan's soft intake of breath as he noticed the swords.

Harry fixed his gaze on the name plate of the engine. A part of me knew what this meant, but I didn't allow myself to think about it. I just let it happen, I just let go.

'My Lord,' I thought Harry said, 'My Lord the King...'

I saw the muscles in his jaw tighten. And his eyes were very wide. He turned to me and he grabbed my hand, holding briefly, tightly. For a moment, I could understand what Polly saw in him. His hand was the hand of a man. A few minutes before, perhaps it had not been. But now it was the hand of a man – a man who'd made up his mind what it was as wanted doing.

He let go and spinning around me, he rammed himself forward and smashed his skull against the ninety degrees of iron at the boiler front.

Then he collapsed to the snow-covered tarmac, growling and thrashing about insanely. Blood was coming from the wound in the front of his head – a lot of blood.

I had my mobile out and was jabbing 999.

'Man in his sixties. Badly injured the front of his head. Just outside Summerhill School, Kingswinford.'

Ryan was all for loading him up and getting him to Russells Hall A & E on the engine, though I couldn't see how we could lift him on to the footplate, or keep him there, struggling as he was. Anyway, we were ordered to keep him where he'd fallen, cover him up and wait for the ambulance crew to deal with things.

As I was finishing the call, Harry gave a monstrous roar and his eyes seemed to drill into the grey concrete clouds above, full of hate and resentment.

Then he raised both his fists and smashed them down into the snow and the tarmac.

And if I'd been in any doubt that there was more here than just a man, the sight of him punching two holes, quite big holes actually, in the tarmac of Lodge Lane Kingswinford – the sight of that would have cleared up any question.

Afterwards, Harry became quieter, though he was still snarling. Ryan had brought a couple of heavy blankets and spread them over him.

It was about half an hour before we saw the flashing blue light through the snow. Harry had remained subdued, comparatively, though I still thought it'd be a struggle to get him into the ambulance. The paramedics looked at me as if I'd gone doolally when I pointed at two potholes in the road surface and told them Harry had put them there with his bare fists. But, when they took a look at him, I think the expression on his face made them wonder a bit. Anyway, they knew what they were doing, and they got him loaded up quickly enough.

He was growling to himself like an ancient sleeping guard dog.

***

Hospital noise, serious business noise. Births, deaths and every ailment in between.

Harry lay very still, still growling. During the course of the evening, besides Ryan and me, he had three visitors.

The first of these I knew only as a lot of high pitched screaming, some way down the corridor.

The second, a grim-faced and tall woman, who, from Dave Calper's descriptions, I recognised as Charlotte Ronsard, came with an explanation of the first.

'That Polly's in a bit of a state,' she said. 'They've had to sedate her.' Then, looking me up and down, she continued, 'You must be Mary Maitland.'

I nodded.

'Thanks for looking after Dad.'

There was quite a bit of affection in her voice. I was surprised.

'Knew something like this might happen,' she confided. 'He's been stressing himself out over stuff the past six months or so, ever since Alice Icement passed away.'

I couldn't keep the look of surprise from my face.

'Guess he looked pretty indestructible to you?' she said, smiling bitterly.

'Guess he did,' I smiled sadly back.

And we were quiet. And stared at Harry's snarling face.

The final visitor was a man none of us knew. Turned out he was something to do with the local Conservative Party. He offered a measure of well-judged professional sympathy to Charlotte, and had a few quiet, serious words with one of the doctors. He left, looking troubled.

'They're gonna be looking for another candidate,' Charlotte sighed.

I didn't know what to say, so I just nodded.

***

It was quite late that night when Ryan got me up on the footplate and chuffed us both back to mine. We slept together, though we didn't want to make love. There'd be time enough for that when I'd got the scent of brimstone out of my nostrils and the damned cold out of my bones.

But we did not have an easy night of it. It must have been about four when I woke up, in freezing agony, the image I'd been dreaming still clinging to my mind's eye like frostbite.

'Hold me, please, love…'

'God, darlin', yer like a lump of ice…'

I nodded.

'What were you dreamin' about?'

I shuddered with the cold and the fear.

'There were… there were two of them. Two Harrys. In a place… somewhere not on this world. The sky was turquoise and the mountains… all sharp and too high… too steep.'

'Hey, love, try not to get in too much of a state about it. Just a dream. Dreams are a load of old cock for the most part.'

'They were fighting each other… the Harrys…'

'Well that sounds like more cock! Harry's never so much as asked

230

himself a question, you can tell. That's half his problem.'

'There was one dressed in brown leather... a bit like a Roman or something... with swords... And there was another, all made of blue fire... cold blue fire and throwing cold lightning bolts... froze everything they touched...'

Minutes passed and Ryan gently, warmly, rocked me back to sleep.

Then, just as it started getting light, we were awake again. Only this time, it was Ryan who was trembling, icily.

'Two of 'em?!' he stammered through chattering teeth, '*Two of 'em?* You got off lightly love. It was... I saw... there were millions of the buggers!'

I clung to him, trying to squeeze the cold out of his bones, as he'd tried to squeeze it out of mine.

'This isn't over yet, is it?' he asked, terrified.

'Not by a long chalk.'

'In the name of God, love, what happened up in that wood?'

'The Devil.'

'Love, you promise me, anything like this happens again, you have me right next to you.'

'I promise.'

''Cause that sod could have killed you.'

'No. He couldn't have killed me. Not really. Though it'd have seemed like he'd killed me to you...'

'Yeah, I know that but you know what I mean...'

'I do.'

I rocked his icy body some more, gradually bringing a little warmth back into it.

'Didn't he..?' Ryan had realised something and, I could feel, the realisation itself had warmed him a little more. 'When he smacked his head against the engine, did he do it deliberately?'

'He did.'

'It was... something about the engine that made him do it?'

'It was. Something about the name.'

Letting go of me, he rose from the bed and went to the window, pulling the curtains apart a little to look out at the black slowly turning to grey.

'Just shows, don't it?' he said, softly. Then he turned to me and smiled. 'A well-restored traction engine can melt the heart of Satan himself.'

Then the scent of brimstone was gone from our nostrils and the damned cold was gone from our bones. And, though we had not intended it to be, that early morning became our wedding night.

***

I made it my business, over the following weeks, to get over to see Harry as often as I could. Christmas got in the way, of course, as did work. To begin with, he was no better. Not cold though. Now he seemed to be running a temperature.

I was alone at his bedside, afternoon of the twenty-third, when it got particularly bad. The heat coming off him felt like a furnace fire and the blood pounded scarlet in his face.

'Flippin' 'eck.'

I turned. It was Sharukh, on duty.

'This is yer Black Audi Bloke, innitt?'

I nodded.

'Still looks pretty scary. What kind of a temperature is he running?'

He stretched out his hand to touch Harry's near-luminous forehead, then snatched it back with a yelp of pain and surprise. Wide-eyed, we both stared at his fingertips, which were blistered quite badly.

Shaking his head, he went away for a bit, coming back with a pair of thick white gloves. With some struggling, he got a thermometer under Harry's armpit, leaving it for a couple of minutes. Finally retrieved, it showed nothing out of the ordinary – bang on 37°C, in fact. This wasn't a heat that could be measured by instruments.

'Just go home and pray, mate,' I told him. 'All we can do.'

'Yeah,' he agreed, 'too right.'

Christmas Day was bright with icicles and blue sky, the heavy cloud blasted away for a while, so that things seemed clear and supernaturally well-defined. That was when things changed. I managed to drop in for five minutes to find Harry had settled down. They'd cautiously stuck him in isolation because they had no idea what was wrong with him. I could see, straight away, that he was different. He wasn't thrashing about or burning up or ice cold. And, as I heard Charlotte's heavy Doc Martens coming clunking down the corridor behind me, his eyes opened.

To my relief, I could see that they were a man's eyes.

***

Charlotte and I wound up getting on quite well. I turned up one evening, a week or so later, to find her talking softly to Polly about what to do with Harry. Polly was determined to get him out and round to her place as quickly as possible where, she declared, he'd be 'taken proper care of'. Charlotte looked surprised to hear Polly talking like someone so used to giving the orders. But she didn't really object.

Later, alone with Charlotte, I knew it was time to level with her:

'You know your Dad's been involved in some... pretty nasty stuff?' I asked her.

She looked at me, hard.

'Has he killed anyone?'

'Yes.'

She closed her eyes and sighed. Then she started crying, silently.

'Been telling myself all these years that I was just imagining it...' she said, eventually, 'but I've been waiting for this all my life, this thing about Dad. Not just him – it's been in the family. I've come close to having it myself and I used to see it see it in Granddad Lantenac...'

'I know, Charlotte but... you know it's probably all got to come out?'

She nodded again.

Since coming to, Harry had looked like a proper old wreck and he could still hardly move, let alone speak. I hated the idea of seeing him banged up, but if people like Mrs Atkinson were going to know what had happened to their sons, I couldn't see any way of keeping it all to myself.

Going back to his bedside, Charlotte spoke to Harry, very softly.

'Do you know me, Dad?'

'Chrr... llll...'

'Can you say your own name?'

'HHH... ssst... ssstrrr...'

That was as much as he could manage.

He raised his two hands and looked at them evenly. Both trembled like those of someone frail and dying. He fixed the left with a very level stare. I think it wanted to obey – but it couldn't. He had more luck with the right; after a couple of minutes under that gaze, it became steady and still. He wriggled his fingers, then looked at me. There was something like pleading in those eyes.

He managed to mouth the word 'Type.'

Understanding, I said, 'I'll get you a laptop tomorrow. I've got a spare.'

Harry Ronsard had a story he wanted to share with us.

***

'That's nine, and we haven't even started looking,' chuntered a copper as yet another appalling-smelling stretcher came down the side passage from Harry Ronsard's back garden.

Standing beside me as we watched from beyond the black and yellow tape, Charlotte made a strange little noise. There were quite a few news teams and a handful of ghouls hanging round; I wasn't sure why they kept their distance from us. Perhaps I looked like I'd've thumped anyone who bothered Charlotte. Perhaps she looked just as fierce.

It was the kind of late January afternoon when the sun makes a decent effort at breaking through the clouds. Though spring's a good way off, you get the sense that winter's not going to last forever. Cally Wood breathed in the wind, strong but restrained.

Polly was distraught, of course, and was round at her mom's. Up the road, the Icements' house looked empty and still. What Shirley was making of this, I had no idea. I knew the 'safe' Labour seat Harry had been about to get his hands on looked like it was going to stay safe after all.

With the exhumation of a tenth body, Charlotte was in tears and I put my arms around her. Turned out, she'd split up with a girlfriend in November, so she was feeling pretty low anyway. And now this.

'Are you going to be alright?' I asked her, after the fifteenth body had been carted out.

She nodded.

Then I had a brainwave – one that took me by surprise, a bit. 'Would you like to come to our wedding reception?' I asked. Because Charlotte was frightened and lonely and she needed friends. Or needed something.

She thought about it.

'S'pose my ex'll be there,' she smiled, with some bitterness.

'She will,' I admitted, 'playing with the band.' I couldn't help another quick glance up towards the Icements' place as I said that. But Martin was long gone.

'I'll come,' Charlotte whispered.

***

'Glad you could make it,' Derek Chiselhurst said, raggedly.

In his office, he looked a state – suit crumpled, shirt not fresh on this morning, hair nothing like as immaculate as I remembered. But it was his eyes that really told the story – sunken, blue-rimmed insomniac's eyes.

And the school was empty.

Even the hushed and crushed shells of teenagers who'd been here last time would have made more noise than this. The whole place had the hollow echoing cold that goes with desertion – glacially quiet, the high, glass-ceilinged foyer as still as a ballroom on the *Titanic* after everybody's scarpered up top deck.

'We've had to close the school,' Derek explained, sheepishly.

235

'Some of the Year Elevens kicked off and put a Science NQT in hospital. Terrible. We've never had anything like it. If some of the ex-students hadn't come in...'

'Lad by the name of Kraygon among them?'

'Yes! How did..?'

'We've met.'

'Oh. Well, it's all down to Shirley being away, of course. And when one of the deputies signed off with stress... well... we just had to close the place down. We really need Shirley back here right now...'

'She won't be coming back.'

He looked at me in despair.

'I'm sorry,' I said.

'I suppose losing... er... whatsname... er... her husband... it must have come as a bit of a shock...'

'It's not to do with Martin. It's Harry Ronsard.'

'Oh, yes, Harry, well that's another terrible thing... There's no one else like Harry-'

'For which you should be profoundly grateful.'

'-and all this rubbish people are starting to say about him. They don't seem to realise how much good-'

'Harry Ronsard has been killing people. That's not rubbish – I've seen him doing it. And we'll be very lucky if we don't find some of your ex-pupils have been killing people on his behalf.'

He looked shocked by what I said, but I wasn't going to spare him the details.

Dave Calper and Neil Haines had gone to Martin's funeral and come back with the story I'd expected to hear. Lee had been more arrogant and obnoxious than ever; they'd wisely given Shirley a wide berth but Dave had described her as 'walking round like one of the bleedin' undead, poor cow'.

'Mr Chiselhurst,' I said, 'Shirley Icement was born Octavia Tolland. She was the daughter of Arthur Tolland – you may have heard of him. He was a sadist and a child abuser, so I'm not one to have much doubt about the kind of treatment he gave poor Shirley.

236

She's been trying to get back at the world ever since, and I'm not criticising her for that – anyone living under the same roof as that bastard would have had a hard job turning out any better. This school has been a part of all that, and so has the bloody teenreich she's been running with Harry Ronsard.'

Derek Chiselhurst sputtered a bit. I didn't think he'd allowed himself to hear very much of what I'd said – he'd certainly tried very hard not to.

'No, frankly, Mr Chiselhurst, I think the lot of you have let things get completely fucked up, here…' This was my first proper swear word for some years. 'And I have no idea how we're going to sort it out.'

He stared at me, horrified. I think he was close to tears.

'I do think we'd better go and talk to Shirley,' I went on, 'because I dread to think of the state she's in. Her revenge on the world has gone pear-shaped, and she'd be in a right mess even if that was all that was the matter…'

'Isn't that all that's the matter?'

'Of course it bloody well isn't!'

I had to pause for a second, because I really wasn't sure what I'd meant. Then I remembered seeing Shirley at Kates Hill Conservative Club – she'd shone with pride that night. And with something else.

'She's in love with Harry Ronsard,' I said, flatly. 'She always has been.'

I stood. 'We ought to go round and see her,' I said.

Dumbly, he followed me out.

***

It was grey again, winter's business-as-usual. The snow still clung in tatty grey rags to the front gardens of Kingswinford, to the roofs of the neat semis and detacheds. A quiet afternoon. Most people at work, except for a few old dears at home. Bit by bit, they'd be getting through the last of the Christmas cake – though by now, first week in February, the icing would be getting pretty steely. And they'd be reading the *Daily Mail*. And they'd be waiting for *Countdown* to come on.

The curtains were drawn in the windows of the Icement house. Poor Martin was dead, but I didn't bother fooling myself into thinking this had been done for his sake.

'Come to check the walking corpse out?'

We were standing at Shirley's front door when the metallic voice sneered behind us. We turned. Lee. Looking beautiful beyond words – the clothes, the face, the posture, the voice. Only the words were hideous:

'I'll let you in, don't worry. She's a great laugh, I can promise you. Oh yes, she fucking rocks!' He mimed the spasmodic movements of someone whose nervous system is packing up. 'Can't see there's much chance of her getting back up your place, Derek! And, what I hear, her little band of teen troopers have been proper kicking off all over the shop! Rivers of blood, as the sainted Enoch promised. Come on in!' He unlocked and opened the door with a flourish, like some unholy ringmaster. 'Roll up roll up! Marvel at the Incredible Kingswinford Fuckup! Like I say – she's a great laugh!'

As we went inside, I looked over my shoulder. One or two faces peered from windows across the road. They vanished, hurriedly, when they saw I was looking back at them.

Shirley was sitting in the back room. She did not look at us. The skin of her face was a mottled ochre, her eyes sunken and her hair tangled and unwashed. The dressing gown she wore was stained and she'd drawn her knees up to her breasts, clutching them with her arms and rocking back and forth on the chair as she gnawed at one knee like a dog with a bone.

Lee, though, wasn't letting up:

'Behold the Twat! The thing that thought it could rule the world through an army of spotty kiddiewarriors! Now reduced...'

'Stop it, Lee...' I attempted.

'Now reduced to a dribbler with hopes of a career as a turnip. You'll note she's acquired the complexion for it...'

'Lee, you don't know what you're doing...'

'Note the spasticated helplessness of the dribbler! Its lack of control over the most basic motor functions! *Has it pissed itself?* I hear you ask. *Very probably*, I answer...'

'You don't know what you're doing, Lee...'

'And all because the lady loves some clapped out old fart –'

'Lee, fuck off! You're as much in love with Harry Ronsard as she is!'

My second swear word of the day. But it shut him up. And woke her up.

The look on her face, when she turned to us, was unforgiving. Big knots and straps of tension were trying to squeeze her eyes out of their sockets and turn her mouth into a lipless scar.

'Shirley,' I told her, 'I understand. I know what your father was like – he tried to do the same to my sister. She's told me all about him...'

A quiet noise of understanding from Derek – finally, he'd got it. A very different noise from Shirley – high-pitched, beginning quietly, then getting louder. Lee took a step back. Shirley stood, tore off her dressing gown and pulled the straps of her nightie from her shoulders, turning away from us as she dropped it to her waist.

Lee flinched a little. Some families think nothing of undressing in front of each other. Not the Icements, though – definitely not. Lee might not have seen the skin of his mother's bare back since his earliest infancy – long before conscious memory.

The scarring on the flesh was very old. Impossible to tell, now, whether it had been done with a branding iron, or if the flesh had been gouged out with a sharp instrument. The word formed was easy enough to make out:

CUNT

Funny how something can come as no surprise, yet it can still shock you.

Lee made a noise. It was an odd little thing, a strangulated choking cry. When I turned to him, his face had the look of someone who's

239

had the ladder pulled from under him when he's a long, long way up.

Suddenly, he'd gone from the room, having shoved an alarmed Derek Chiselhurst out of his way. The front door crashed open as he sped out.

I went outside and looked in either direction. He had disappeared.

24: Dave Calper

In the first few weeks of 2011, things kicked off in the Black Country, good and bleedin' proper, like a dragon with its head chopped off, thrashing about as it died.

You had bunches of grim-faced greyshirts on the streets, looking for anyone a bit dodgy to slap around. They'd got the idea that there was a conspiracy on the go and they were sure somebody'd tried to bump off their Beloved Leaders. So, of course somebody had to pay!

It didn't necessarily have to be the 'somebody' who was to blame, though. It so rarely does.

Some of little buggers went further afield and decided they were going to 'root out the rot' from one end of the country to another. Dangerous time to be caught reading *The Guardian* or suggesting we stay in the EU! One poor sod who worked for the European Court of Human Rights had been on his way back to his flat in Wimbledon, when he'd been cornered by a bunch of neat but acned goons with what a lot of people suspected had been West Midlands accents. He never made it home, and his killers never got caught. Poor bastard! They tied him to a lamppost, poured on the kerosene and... well, you know... that's fucking evil, that is...

Things got worse when such of the drug mobs as Harry hadn't wiped out sniffed a power vacuum. In February, there was this bloody great ruckus in Tipton – five dead, according to the papers, and a lot more in hospital. I turned the telly on and there was this smashed up row of houses with one of Lee's murals painted on the end of it. Arthur Tolland's face was staring down, through a plume of burning tyre smoke, at a pile of blazing cars.

A big spike of metal was sticking out of the cars and somebody was impaled on it.

'Kraygon Boswell, sixteen years old,' said the newsreader.

One of Harry Ronsard's lads.

There was an interview with one of his 'comrades,' a big young

Asian bloke called Mohammed and, this Mohammed, he made me cry. The thing was, although he came out with the usual load of bollocks about how the guys who'd done it were 'going to pay', he still looked into the camera and said this Kraygon had been 'a brother' – like he meant it.

And Arthur Tolland stared down on his handiwork from his grandson's mural.

You've won this one, I thought. *Thanks a fucking bunch, Arthur.*

Nobody saw Lee after Mary went round to his mother's. They'd dragged Harry Ronsard out of Polly's and banged him up, pending the trial. I heard he'd not seemed too bothered – turned out, he was spending most of his time tapping away at a computer keyboard with his one hand that just about still worked. Doctors still couldn't decide what was wrong with him. Bit by bit, he was coming up with a few fragments of an autobiography, which you've read, of course. Polly married him early in February – in the nick, but she still looked as pleased with herself as a hamster with two full pouches. Don't think many people were there – just the couple, Polly's mum, who was in a right state, apparently, and Charlotte Ronsard.

Shirley Icement wound up in a psychiatric unit. There was a bloodbath going on round her old school. No chance of getting it reopened, so most of the kids got shifted to other places, where they did not fit in at all well.

God knows what happened to Graham Tolland. There was talk he'd tried to bump himself off. And I don't suppose his bosses were too keen on him having backed a horse that had fallen at the first hurdle. To my knowledge, nobody saw him after that, least of all Shirley or Lee.

***

April 2011 and we'd booked a big field near Greensforge for Mary and Ryan's wedding reception. The rain held off and it wasn't too cold. Dunno who they'd got in to run the food and drink tent but the beer seemed to flow freely enough. And the music, of course, was brilliant. Big sound stage, we got Viv Jones in to DJ and we played the best set we'd done in bleedin' ages. Came out on CD later in the year, and it's a pretty decent live album by any standards; drop round mine, if you want one – only a fiver and I've still got loads of copies.

Charlotte Ronsard was there before most other people turned up. I had a bit of a natter with her while we were waiting for everybody to come from church.

'Dad's still in custody,' she said. 'Seems a shame. Polly only had him for a couple of weeks and she loved taking care of him.'

'Yeah. I heard. Sorry.'

'No "sorry" about it. A pile of corpses in your back garden, you can't really talk your way out of that, can you?' Her voice trailed off for a bit, then came back. 'Funny thing is, he never laid a finger on me. Never so much as a smack. Can't understand why I was always so scared of him.'

'He was a scary bloke.'

'He isn't now.'

'No.'

She was quiet for a bit and looked at her feet. Harry Ronsard's daughter – spent all her life just being scared of Harry Ronsard. A lot of anger and a lot of waste and a lot of loneliness in her face.

'One of his lads has been round to see me,' she said, quietly. 'Lad they call Big Mohammed.'

'Ah, yeah. Seen him on the telly.'

'Nice lad. Telling me how much they respected my dad and how they'd always look after me for his sake.'

I turned to her and looked at her very hard. A bit of life seemed to come back into her as she said that – only not in a nice way. She was a tough looking bird, in leathers, over forty but still a hard number. She looked like she could handle herself. Frankly, more than that, she looked like her dad.

At that moment, there was a loud squiggle of really wild noise from the stage and we both looked up. Madame la Keyboard was soundchecking her synthesiser. Her eyes and Charlotte's met and they waved at each other – kind of embarrassedly, which I thought was a shame.

Once Mary and Ryan showed up on that great chuffing traction engine of theirs – Mary's dress already a bit soot-smudged – we kicked the gig off.

Luke and Mattie were in the front, their mum's kung-fu-hardened hands on their shoulders, their four eyes fixed, as one, on their dad. He got it going in his usual style – a fresh burst of snare and cymbals, meant to sound a bit like waves on rocks, or thunder. Something cleansing, clearing a space for new life to begin and to grow. Then in came a warm, gently pulsing pattern on the toms. Life stirred. This all gave Neil and me plenty to work with on guitar and bass. Things got well sexy pretty quick. Then it broke through all the barriers when the flute went crazy, courtesy of old Wilf's Andy, and the keyboards…

Lon had got herself a new Korg Microsampler and she was blasting out sounds of birdsong and power stations and wind in the trees – all tuned to sound like otherworldly orchestras and choirs and gods-know-what. Beautiful! Beautiful! Beautiful! And I knew it was all the stuff off Martin Icement's tapes and I looked around, crazily, half thinking that he'd be there, in a corner of the stage, behind his nest of cassette decks and reel-to-reels and samplers and minidiscs. My head turned out to the audience, hoping more realistically that Martin's son would be there, because I knew Lee needed to hear this music!

But he wasn't. Neither of them was there.

At the back of the crowd, Charlotte was looking up at the stage, and at Lon in particular, but it was like she was looking at an old photograph.

After a few minutes, she turned and walked slowly to where she'd parked her Harley. Loud bastards, those Harleys so when she got it started, I could hear it even over the noise we were making. The only time I ever heard a Harley engine sound sad. I didn't think many people noticed her go. Mary, perhaps, but probably just me and Lon. As she rode out on to the Mile Flat, I guess we knew that, the next time we saw her, she'd be in front of a mob of scowling kids in grey shirts.

Stick the album on now, if you've got it. Track three, 'That's One Big Ass Dragon You Got There', three minutes and twenty seconds in... Hear that? That bit where the keyboard solo goes a bit wonky? That was it.

Lon had other exes she was playing to so she didn't let it stop her. Martin's sounds blasted out of the speakers and we, the band, all knew he should have been here with us, with Alice and with Lee – and with Lee's arm draped over the shoulders of Lewis Gladrell. But that wasn't how things were. And Shirley wasn't off somewhere getting telescopes ready to show little Luke and all the kids like him the way to the stars. Things weren't like that and we, the band, wanted to cry our guts out over things not being like that. So we did the one thing we could do about it...

We put it in the music.

Because, when some things get broken, it's the music that comes closest to putting 'em back together.

Mary and Ryan had a caravan hooked up to the traction engine and were getting ready to go. Lots of soot on the wedding dress by now. Mary didn't seem worried, bless her. Ryan grinned and there was a big hoot off the engine whistle and Ryan and Mary Sheepshanks stood happily on the footplate as they were hauled off into marriage by that great chuffing EXCALIBUR.

25: Satansfist

'Oh.'

'Hello, Polly.'

'I didn't think you'd be here.'

'Harry gave me a key last summer. You can see what's been done.'

'Yes. I always thought it was funny.'

'Funny?'

'That you'd never done any murals in here... in the bathroom.'

'It's a tricky space. Lots of condensation. It's had chance to dry out a bit now, so...'

'Ah. I see. Good time to get it done.'

'Exactly.'

'I hope Harry gets to see it.'

'Well, Polly, that depends on how the trial goes. And that might well depend on whether things calm down on the streets of Sandwell and Birmingham – and other places.'

'I see.'

'You might want to talk to Charlotte about it. I believe you have some... influence in that quarter.'

'I will. Charlotte listens to me. So does Mohammed... They call me "The New Cimourdain."'

'What's that mean?'

'Cimourdain was the... stepfather of an... ancestor of mine. He was one of the guys who ran the French Revolution. People listened to him. They didn't muck him about.'

It was hard to put a name to the cold burning that flared up in her eyes then. But it only showed itself for a moment. After, she was just Polly again:

'Oh Lee...'

'Yes?'

'I wish Harry was still at my house. We could get some privacy

there…'
   'Ah.'
   'Lee?'
   'Yes?'
   'I'm pregnant.'

There was a pause.

   'Really?'
   'Yes.'
   'By Harry?'
   'Yes.'

There was laughter.

   'Well who'd've thought it? Pretty preggie Polly! Well done you!
Pretty Pol's hard-working little fanny squeezes something halfway
useful out the old ruin!'
   'Don't, Lee. Please.'

There was silence.

   'Lee?'
   'Yes?'
   'Have you been… staying here?'
   'Yes. Seemed a good place to lie low for a while. Didn't want to
go back to the flat. Didn't… feel quite ready to bump into The
Cunt.'
   'Lewis Gladrell?'
   'Call him that if you must.'
   'I don't think he's been there much, either. I met him, the other
week. I got it out of him that… after you beat him up the last time…
Lee… he had to go into hospital.'
   'Oh.'
   'There was internal bleeding. He nearly died.'

'That must have got his rocks off.'
'It didn't, Lee.'

There was a pause.

'He's really angry with you, Lee.'
'Will wonders never cease?'
'I think, if he sees you again, he might... kill you...'
'Well snort my ashes and dance the Macarena if he does.'
'Is it that you miss Alice, Lee?'

There was silence.

'Because I do, Lee.'

There was a pause.

'Polly.'
'Yes?'
'I miss a lot of things.'

There was a pause.

'I understand, Lee. Are you going?'
'I think it's time to.'

There was sobbing. Polly's sobbing.

'Lee!'
'Yes?'
'Don't go!'
'Why not?'
'Because... Lee... I don't know... I thought you'd created Harry to be indestructible!'
'Polly. I wish I could have done. But nothing's indestructible.

Everything's always far too bastard fragile…'

***

The bathroom mural: ceiling and half the wall utterly black. Walls divided diagonally between darkness and a confused, uncertain, greyish light. No myths or heroes or dragons. But there is the possibility of them among the greyness, among the clouds and the vapours and the shadows. No such possibility in the black. There is something universal, final and all-consuming about this particular darkness. It is a darkness in the face of which no re-emergent light ought to be possible. It is a darkness that ought to be the end of all things.

***

Outside the flat. Memories of a time when it was shared. Not pleasant memories. Home? *'Home!'* Stupid! Self-indulgent concept for self-indulgent people! Call it by its proper name: the place where sleeping and fucking used to happen.

***

Later. Inside the flat. Collapsed on the sofa and failing completely to get up and make a cup of tea.

There was a noise. In the kitchen. The plumber had been due to come in, a while back. He was supposed to rip out a length of lead piping that had somehow got overlooked through the years. That should all have been done and dusted by now, though.

The kitchen was lit by soft spring light.

'Oh.'

Not the plumber.

'You.'

'Me.'

'I...' I wasn't sure what to call him. Nothing seemed right. 'Didn't

249

think you'd come back here.'

'Just collecting some things.'

'Oh.'

Another long silence. I tried to say something. I really did. But it just wouldn't be said. Eventually, he went on:

'I wasn't sure whether or not to come here. I thought we might get into a fight.'

'Congratulations on your perceptiveness.'

'Don't be so fucking patronising!'

On the work surface, a foot long dildo of old metal, flecked and stained with paint and muck, left behind by the plumber. Suddenly, it was in his hand, waving threateningly in my face. I could have laughed and mimed giving the thing a blow job. I really could have done that. But if I had, he'd have lost his temper; he'd have done what there was to do without thinking about it. I'd have been making it easy for him. And I was not in the business of making it easy. So, instead:

'In the kitchen? With the lead pipe? Ooh, Miss Scarlet, you brazen hussy, you!'

A silence.

'So,' I continued, 'are you going to kill me?'

Another silence. Then:

'I haven't decided yet.'

26: The Cunt

I haven't decided yet.

The En

27:

I haven't decided yet.

28: Lewis Gladrell

I haven't decided yet.

The End

Luke and Mattie Cayle will be back in
Cooper's Ducks for Planet Earth???!!!

Previous Maitland family troubles are told of in
Both